'I shall remember while the light lives yet
And in the night-time I shall not forget.'

SWINBURNE: *Erotian*

ALL FOR YOU

Finella Wood met Darley Martington, a handsome young subaltern, at a Sandhurst dance. They fell in love immediately, and on a golden October day barely three months later, they were married. But two hours after the wedding Darley was recalled to his regiment. He was to spend the next five arduous years fighting overseas. Meanwhile Finella was growing up. She was no longer the nineteen-year-old innocent Darley had married—she had done four years' service as a driver in an Ambulance Corps; she had met and become infatuated with the attractive and forceful Gilfred Bryte. Now Darley was on his way home . . .

ALL FOR YOU

Denise Robins

'All for you
The world can never sever
Our perfect tie,
All for you and I will love you ever
Until I die.'

A Lythway Book

CHIVERS PRESS
BATH

First published 1958
by
Hodder & Stoughton Limited
This Large Print edition published by
Chivers Press
by arrangement with
Hodder & Stoughton Limited
1984

ISBN 0 7451 0071 6

British Library Cataloguing in Publication Data

Robins, Denise
  All for you.—Large print ed.—
  (A Lythway book)
  I. Title
  823′.912[F]   PR6035.O554

  ISBN 0–7451–0071–6

IN MEMORY OF
MURIEL
AND FOR MY FRIEND
ANDRÉ RIESE

ALL FOR YOU

CHAPTER ONE

'Now that it's all over and I know he'll be back at any moment—I just can't believe it's true,' said Finella.

And her lovely, long-shaped eyes which were so thickly black-lashed, held a look in this moment which might almost be called 'dazed'. A pathetic, childish look. The big, heavy built man sitting beside her on the red-plush sofa in the Mirabelle Restaurant where they were dining, saw that look but was unmoved by its poignancy, its defencelessness. That childish quality in Finella—the slenderness of her, the fragility of bone—her small wrists and ankles, the tawny mane of hair curving to her neck—all that was so very young about her—appealed to Gilfred Bryte's senses but did not touch his pity. He ought to leave her alone. He knew it. He ought never to have started the affair with her, knowing that she had a husband in the Forces; a Regular officer fighting abroad whilst he, still in the middle thirties and only a few years older than Finella's husband, held down a 'cushy' job in a reserved occupation. He ought, now that he knew Darley Martington was coming home, to make his exit. Give the young couple a chance.

Finella herself wanted that chance. She had told Gil Bryte that many times.

She was telling him so again this moment. With that 'lost', forlorn note in her voice, she said:

'Gil, we ought not to see each other any more. I'm terribly fond of you. But I'm fond of Darley, too. And he's my husband. You've no idea what sweet letters he writes ... how he's looking forward to seeing me again, to beginning life with me. Gil ... I must give him—and myself—a chance. I *must!*'

The man raised his brows in a deprecating way and blew a cloud of cigar smoke through his nostrils. The wide, strong nostrils of a strong, selfish man who liked to get his own way in all things. He did not move a muscle when Finella touched his arm and repeated her almost piteous cry.

'I *must*, Gil ... you understand, don't you?'

Then he turned and looked at her; for an instant examined critically the almost flawless young face upturned to his. She was ravishingly pretty, this girl who was twenty-four and looked seventeen; had done four years' service as a driver in an Ambulance Corps; driven through blitzes, winter ice, summer heat, and stood up to it; strong despite that delicate appearance. She was lovely with that golden glow to her skin and the bronzed hair that had red lights in it; the smoke-grey eyes and full sweet mouth. As for her throat—so long and white and slender—he had a mad desire to kiss it now in front of all

2

these people sitting around the restaurant. But he pulled himself together and called abruptly to a passing waiter to bring him another double whisky.

A slight feeling of despair settled upon Finella. Gil wouldn't answer. He was cross. She could see it. She knew him so well. After all, they had been going out to parties and dances and lunches pretty continually for over six months now.

She had grown accustomed to his 'black' moods. She knew that he was a ruthless egotist. Spoiled, because a great many women ran after Gil Bryte. He had a 'way' with them. He was not too easy; a little insolent, often casual. Women liked that. He had intrigued Finella, so used to easy conquests. Admirers could be two a penny to a lovely young married woman like herself with a husband overseas. Until she met Bryte, Finella had skimmed the cream off existence; flirted a bit here and there. Nothing more serious. Darley, her husband, had been her most serious consideration always.

She wished now, in a queer perverse way, that she had never met Gil Bryte nor fallen victim to his strange fascination. She had tried once or twice to get away ... like a fly struggling helplessly in a spider's web. But he kept his hold on her. Perhaps because he did not always spoil her and indulge her every whim. Or because he made her want to please *him*. Strange Gil—when

3

he was in a good mood he was delightful. Intelligent, amusing, ambitious. His father, old Tom Bryte, Labour M.P., had risen from nothing. Gil was self-educated, self-made. The day of the idle rich was over ... the Brytes meant to see to that. Gil was an engineer. He was considered a brilliant man. He had already made a lot of money and he would make more when he switched over from his war job to factories of his own. And he had ambitions towards a Parliamentary career for himself.

It was Gil's immense enthusiasm for work, his terrific reserves of energy which fascinated Finella. Something in that rugged face of his with the cold, critical eyes, the mop of dark curly hair, the square dented chin. She had to confess to herself that it was more than a little thrilling to feel that this powerful man was in love with *her*. Wanted her to put an end to her marriage with Darley and marry *him*.

She shivered a little and hastily, with slender fingers shaking, lit a cigarette for herself. She was smoking too much. Bad for the nerves. She *had* 'nerves' at the moment. Everything was crowding down upon her. Her deep-rooted affection for Darley; her infatuation for Gil Bryte. Four years of hard driving and leaves, mostly spent with her mother-in-law, Lady Martington, in Darley's lovely home. Difficult leaves, a difficult association with a proud, possessive woman who adored her only son and

4

had disapproved of the wedding right from the start.

Suddenly, Finella uttered a sound that might have been a sob. The band was playing an old tune which she liked: 'Strange Enchantment'. There were many happy-looking couples on the floor. Finella loved dancing, and she, too, wanted to be happy. But tonight she could not have danced if she had been paid to do so. She felt utterly depressed. Yet London was mad with joy, dancing, gasping with relief because the war was over ... and there was peace in Europe again. Lots of these women on the dance-floor were probably mad with joy, too, because their husbands or sons or lovers were coming home. *She* should be on top of her form with the rest ... delirious at the thought of seeing Darley.

That was what she had wanted; what she had intended. But it was too late. She had grown tired of the waiting, the strain; the endurance test had been too much for her. And Gil Bryte had finished things.

She was desperately unhappy.

'I want to go home, Gil,' she said in an undertone.

He gave her a compassionate look now and took her hand.

'Tired, darling?'

'Yes,' she said. 'Of everything.'

He smiled at that and helped the slim young

5

arms into the small ermine bolero.

'Silly child,' he murmured. 'Don't worry so much. It's a great life if you don't weaken, you know.'

Finella's great eyes stared up at him desolately.

'But I *am* weakening . . . that's the trouble.'

'Tired of me?'

'You know I'm not. But the position is so hopeless. I tell you, Darley will be back any day now. His letter to me this morning said it was only a question of a week or so at the most. His mother has heard the same. She rang me up. I've got to go down to the Manor tomorrow for the week-end.'

Gilfred Bryte frowned. He paid his bill and followed Finella's graceful figure from the restaurant. In the foyer, whilst they waited for a taxi, he said:

'Do you know where Martington is now?'

'Oh, the usual—*somewhere* in Italy.'

'H'm. And so you want to be here to meet him . . . the eager little wife ready to crown the brow of the returning hero with laurels, eh?' said Gil, in a voice of some bitterness.

Finella coloured and withdrew her gaze from him.

'That isn't very kind of you, Gil.'

'I'm not kind—you ought to know that by now. But I'm crazy about you, my dear, and I'm not going to find it easy to stand aside and see

6

you walk into another man's arms.'

'But I'm married to him, Gil.'

'You made some vows and signed a document, yes. An hour or two after which, he left you. Whereupon you called yourself Mrs. Darley Martington but remained, in fact, Miss Finella Wood. You are no more his wife than you are mine. If as much ... because you love me and you don't love him. Am I right?'

The girl looked desperate again.

'Not altogether, Gil. I love him, too. Oh, it sounds awful of me ... you may not understand ... nobody could. But I was once terribly in love with Darley. If he had stayed with me I would never have altered. I know it. But five years is a long time. I was such a child when he left. I'm a woman now. I've been through so much. And I've almost forgotten him. But I haven't forgotten that I did once love and marry him. And it is my duty to be here when he comes back.'

Gil Bryte's cheeks reddened with annoyance.

'It all sounds heroic, my dear. Perhaps if that's how you really feel, I ought to back gracefully out. Shall we call it a day after tonight?'

She threw him a moist, reproachful look, her lips quivering. They did not speak again until they were in the taxi driving Finella to Church Street, Kensington. She was staying there with her married sister, Barbara. Barbara, who was

7

two years older than Finella, had a husband in the R.N.V.R. Jack Stevenson was not yet demobilized. Barbara lived in one of those small, charming little Georgian houses at the top of the hill, alone at the moment with her small boy of two. She was just as happy and settled and complacent as Finella was the reverse.

Finella thought now of her sister. She always envied Barbie because her life was so smooth ... she had never really been parted from Jack. He was older than any of them. A chartered accountant in civilian life, he had been doing a paymaster's job in the Navy most of the war, and had only been at sea for one year, then held shore jobs. Barbara was devoted to him, and there were no complications in her life. *'But in mine,' thought Finella drearily, 'there are endless ones. I can't give Gil up altogether. I can't...'*

He was holding her now in the curve of one strong arm. His lips brushed her hair.

'Nella, little Nella,' he said, using his particular name for her. 'Don't leave me. I'm a gruff brute and a beast to torment you and I've no right to sneer at Martington, who has done a fine job in this war. He deserves a break, I know. But I love you. And I can't give you up without a struggle.'

She crumpled a little in his embrace. He could always win her back like this when he was tender, tolerant, charming. She was so lonely and in need of his tenderness. His lips found

8

hers and the passion he always lit in her flamed up. Yet in the midst of that kiss, she remembered something Darley had written in his last letter. At once it destroyed desire and made her ashamed.

I think only of the moment when I can take you in my arms again and kiss that wonderful mouth of yours, my darling ... all through the long weary waiting I've dreamed of your lips and our remembered kisses. Lips that are mine, and waiting for me. My adored wife ...

Lips that were his ... waiting for him ... that was tragic. It *should* have been so. It was what she had meant it to be. But he had been away so long, fighting ... in Libya, in all those dreadful battles against Rommel ... in Italy. Once wounded slightly and sent to Alexandria and Cairo to recuperate. But never home. Five long years away, gradually losing touch with her ... oh, the long agony, the waste ... the pity of it all!

Finella tore herself out of Gil Bryte's arms. She was weeping bitterly. He had only seen her cry once before and that was a touching incident when she had seen a dog run over while she was with him. She had burst into tears then. She was so young and soft-hearted. So indeterminate in her emotions. He knew that he ought to have pity but he couldn't leave her alone. And he was

9

afraid that the nicest side of her, her real intrinsic wish to do the right thing, would control her final decision.

'Darling, don't upset yourself,' he said. 'It'll be all right.' (Damn the taxi. They were already pulling up in Bedford Gardens.) 'I'll phone you from the office. What time do you go down to Godalming?'

She sat up, blowing her nose forlornly.

'On the ten-ten.'

'I'll ring you at nine. You won't walk out on me, will you, Nella?'

She shook her head. For an instant she pressed her wet cheek to his.

'I couldn't. You're so much a part of my life now, Gil.'

In the dimness of the taxi his eyes narrowed with triumph. He knew it. He was necessary to this child. His strong personality, his clever love-making, even though he was only the son of a man who had started life as a coal-miner.

The Brytes were Lancashire folk. Rough and ready; shrewd. Gilfred . . . it was a queer name, a whim of his mother's. Gil, after his paternal grandmother, Gillian and Fred, after her father. He had all their inborn roughness, their real dislike of the 'upper classes'. But he had acquired a certain polish. He used it for Finella's benefit. He wanted her as his wife. He didn't like the hearty, self-reliant type. And he had no compunction about taking her (if he

10

could) from Darley Martington. Darley, who was Wellington, and Sandhurst, and 'Army', son of a Cabinet Minister, a rigid Conservative, knighted in the last war; now deceased.

Finella was thinking:

'I rely so much on Gil now. His advice, his friendship. He's so clever and wise, and if he went out of my life, I'd miss all the mental stimulus of it, the thrill of the telephone calls, our companionship, everything we've built up.'

But what about the things she and Darley, her husband, had built up five years ago?

She kissed Gil briefly and stepped out of the taxi.

A few moments later she was in the house. It was wrapped in darkness and silence. Barbara and little Mark, her son, were asleep. By the light of a torch, Finella tip-toed up to the spare room, switched on the light and stood a moment, staring around her.

It was all tidy; dear old Barbie must have come in and put away the disorder Finella had left. (Tidiness was not one of her strong points.) Barbie was domesticated and good at all things in the house. Finella was the artistic one; had, when she left school, wanted to devote her life to painting. She used to paint quite well ... do clever little sketches of people. But the war had knocked all that on the head. At nineteen she had, of her own accord, abandoned art and joined a Red Cross driving unit. A job she had

11

stuck to even after her marriage. She never had time to paint now. Only to draw occasionally . . .

Her gaze lit on a photograph standing in a leather frame beside the bed. Darley in his Captain's uniform. It had been taken in Cairo two years ago. (He was Acting-Major now.) She moved across the room—picked up the photograph and looked long and earnestly at it. How good-looking he was! His was a chiselled face with a sweet good-tempered mouth and frank eyes. The antithesis of Gil Bryte. Darley was slim built, boyish in type. Brown hair, fair skin, hazel eyes. A typical Army officer in some respects, Finella mused. Disciplined, concise, a lover of outdoor life. Darley was wonderful on a horse; had won cups at many Point-to-Points; was a good shot, a keen fisherman. Thoroughly *English*. But sensitive to the artistic things of life. He knew little about painting but had adored and fostered Finella's gift in that direction. And he loved music almost as much as she did.

They had fallen in love as soon as they met. It was at a dance down at Sandhurst. Finella had gone to it as the guest of a boy whom she and Barbara used to know at their old home. He had introduced her to the handsome young subaltern, Darley Martington, earlier on. It had proved fatal. Darley had claimed most of her dances . . . and Finella's unfortunate escort had

12

retired ruefully from the contest. It was a 'go' right from the start between Darley and Finella.

Her thoughts winged back to that night . . . what an exciting night in her life . . . she had been nineteen, unspoiled, happy-go-lucky, still living in a world that was untroubled by war.

She wore a rose-pink chiffon dress and a cluster of rosebuds in her hair. Shining hair, shining eyes, fresh and perfumed as her roses, deliciously young. Darley had fallen for all of it at once. She was the first girl he had wanted to marry. At twenty-six, in the Regular Army, it was considered foolish to marry. But he had money of his own, which made a difference. He decided that he must become engaged to Finella . . . there couldn't be another girl in the world to equal her. He couldn't risk losing her.

Finella sat down on the edge of the bed . . . caught in the web of her memories . . . her head dropped . . . her lashes were still wet with tears.

CHAPTER TWO

That had been at the beginning of August 1939.

Darley and Finella emerged from the dance at Sandhurst madly in love. Two young things deeply conscious of their youth and inexperience, new to the intense emotion they evoked in each other, but certain it was everlasting.

He took her, straight away, down to the Manor House which was his home and inheritance—six miles out of Godalming, in lovely wooded country—to see his mother.

Lady Martington did not approve. She received her son's lovely girl-friend with mixed feelings. She admitted that Finella was beautiful and had charming manners and although not 'anybody' in particular, was the daughter of a doctor (that helped!) And incidentally that she had artistic talent. But Darley was much too young to *think* of marriage. He had a career to make in the Army. Besides, Lady Martington had other plans. Knew another girl whom she wanted for a daughter-in-law.

But all Lady Martington's little hints and little lectures and little efforts to prevent her son's marriage failed. The outbreak of war settled the question ... spelt ruin to Lady Martington's hopes as well as the hopes of a great many other millions in the world. Darley insisted on an engagement immediately. Then when, in October 1939, he was ordered abroad he insisted upon marriage.

Finella, sitting in her bedroom on this warm April night ... so changed from that *other* Finella ... felt a deep pang, akin to real grief, as her memories took her to the day of her wedding.

It should have been down at Christchurch, in

her home. But Barbara, then only engaged to her Jack and still living with their widowed mother, was tactless enough to develop mumps a week before the wedding. Everything had to be altered. Lady Martington, resigned to the affair but no more pleased than she had been at first, took command. (She was a very commanding woman, Finella had since learned that to her cost.)

Mrs. Wood was left to nurse the unfortunate Barbara. Her ladyship arranged a hurried wedding and reception in London. Finella and Darley, more than ever enamoured of each other, allowed themselves to be swept along on the tide of Lady Martington's imperiousness. The bride stayed with an aunt in Kensington and her uncle gave her away.

Oh, that unforgettable morning. A golden autumn day in London ... a day of mild temperatures, slight mist, red and brown leaves; that hint of melancholy that always settles over London in October.

Finella was a white bride. She had wanted that so badly, for Darley. He had wanted it, too. It was to be his last memory of her; a slim figure in creamy satin wearing the double row of pearls which was his wedding present; and a Russian head-dress on her tawny head; a foam of delicate lace (the veil was lent by Lady Martington). A sheaf of lilies, an ardent, rapt young face, exquisitely beautiful in its intensity.

She had *felt* intense ... bewildered by so much sweetness in life ... Darley's love and longing ... her own warm impulses towards him. Oh, she had meant every word she said when she took those marriage vows. She had *wanted* to make Darley a good wife. She had *meant* to be loyal ... for ever ... until death parted them.

She had come out of the church ... Holy Trinity in Brompton Road ... smiling adorably for the photographers. (It must be in the Society journals ... her ladyship had seen to that.) She had felt that life was a miracle. Even though Darley had to go away and fight for his country, they were to have a whole week together first. And everyone said the war wouldn't last long. Darley would soon be back.

How it hurt to remember how confident she had been, how pathetically proud to stand beside the young officer in his khaki uniform, with his sword at his side and his hazel eyes brilliant with passionate love for her.

It was in the middle of the reception that the blow fell. Telegrams were pouring in ... from the Martington's many relations and friends; from hers. She was just about to cut the cake with Darley's sword, when the message was brought to him by a despatch rider from his regimental depot.

Then it was all over ... the gay, glorious reception ... all happiness over for *him*. He had

16

been recalled. He must go at once. And although he could not tell anybody ... he knew that it meant that he would be at a port 'somewhere in the North' by this time tomorrow ... awaiting convoy overseas.

A bitter blow for the bridegroom. Finella knew how bitter. It had wiped all the boyishness from Darley's face. And when he broke the news to her, she felt her heart sink like a stone. He had gripped her hand ... the one wearing the new slim circlet ... very tightly and whispered:

'Be brave, darling. I've got to be, too. It's grim ... but I'm a soldier and you're a soldier's wife, now. Chin up, sweetheart. Smile ... let the others see you smile.'

She had done as he asked. But she had felt her heart crack a little. Almost at once she had slipped away to change from her gleaming bridal clothes into her going-away suit and hat. But the light had gone out of her eyes ... as it had done out of his. There was to be no wedding-night, no honeymoon ... just nothing. It was a cruel war. For the first time, really, the war struck at Finella, and life struck too ... warning her that it was not to be all roses and moonshine and kisses.

She was brave because Darley asked her to be. She guessed that this meant that he was 'off' into the blue. She might not see him again for long weeks and months. (*Oh, but she hadn't realized*

17

that it was to be years ... nearly five years ... before she saw him again!)

It had all been a nightmare ... their last frantic embrace ... his departure ... Lady Martington in tears ... but not too tearful to say in Finella's hearing: '*I always knew he ought not to have organized this wedding. Going off like this ... leaving a young wife behind him ... such a responsibility for me.*'

It had been a responsibility for the young wife, too. She was a married woman. Yet not married. She had to go back to her own home. Nothing was left now but letters ... dozens and dozens of letters ... by air, by sea ... from her to him. From him to her. Endless correspondence. Never really knowing where he was or what he was doing. Hints ... rumours ... guesses. He was in Egypt. He was at Benghazi. He was in Persia. He was back in Cairo.

M.E.F. That was what one put on all the letters. *Middle East Forces*. It was all she ever knew. Sometimes he sent descriptions of the desert, of leave in Cairo ... of a hurried flight to Palestine to take a staff course ... of leave again in Beirut or Damascus. Then the old routine ... desert.

Snapshots. Darley in shorts and shirt with sun-glasses and topi. Darley with a moustache (she begged him to take that off at *once*). Darley on leave. She studied every pictured face ...

trying to keep touch ... to *know* something about him as he was these days. And she sent him her latest photographs; books, magazines; Christmas presents, birthday presents, presents to celebrate the anniversary of their wedding. *One, two, three,* oh, God, how slowly the years crawled by. And still Darley fought in this battle and that ... and Finella lived through a continual strain of anxiety. Dreading to see a poster with bad news or listen to a broadcast on it ... scouring the papers, following the maps, trying to follow *him* ... celebrating if the day was victorious ... holding her breath for fear when it was going badly ... suffering as only the very young can suffer ... exaggeratedly ... pathetically. Feeling always that it was *her* husband against Rommel, himself. Longing for cables which said '*all well and all my love*'. Dreading the telegrams.

Weeks, months, *years* of it.

Finella grew up. She no longer devoted her time to art or music or dancing. Her sister, Barbara, became engaged and married. But she had her husband with her a great deal, and a baby by the end of the first year. Lucky Barbie. To have a child to love and look after when Jack went away; to have a home of her own.

Their mother died in the winter of 1940, and the old house in Christchurch disintegrated. Finella was thrown more and more on her own resources ... and on her mother-in-law. Of

19

course Darley's mother insisted on her going down to the Manor often. She did not like Finella any more than the girl liked the older woman ... but the existence of Darley held them together ... and Lady Martington was conventional, always correct. Finella was Mrs. Darley and Mrs. Darley had a right to live, if she wished, at the Manor which was Darley's home.

As the time went by, things became more difficult between Lady Martington and Finella. The girl was growing independent; in uniform, leading a 'tough life', and Lady Martington could not control that life as she wished to do. When Finella arrived at the Manor, worn out, nerves frayed by mental and physical strain, the older woman was often unsympathetic. She accused Finella of going out with other men, of enjoying herself whilst 'poor Darley' fought for her. Finella protested wildly. It was Darley's wish that she should go out and enjoy herself. He said so in his letters. She was young and the war looked like dragging on endlessly. She couldn't be expected to sit at home like a recluse.

But Lady Martington was acid and disapproving. So Finella withdrew more and more into herself. She grew introspective. She began to refuse invitations. And that was bad for her. It was when she was in her most vulnerable condition of mind, lonely, desperately longing for her husband, that Gil Bryte entered her life.

The more she saw of Gil and the more attracted she became, the more she tried to revive her old feelings for Darley. She went on writing to him ... feverishly ... pages and pages. He wrote back, always the same devoted young man. His love for her had not diminished. She was his dream ... all that mattered to him ... all that he was fighting for and coming home to.

He wrote:

Out here, always amongst men, one grows a bit morbid and short-tempered and to each one of us, the memory and thought of our wives becomes of increasing importance. In you, my darling little Finella, lies my hope of life itself. I want to live ... to get through this war ... for you. We had so little time together. But thank God we are both young and can make up for it all in the future ...

On one occasion she wrote:

Miss you dreadfully ... wherever I go and whatever I do. Oh, come back soon, darling Darley. Sometimes I look at my wedding ring and wonder if I really am your wife.

She had never sent that letter. She had torn it up, afraid that it might worry him to know that she did not feel *really* married to him.

He was a captain now. He had won the Military Cross at El Alamein and been mentioned in dispatches. He was a fine soldier and she was desperately proud of him. But he was no longer the gay young subaltern who had danced with her at Sandhurst and married her in the second month of the war. He was a man . . . who had been living among men, living dangerously, under fire . . . under strain.

What would he be like when he came back? Changed, like herself? She was more critical. Not such a child. Gil called her a 'child' but she knew that she was much more mature than the Finella whom Darley had married. She had faced big blitzes, seen awful sights, and carried on . . . sometimes forced herself to carry on when she was exhausted in body and mind, sick to death of it all.

Now she was half in love with a man older than Darley, and much more forceful. (At least she could not remember Darley as being forceful.) That was the trouble. She could only remember him dimly. His letters . . . his impersonal descriptions of foreign countries . . . his parcels . . . brocades from the East, silk stockings, cosmetics . . . what did they mean? Nothing. There was no *real* link. She couldn't go to Darley with her little troubles (one mustn't worry a man who is fighting) . . . she couldn't tell him how bitter was the antagonism between her and his mother . . . she had not even told him when she was so ill with 'flu last winter.

She could only write the same old words ... endless repetition ... it had become almost monotonous, no longer genuine or from the soul:

Darling I miss you ...
Darling I'm longing to see you again.
Darling I live only to get you back ...

And now, when he was actually coming, she had lost touch with Darley completely and wanted to run to Gil Bryte and be lost to the rest of the world; wanted never to have to face Lady Martington again; nor worry about anything. One wouldn't worry with Gil. He'd do all the thinking for *his* wife.

Yet she couldn't behave as Gil wanted and walk out on Darley now ... at the last moment. It would be beastly of her. Unfair. She hated unfairness. Barbara, too, had begged her to wait. When she had discussed things with Barbie last night, she had said:

'There's something about that Bryte man which repels me though I admit he's fascinating. I liked Darley so awfully much. You were mad about him once, Fin. Wait and give him a chance.'

Finella had been saying that all the evening.

But she was sick with worry. If only she could feel thrilled because Darley was coming home.

23

She groped in a dressing-table drawer and found the air-letter from Darley received this morning.

It is so wonderful knowing that I may be able to get back to England and to my wife within the next few days, that I can hardly believe it true. Finella, my adorable darling, I try to imagine what you will look like ... what you will say to me ... God, what a thrill for any fellow. Keep your fingers crossed, darling ... it may be any moment now ...

Boyish, eager ... rather like the Darley she had married. But between them lay five long bitter years ... They had become strangers ...

Finella dropped the letter and covered her face with her hands. It was the face of a woman in torment ... not of the laughing child of nineteen whom Darley Martington had married and whom he would expect to find.

Yet the same words went on echoing grimly in her head.

I must give him—and myself—a chance ...

Then, if when she came face to face with him she felt the same ... the same deep longing for Gil ... she would tell Darley the truth and ask for her freedom.

CHAPTER THREE

In the grounds of the manor house the daffodils made a brave golden border on either side of the drive. The first delicate green of the spring showed itself in bud and leaf. The fine unspoiled façade of the early Georgian house looked its best on an April day like this, and Finella felt almost happy as she walked toward the portico which in a short time would be covered in purple wistaria.

She loved Darley's home. She felt all his personal pride in the fine house in which he, and his father before him, had been born; in the green velvet of the lawns; the famous herbaceous border; the even more famous yew hedges.

Even five years of war had failed to ruin the Martington home completely, despite the lack of gardeners and servants, and a family of evacuees who had lived down here since 1940. But now the evacuees had gone back to London.

There was peace—quiet again—privacy. And Lady Martington could boast of at least one good cook and a 'daily'. Not, she said, that things could ever be quite the same as when Darley was a boy and in the days of Sir George, when they had kept a huge indoor and outdoor staff.

It was lovely here, thought Finella, and one day she would be mistress of it all ... strictly speaking, she was its mistress now. Darley had inherited the estate. When he came home, his mother must find another house. But at the moment she continued to reign supreme—by Finella's wish as well as her own.

Finella did not mind her mother-in-law dominating over her own household. It was when she tried to dominate *her* that things became so awkward. And she would smile all the time that she was saying nasty biting things. That got Finella down ... that fixed smile which belied the acid tongue. Only this morning—almost as soon as Finella arrived— Lady Martington had said tartly:

'I think you should stay down here now until dear Darley arrives. Why must you go up to London again? Your sister doesn't need you.'

Finella had felt like saying 'Nor do you.' But she had merely remarked that she liked to stay with Barbie during the week, and come here for week-ends. Whereupon Darley's mother had looked at her with icy suspicion behind the inevitable smile and said:

'You must go gadding about, I suppose. How I detest this modern craze for enjoyment. No repose. No love of the country which, I may say, is what *Darley* loves best. You will disappoint him if you are not careful.'

Again Finella had longed to retort; to say

26

'Perhaps *I* shall be disappointed, too. Why must it all be on *his* side?'

But because she felt more than a trifle guilty about Gil Bryte, she kept silence.

Then Rachel Webb came, and from that moment onward Finella had been even more silent and more unhappy. If she had an enemy in the world, she knew that it was Rachel— Lady Martington's god-daughter and daughter of General and Mrs. Webb who lived at Ashleigh Hall about two miles from here. She was a tall, thin, good-looking girl, with none of Finella's delicate beauty or charm. But she had a pair of dark sparkling eyes, a ruddy skin and dark curly hair which she wore short. She nearly always dressed in sensible, well-cut tweeds; rode hard to hounds in peace-time and was noted in the district for being a fine all-round sportswoman. She got on a great deal better with men than with women. But Aunt Margaret, as she called Lady Martington, had always been fond of Rachel, and Rachel had adored Darley since they played together as children. An adoration which later had developed on Rachel's side into a passion which Darley could not reciprocate. He admired Rachel but could never love her.

The day that Darley brought Finella back to the Manor as his promised wife had put the end to any hopes Rachel had entertained of winning him. But she did not stop coming as frequently as ever to the Manor. And she was gratified by the knowledge that Aunt Margaret was a great deal fonder of her than she would ever be of Finella.

Rachel waited and watched. She had gone on waiting and watching all these years that Darley had been away. She did not think the marriage would last. She entertained a wild hope that in the long run Darley would turn to her, his old friend. Meanwhile she loathed Finella with a maliciousness undreamed of by people who knew Rachel and thought her such a 'sport'. There was nothing sporting in Rachel's attitude towards Finella. Nothing. Outwardly she was friendly to the girl who was some six years younger than herself. But all Finella's feminine instincts warned her against Rachel, and she had at times great difficulty in not showing her own hostile feelings. Rachel was malicious in a sly way; took delight in making 'digs' at Finella in a roundabout fashion, capping what she said by a 'dear' or 'darling'. Last week-end Finella had made a poor effort to play family bridge and let her partner down several times, unable to concentrate in the unpleasant atmosphere which was always put up by the presence of both Darley's mother and her god-daughter.

'Darley loves bridge—you really ought to learn to play,' Lady Martington had said. And when Finella had stammered that she had no 'card-sense', Rachel Webb had cut in and said:

'What sort of sense *have* you got then, dear? Do tell us,' and capped the remark by patting Finella playfully on the back; but Finella had hated her ... the friendly pat held nothing in it of real playfulness. Finella knew that Rachel knew herself to be expert at contract bridge and a fitting partner for Darley.

There were so many petty, horrid moments like that down here.

And today Rachel was staying for lunch and possibly the whole afternoon. Finella wished she could go out by herself, take a long walk in the country with Darley's old springer spaniel, Sue. Poor old Sue. Still alive. Waiting for her master to come back ... like all of them. Or would old Sue, like Finella, have forgotten a little? How sad it was ... this fading of memory ... with the march of time. Finella was still worried to death after last night at the Mirabelle with Gil. His 'phone call early this morning had brought no happiness. She had been miserable and he had grown irritated and rung off abruptly. All the way down to Godalming she had thought about him, and realized to the full how she would fret and grieve if he stayed away from her altogether.

During lunch Lady Martington eyed Finella with some genuine concern.

'You look very pale. I hope you're not going to be ill just as dear Darley is coming back,' she said.

Finella coloured and said:

'Oh no, I'm all right—really.'

'I should cancel your plans to go back to your sister and stay down here next week if I were you,' said Lady Martington.

Almost Finella decided to do so; to try at least to strangle this longing to get back to Gil . . . to wait in Darley's home for him. Most certainly she would want to be here when he came. She would not dream of doing anything else.

But Fate—and Gilfred Bryte—had other plans in store for Finella. For after lunch, Lady Martington, feeling a fresh stab of conscience about her young daughter-in-law, ordered the local taxi to take them into Guildford.

'We'll do some marketing, have tea there, then come back. Shall we, my dear?' she suggested.

Finella in her despairing mood did not mind whether she went or stayed. She accepted the invitation listlessly. Rachel was asked to accompany them. To Finella's relief she refused. She would like to stay here and pick some daffodils for her mother, she said, as all their bulbs were over. Then she would cycle home.

The afternoon with Darley's mother was one of the most pleasant Finella had ever spent. Her ladyship was in a good mood. And Finella had quite made up her mind to remain at the Manor from now onward. She would ring Gil up and tell him so. But when they got back to the Manor they found that Rachel Webb had not cycled home after all. She was still here, smiling in a rather curious way. When Lady Martington went upstairs to take off her things, Rachel called the younger girl into the morning-room.

'I want a few words with you, dear,' she said.

She said it in such a friendly way and with such smiling eyes that Finella was confused. What on earth had Rachel to speak to *her* about?

She soon knew. Rachel had been about to go home when a large car had driven up to the Manor and a big, imposing man, as Rachel described him, had stepped out and asked for Mrs. Darley. He had given his name as Mr. Gilfred Bryte.

'From some Ministry or other, on his way back from visiting a factory they're just closing down in this district, he said,' Rachel Webb announced, watching Finella closely. 'He said he was an old friend of yours.'

Finella could not prevent the burning colour from staining her face. She tried to appear nonchalant but inwardly she was furious that Gil should have come here and introduced himself to Rachel ... to Rachel of *all* people. Besides, she had asked him never to come to the Manor. Never. She could only suppose he had regretted his abrupt dismissal of her on the 'phone and had come to make amends. He could not stay, Rachel went on, but left a message asking

Finella to meet him in London on Monday night. It was to celebrate something or other (Rachel didn't quite know what) ... but she was to meet him at the Berkeley at eight o'clock.

Finella lowered her lashes.

Her heart was thudding. Oh, it was maddening ... to feel this way about Gil ... but she always did. Having decided not to go up to town on Monday ... here he was, throwing temptation in her way again.

Rachel, humming under her breath, watched the girl change colour, noted her agitation. She said nothing. But she knew ... quite a lot. She knew from remarks Mr. Bryte had deliberately made ... that there was an affair between these two. All to the good. Darley would be livid. Darley wouldn't stand for it, if Rachel knew him. He'd get rid of this girl once he got back— just as quickly as he had married her.

Aloud, Rachel said:

'Look here, my dear, I know what you're thinking. You are allowing dear Aunt Margaret and her old-fashioned ideas to get you down. But I know Darley, too. He's broad-minded— he wouldn't want you to sit down here and play bridge when you hate it. I may seem unsympathetic, but I do sometimes feel for you, really. You're so young and pretty. Mr. Bryte seems a good, sensible friend. Go out with him, my dear. Enjoy yourself. That's my advice.'

With pathetic eagerness Finella looked into

Rachel Webb's cool, dark eyes.

'Do you really mean that, Rachel?'

'Of course, silly. You needn't tell Aunt M. One has to make allowances for the older generation. I shan't say a word. But I just advise you to go and be happy—while you can. It's only natural.'

That was what Finella once thought . . . what she wanted to think now. It was only until Darley came home. *But was it!* She was in a fever of doubt and longing again . . . longing for Gil and his never-failing efforts to cheer her up . . . to make the world seem a little less lonely and difficult. And Rachel Webb was being quite human—much nicer than she had ever been. Finella suddenly smiled.

'Okay,' she said breathlessly. 'I'll go up on Monday. I do adore dancing, I admit it. You are a sport, Rachel. Darley always said you were.'

Rachel Webb looked away from the beautiful shining eyes and felt a trifle uncomfortable under Finella's praise. For she knew that on Monday—as soon as Finella had gone up to town—she meant to 'phone Aunt Margaret and tell her all about Mr. Gilfred Bryte. All about the affair Finella was having with that big, bumptious fellow, who had had the nerve to come here this afternoon to see Darley's wife.

CHAPTER FOUR

Acting Major Darley Martington arrived in England by plane from Italy late that afternoon with one or two other staff officers, and put a telephone call through to his home from the aerodrome at which they landed.

Whilst waiting for that call he sat drinking the first good cup of English tea he had tasted for a long time. His left arm was in a sling. That wound—he had 'stopped one' during the offensive of last autumn—was still not right. They kept getting bits of shrapnel out of it and it would keep on refusing to heal. But on the whole he was well. Well, but tired. His bronzed face was haggard for one so young. His eyes looked strained ... but full of eagerness and pleasure as he regarded the fine spring afternoon. God, it was incredible being on English soil after five years of foreign service. Active service at that. Grand to see the old country again. And quite unbelievable to think that tonight he would be with Finella ... with the lovely young wife he had left a few hours after their wedding in 1939.

Since then he had seen hell let loose ... and passed through it, not altogether unscathed. A man could never forget some of the sights he had seen or the sounds he had heard. But at least he had come out of it with his life, and whole in wind and limb except for this rotten arm. But that would soon heal up and he was still fit enough to do a job. But just now, thank God, the long struggle against Hitler was over ... and so far as he, Darley, was concerned, the old Jap show could wait. He was going home on long leave ... going back to his mother ... and to *his wife*.

Wonderful women, those two. Mother had been marvellous about Fin ... his little lovely Fin ... looked after her when her own mother died; made her welcome at the Manor. And Fin had been more than wonderful. Driving through all that hellish *blitz-krieg at home* ... writing to him every day ... waiting for him.

Darley Martington felt an almost choked sensation in his throat. His fingers trembled as he pulled his pipe from his tunic pocket and lit it. He could not always control that nervous trembling when he thought of Finella. How madly in love they had been just before he left; how glorious it was to get back and start, tonight, that honeymoon he had had to forgo.

He had visualized it all so often out in the desert and later in the desolate mountainous country of Italy ... where they had fought many hard battles. Visioned this day and this night ... with Finella. He had got it all fixed ... all organized ... (Darley liked organizing things in an orderly manner.) He had forgotten

35

no detail, he hoped. Sent cables flying right and left. To Finella ... to mother ... to the Berkeley. That was where he had booked a suite for his wedding night five years ago. Since then he had dreamed of it ... often with hopeless yearning ... wondering if he would ever come through the ghastly show, ever see his wife again. But now he could make his dream a reality. The same suite was booked again ... there were to be flowers in it ... masses of them for Finella. She had been his wife all these years but tonight she was his bride.

What a lot they would have to say to each other! Of course, they would have to get to know each other all over again. He realized that. Her letters had been a little impersonal ... yet always sweet and devoted. He had no fears that he would find her still the girl he had loved and wanted so madly before the war separated them.

But of course, he *was* a little vague about her life today. What could he really know of it? She went to parties and met people he did not know and in whom he was not interested. She mentioned names which held no meaning for him. Sometimes he had felt an absurd, agonizing jealousy of the men who were able to touch her hand ... dance with her ... look at her. But he was not too selfish, he hoped; he told her to enjoy life while she could. Of course she would never be serious about any other man. She wasn't like *that* ... his Finella.

His call came through. Darley sprang to his feet—every nerve throbbing—and put the receiver to his ear.

'Hello,' he said huskily. 'Hello.'

A woman's voice answered:

'Her ladyship is out, sir. Who shall I say?'

A new maid, Darley thought. Lord, how little he knew about home . . . about anything back in the old country. He said: 'Is . . . Mrs. Darley there?'

'No, sir. She's gone sir. But her ladyship will be back for dinner, about six o'clock I believe.'

Darley said sharply:

'Where has . . . Mrs. Darley gone?'

'I'm sure I don't know, sir. She generally only comes weekends.'

Darley's face fell, and the loud hammering of his excited heart died right down. It was as though a douche of cold water had been thrown upon him. He persisted:

'Hello . . . hello . . . there . . . can you possibly tell me where to find Mrs. Darley?'

The woman hesitated, then answered:

'I don't really know, sir, except I heard her tell her ladyship she would be at her sister's, but I don't know the address. Who shall I say telephoned, please, sir?'

'Tell her ladyship that Major Martington called and will 'phone her again later tonight,' said Darley slowly, and hung up the receiver.

As he rejoined the little group of officers with

37

whom he had flown from Italy, he was frowning. He was a disappointed man. And a perplexed one. He had so hoped to hear Finella's voice . . . or at least his mother's. Well, his mother was only 'out'. But Fin wasn't there . . . wasn't staying at the Manor. She had gone away . . . to her sister's.

Darley realized that he had not the least idea where Barbara lived. Somewhere in Kensington. Fin had mentioned an address in one of her letters but he could not remember it. Of course Barbara was married these days . . . had a child . . . the old Wood household had broken up while he, Darley, went away.

Where was Fin to be found? Why hadn't she waited for him at his home? She must have got his cable. Or had it been hung up? He could not *believe* that she would have left the Manor like that . . . so casually . . . knowing that he was on the way home.

Darley was a man whose nerves were already frayed by the long years of strain. The wound in his arm was beginning to throb (it always did that when he was upset). He felt wretchedly disappointed. His home-coming had not started off on at all the right note. He told himself, cynically, that it was always fatal to set one's hopes too high . . . expect too much. But when he thought of meeting his lovely young wife, of her rushing into his arms tonight . . . it was a little disheartening to a chap to say the least of it.

He decided that he could not possibly get down to the Manor tonight. Better go straight to the Berkeley where he had booked the 'bridal suite' and grin and bear it . . . alone if need be. He wanted very much to see his mother. He was devoted to her. But tonight he had set apart for his wife. If he could not be with her he would rather be alone. Besides, that woman at the Manor may not know everything. Possibly Finella had got his cable and gone up to meet him. Yes, he would find her waiting for him at the Berkeley.

Hope revived in Darley Martington. He found and lit a cigarette (he was getting adept at it with one hand) and waited as patiently as he could for the train to town.

Everything from then onward combined to fray the edges of his usual patience and amiability a little further. A long wait for the train; a rotten journey in a crowded apartment; and it seemed an eternity before he finally walked into the vestibule of the Berkeley Hotel.

It was certainly too late to get down to Godalming now. Even if he did not find Finella here, he was too tired and disheartened to travel another mile.

But he would find Finella. He must.

His first enquiries had disappointing results. No Mrs. Martington had been here or asked for him. He let his luggage be taken up to the rooms booked, washed and walked into the restaurant where the dancing was now in progress.

It seemed a very long while since he had been in a London restaurant! Seen so many lovely, well-dressed women. Listened to such a good dance-band. But he was not a happy man. He was an anxious one. His gaze searched feverishly for the figure of his wife.

'Darling...' he thought. *'Darling ... you must be here ... for me ...'*

One or two people looked twice at the slim figure of the man in uniform with the crown on his shoulder and the arm in a black sling. Another wounded hero back from the war ... there were thousands of them. All over London.

Then Finella saw him.

Finella who on Rachel Webb's advice had come up to have this dinner-party with Gil Bryte and had left just an hour before her husband's cable had reached the Manor ... saw that familiar figure in the doorway and stopped dead in the middle of the dance-floor. Her slight body went stiff in Bryte's arms. Her face turned a bright crimson.

'What is it, Nella?' asked the man.

She almost choked the answer.

'It's Darley ... good heavens ... it's *Darley!*'

Her large luminous eyes stared at the slim khaki-clad form ... at the injured arm ... at the thin bronzed face so changed, so much sterner and older.

Then Darley saw her too and a great light sprang into his eyes.

He edged his way quickly in and out of the dancing couples and stood an instant beside Finella and the big man in the grey suit who was with her. (He had not the vaguest idea who the chap was and did not care!) His whole gaze was fixed with an almost pathetic absorption on the lovely face of his young wife; noting the perfect grace of her figure in the long black dinner dress; the orchids on her shoulder. (He had meant to give her orchids tonight. Pity another fellow had already done it!)

Darley turned to Gil Bryte. He said with excitement:

'Sorry to interrupt, but this is my wife and my dance—you understand . . . ?'

Gil Bryte raised an eyebrow and glanced at Finella. She was obviously startled, speechless for the moment. Gil looked and felt an almost murderous irritation at this finale to his evening. But he had no other course than to make his exit.

'Oh, hello . . . good evening, Major Martington . . . of course I'll make myself scarce. So long, Nella . . . see you soon, I hope.'

She did not reply. He moved off. And Darley, his mind and body one flame of thrilled appreciation of his wife's loveliness, put his uninjured arm about her. Automatically they began to dance. He held her so close that she

41

could scarcely breathe, drinking in the fragrance
of her . . . adoring that tawny silken hair curling
to the creamy neck. (A new way . . . not as she
used to do it . . . but he liked it.) He said:

'Fin . . . my darling . . . my darling . . . then
you knew I was coming here . . . that I'd booked
our rooms. You were just filling in time with
that fellow . . . what's-his-name . . . Bryte . . .'

She found her voice . . . she could not lie so
unblushingly as that. She said:

'No . . . I didn't know you had booked
rooms. I . . . was spending the evening with . . .
with Gil.'

She felt his grasp slacken a little and saw the
hurt surprise flash into his eyes.

'But I cabled you . . .'

'I . . . didn't get the cable. Where did you
send it?'

'To the Manor. I thought you'd be there.'

'I'm sorry,' she stammered.

'Oh, it doesn't matter,' he said, feeling both
himself and the remark to be ridiculous.

But once more Darley Martington's world of
illusion crumbled a little. He stopped dancing
and led the lovely figure of his wife into the
hotel vestibule.

'I'm rather a broken reed at the moment,' he
said abruptly. 'This arm . . . makes dancing a
bit awkward . . . look here . . . lucky running
into you like that, but sorry if I broke up the
other fellow's evening.'

She went scarlet. She was horribly embarrassed and sorry for Darley ... and utterly unable to cope with her own emotions. She only knew that she had hated to see Gil walk off like that ... that this paralysing sudden appearance of her husband was more of a shock than a pleasure. And yet ... she ought to be thrilled ... ought to show that she was thrilled. (Oh, God, how difficult it all was.)

Darley was speaking again:

'Look, I've booked these rooms. We may as well use them, darling. Let's nip into a taxi and fetch your luggage from your sister's place and come back here, shall we?'

She did not answer for a moment, but stared, half fascinated, half afraid, up into the face of this man she had married ... and with whom she had never yet lived.

CHAPTER FIVE

Darley spoke again.

'Will that little fur thing you're carrying be enough? You won't be cold? No—I think it's fairly warm out. Well, come along, we'll get cracking.'

Finella swallowed hard. *'Get cracking.'* Heavens, how that typical Army phrase flashed her back to the old days. She could see Darley—

the Darley of Sandhurst days—his merry hazel eyes—his boyish grin—hear his voice: 'Come on, Fin, let's find the car and get cracking—I want to get away from everyone else and be alone with you. Okay by you, sweetheart?'

He wasn't exactly saying that now; he didn't seem quite the sort of man to wait for a woman's orders. He was so very changed and decisive. That was what five years of hard campaigning had done for him. Major Martington was obviously used to giving orders and having them obeyed.

She was still so stupefied by his unexpected appearance tonight that she could not yet find the right things to say, nor know what she meant to do. But she was conscious of a slight and ever-increasing resentment against him. If his cable had missed its way, it was not her fault. But it was just the strangest coincidence that Gil should have brought her here to the very place where Darley had asked her to meet him. Not only was it a coincidence, but most *awkward*.

She found her voice:

'I . . . I don't think you know what London is like these days, Darley. One doesn't just hop into taxis all over the place . . .' she laughed nervously . . . 'one waits for them.'

'Right,' said Darley. 'I'll tell the chap to get us one and we'll wait.'

'But—' began Finella, then stopped helplessly.

'But what?' he asked.

His gaze searched her face. She was flushed and unsmiling and, he thought, worried. Worried about what? Wasn't she glad he'd come back? Was she by any chance annoyed because he'd broken up her evening with the other chap? Now he came to think of it, Bryte had walked off rather hastily and in a 'huff'. Good lord! Wasn't one permitted to claim one's wife the first night one got home after five years overseas?

The flame of Darley's enthusiasm flickered down somewhat. He felt aggrieved. He said, shortly:

'As a matter of fact I've changed my mind, if you don't object, Finella. I haven't eaten a bite since lunch. Think I'll get some food in me before we take that drive. Have you dined?'

'Yes. We . . . had just finished.'

'Do you mind watching me eat?'

'Of course not . . .' She gave her nervous little laugh again.

'Maybe you'd like to put a call through to Barbara and warn her we'll turn up later to pick up your luggage?'

'Y . . . yes . . . maybe that would be a good idea,' she stammered.

He walked into the restaurant. Finella moved like one in a daze toward the telephone boxes. Again her gaze searched frantically for Gil. But he was nowhere to be seen. He must have left the hotel. Perhaps he was so fed up with what had happened tonight that he would never see her again. He would finish with her finally. It was quite right if he felt that way. After all, her husband had come back and she had asked Gil a great many times to let her give Darley a chance. Yet now that chance had come she felt nothing but a sense of panic as though she had been caught, suddenly, and flung into a prison. And Darley, her husband, was the gaoler. He held the key. They key to her freedom, her independence, all that she had built up while he was away.

She could not think straight. She wanted to go back to Barbara and stay with her tonight. She couldn't stay here with Darley. Oh, but that was mad, of course. She *must*. She was his wife. She must give him some sort of a welcome home. She must forget Gil Bryte and that devastating effect which he had upon her.

She was in the telephone booth before she remembered that it was futile ringing up Barbie. She was out tonight with her in-laws. Mrs. Jennings, who did the cleaning, was sitting with little Mark.

Slowly Finella turned away and walked back into the restaurant. She found Darley ordering his dinner. She looked at him, wide-eyed, critical; thought, as she had done when she first saw him, how changed he was. So *matured* . . . so solemn. Only when he smiled was he the same young, enthusiastic man she had married.

He rose politely as she joined him. She sat down and explained about Barbara being out.

'But I have a key,' she said. 'I . . . can get in.'

The waiter brought Darley's soup. He crumbled a roll in thin, nervy fingers, and kept glancing at Finella. *His wife* . . . he was sitting here in the Berkeley beside his wife and she was the most beautiful girl in the room. It was part of his dream-come-true. Yet somehow it was hollow . . . an elusive happiness. There was nothing that he could grasp. She seemed miles away from him.

He said:

'I really feel I owe you an apology for dashing in on you like this, Finella. Damned unfortunate you didn't get my cable. Just luck, of course . . . finding you here at all. Do you come here often?'

She could not tell him that the Berkeley was one of Gil's favourite 'haunts'. She stared at her evening bag and said:

'Quite a bit.'

'I thought you'd like to be here with me tonight . . . because we chose it . . . for our wedding.'

'Yes,' she said, her cheeks burning pink.

'It's . . . pretty wonderful, seeing you again after all this time.'

She made a desperate effort to play her part.

'Absolutely wonderful. It's been so long . . .'

Now he looked at her and she looked at him. Both were nervous and glanced away again almost immediately. He muttered:

'I can't quite believe it . . . yet . . .'

'How is the arm? Where did you get the wound? What treatment are you getting?' She plunged into conversation about his arm and he answered all her questions.

He had first been wounded in the advance on Rome. Didn't she remember . . . he had written from hospital . . . then it had healed and he'd gone back into the field . . . but it broke out now and again and he had to have a splinter removed. He had one taken out three weeks ago. The arm was in process of healing now. He had indefinite leave but must attend a military hospital . . . near Godalming if possible . . . for final treatment. He couldn't use the arm properly yet. And so on.

Finella sympathized . . . genuinely concerned for him. She had time now to see how tired he looked; there were lines under his eyes; his bright brown hair had darkened and thinned a little on the temples. His movements were jerky . . . self-conscious. He was a man with 'nerves'. He had nothing in common with the care-free boy with whom she had fallen in love . . . she and that boy had done nothing but laugh, dance, spin along in fast cars, think of themselves and their pleasures. War . . . foreign service . . . terrible things had altered Darley.

She knew he must find her very changed, too. Much more difficult.

How difficult he was finding both his wife and this critical moment in their lives, Darley could not have told her. But he took his cue from her and talked ... They went on talking about their families, their old friends, snatching feverishly at any subject that they could share.

When that meal ended Finella felt almost hysterical. It seemed so ... so *absurd*, she thought ... that her husband should have been with her already over an hour and they had not exchanged a single kiss. She was grateful for that, at least. She had kissed Gil when he called for her at Barbie's house. Kissed him and felt her pulses stir. (Oh, Darley, Darley, you have been away too long, my dear ... and come back too late ...)

The farce continued.

Laughing a little over some forced joke, still chatting, the Darley Martingtons took that taxi out to Bedford Gardens. Driving through the starry spring night ... warm, freakishly warm for April ... they sat quite a distance apart. Darley was smoking. Finella in her corner watched the red point of his cigarette glow as he inhaled the smoke. She plunged again into conversation. Even that seemed unreal to her. It was as though she had not said one sincere thing. When he had questioned her about his mother she had said 'how kind she had been'.

She had not been able to say *'She hates me ... and your friend Rachel hates me, too. I've been so unhappy down there'* ... She might have said it to a husband she knew and who understood her. But what understanding was there between Darley and herself? Only the faint sad echo of a hurried engagement and wedding five years ago ... and those endless, futile letters which had become more of a habit than a pleasure.

Suddenly Darley flung away his cigarette. He leaned nearer Finella ... his senses stirred by the scent from her hair ... her nearness. He said:

'Fin ... we're together again ... do you realize it?'

She caught her breath sharply.

'Yes...'

'It was cruel having to leave you that day ... I loathed it. It's been a damnable affair ... all those wasted years of our marriage,' he said, his voice rasping with sudden pain. 'But now I'm back. You've waited for me all this time ... I know you have ... Fin, my darling...'

She shrank back a little. Her heart pounded. She was by nature frank and open. She did not like deceit. Yet she could not say to this husband who had come back to her ... *'I got tired of waiting ... Gil came ... Gil made me love him ....'*

Then she felt Darley's strong right arm go round her, pull her roughly to him.

'Oh, God, darling . . . *darling*. . .' he said.

He kissed her mouth like a man dying of thirst. She leaned against him weakly, more frightened than thrilled by his desperate kiss . . . yet with all the woman in her wanting to show some kindness, some mercy, to the soldier who had returned. But for herself she saw no mercy and no hope. she was in a trap . . . laid for her by her own youth and inexperience. The long waiting had thrown a wall between her and her first love.

He found her lips almost unbearably sweet in his aching need of her . . . his desperate wish to make incarnate his old recurrent dream of reunion with his wife.

He did not release her until he felt her straining away from him, gasping. He heard her whispered appeal:

'Please . . . no more . . .'

He let her go then and, half ashamed of his lost control, laughed a little.

'Sorry darling. Can't quite keep my head . . . tonight. I'm crazy with happiness . . . getting back to you.'

She said:

'Yes . . . of course . . . I . . . I . . . it's all a bit startling really, isn't it?'

And she, too, laughed . . . but in the darkness her face was a pale mask of misery with woeful lips and troubled eyes. An almost ridiculous prayer surged up from her heart:

'God, make me *want* to be sweet to him . . . help me to forget Gil . . . and all these years between us . . .'

Darley did not touch or kiss her again either then or on the return journey. They talked once more of petty, unimportant things . . . anything but themselves . . . while Finella packed her case and left a note for Barbie and wondered hysterically if Barbie would believe it . . . or half think she had gone away with Gil. But she would never have done that . . . never. She had always wanted to play the straight game with Darley.

She must play it now.

But when finally she stood facing her husband in their beautiful bedroom in the Berkeley . . . all the old embarrassment and confusion of spirit returned to her.

Darley was walking restlessly round the room, looking at the flowers . . . there were vases of red carnations on the dressing-table and mantelpiece. Glorious carnations and delicate green fern.

'I cabled to them here to have these waiting for you,' at last he blurted out, stopping to face Finella. 'I meant to buy you a spray to wear, too . . . you always loved flowers . . . I always gave you orchids when we went out to dance . . . didn't I?'

Finella nodded.

'Yes . . . marvellous of you . . . the carnations

are wonderful, Darley . . .' she said. But she felt her husband's gaze rest resentfully on the orchids she was wearing. Gil's present. With cold, nervous fingers she suddenly unpinned the spray and tossed it on to the bed.

The room was warm, luxurious, charming; golden with soft-shaded lights, and through the half-open door she caught a glimpse of the pale green bathroom; the little hall with its big hanging cupboards. She remembered how she had as a girl always longed to stay in this hotel and it was because she had once told Darley so that he had meant to bring her here on their wedding night.

If only that *other* Finella could come back, she thought in despair; that immature, happy-go-lucky girl who had thrilled madly to a young subaltern's kisses. Between them now lay inexplicable shadows.

She was here tonight with a *stranger* . . . a tired-looking, nervy man in shabby khaki uniform and his arm in a sling. A man who had kissed her in the taxi with a fever of longing that she wanted to assuage . . . but could not.

Suddenly Darley took her hand and drew her to one of the beds which had been neatly turned down for the night. They sat on the edge, gingerly, uncomfortably. He said:

'Darling, I'm afraid this homecoming has been a bit . . . too sudden for you. It's all . . . rather bad luck . . . you not getting my cable.'

53

'Oh, it's . . . all right . . .' she stammered.

Darley persisted:

'That chap you were with . . . is he . . . an old friend? I don't think you mentioned him in any of your letters.'

'Didn't I?' Finella looked at the tip of her shoe, struggling for composure. 'Oh, I . . . know him quite well . . .'

Darley saw the swift scarlet run to the roots of the tawny hair . . . and immediately a thrill of pure jealousy smote him. The first unformed suspicion that in his absence this lovely wife of his might . . . *might* conceivably have grown fond of some other man. *This* man who had been dancing with her here tonight, for instance. But such a suspicion was too dangerous to be fostered for an instant. No, he dared not let himself think that way. He'd be a fool to spoil tonight by a jealousy which probably had no foundations. Oh, damn it all, this was not what he had meant this night of love to be. There was no spontaneous rapture between them. Since he had kissed her in the taxi his whole body had been fired with passionate longing that he had kept under iron control. He kept telling himself that she was still very young and inexperienced and that he must be patient . . . tender with her . . . a fellow who had lived amongst other men for so long was apt to be rough . . . to forget the old subtlety and polish and good manners . . . all part of an English gentleman's training.

Gentleman! 'Good lord...' thought Darley Martington ... and smiled a crooked sort of smile ... knowing that he felt the most primitive desire to pick this wife of his up in his arms, get out of this civilized hotel, this crowded city, and disappear with her into some wilderness where he would have his woman to himself ... demand from her complete, absolute surrender.

Instead, he played gently with the long slim hand he held, looking thoughtfully at the ring he had placed on it five long years ago.

'I used to imagine this moment ... out there in all the dust and heat of the desert...' he said. 'Or waiting in a trench in the mud and rain ... for an advance ... or listening to the whine of shells coming over to our lines. And in the hospital, too ... where it was quiet ... I used to think of you and our marriage. You've been my wife for a long time ... and yet we don't really know anything about each other, do we?'

She looked at him piteously.

'No, Darley ... we don't.'

'We'll just have to start learning, my sweet. We'll have to help ... each other ...'

His eyes ... brilliant with suppressed emotion ... held hers for a moment. She felt herself trembling from head to foot. She seemed to hear Gil speaking ... Gil, who only this evening during dinner, had said:

'If and when that husband of yours comes

back . . . couldn't you stave off living with him . . . I mean . . . give me a chance as well as him? You don't love him. Why not face up to it . . . ?'

But she couldn't face up to it. Now that the crisis had come she felt helpless and weak. She was *in love* with Gil Bryte. But she loved Darley . . . or *had* loved him once very much. He was her husband and he had come back to her as a lover. She was up against something stronger than her own personal desires . . . something elemental . . . almost frightening in its intensity.

Darley was speaking, a new rough note in his voice:

'Tell me you still love me, Fin. There isn't any other fellow . . . is there?'

For the life of her she could not answer. And the man, seeing what lay in her eyes, felt the blindness of rage and jealousy overcome him again. He said, through his teeth:

'Don't answer. I don't want to know. I've been through hell . . . and come out of it, back to you. I want my wife. Finella, darling . . . *for heaven's sake* . . .'

His arm was around her again. She shrank back just for a moment whispering:

'Darley, Darley . . . try and understand . . .'

But the moment for understanding . . . for plain speaking . . . for actual recognisation of the fact that the years had come between him and this wife of his . . . was not now. Once more his lips touched hers . . . and this time there was no turning back. She lay quiet—her satiny hair spread on the pillows, drowned in the relentless tide of his passion. She did not fight against him. This was Darley's hour. And while his uninjured arm was thrown across her breast, imprisoning her, and his lips, rough, urgent, bruised the creamy whiteness of her throat, he whispered incoherently . . . words she only half heard:

'Mine . . . darling, darling . . . you're so lovely . . . Fin, Finella, kiss me . . . kiss me as you used to do . . . Fin, my darling, it's the beginning of a new life for us . . . oh, darling, *darling* . . . how I've wanted you . . .'

Till, gradually, his passion lit some semblance of fire in her . . . and her lips returned the kisses and she was warm and yielding in his arms. He was charming. His desire, his tenderness could not fail to disarm her . . . to draw her for a little while into his own world of illusions and dreams.

Later . . . so much later . . . while he slept like a child . . . his arm still imprisoning her . . . she lay awake staring into the darkness and felt, incongruously, a hateful disloyalty *toward the other man*. In a hopeless confusion of mind and heart, the tears rolled hotly, silently, down her cheeks. But Darley . . . the husband who had come back . . . did not stir . . . unconscious that his wife wept desolately all through the night.

CHAPTER SIX

Finella sat at the dressing-table in the hotel bedroom 'doing' her face. She decided that it needed rather a lot of 'doing' this morning. She looked deadly pale and her eyes were heavy-shadowed from crying. She had already smoked three cigarettes since she woke up. She knew it was too many. Darley had commented on it.

'I can't get used to the sight of you smoking, darling. Like a little chimney-pot, too. You never used to.'

No—she never used to. She used not to do so many things that she did now. And most decidedly she was not used to this incredible business of having a husband and sharing a bedroom with him.

She put down powder-puff and lipstick—turned round and stared about her. So many evidences of 'a husband'. Darley's pipe and oblong-shaped wrist-watch on the table between the twin beds. His brushes and hair cream on the chest of drawers. His uniform thrown over the back of a chair.

The April sunshine filtered through the filmy net curtains, making the carnations glow a burning red. It was not quiet here, for there came the steady roar of traffic in Piccadilly. London was very much alive at this hour ...

eleven o'clock. But Finella did not feel alive. She was too numbed mentally; amazed at Darley, at herself, at last night which had held so much sweetness and bitterness, too ... held the broken laughter they had shared ... the tears that had been hers alone.

Finella heard the sound of cheerful whistling from the bathroom. A little lump came into her throat. She covered her eyes with the back of one slim hand as though the sunshine hurt them. She whispered:

'What a hopeless affair. Oh, what, *what* shall I do?'

The door opened. Darley came in. He was freshly shaven and looked much younger this morning; his brown hair curled like a boy's, before he flattened it down. He approached Finella with an almost touchingly shy expression in his handsome eyes, and said:

'Darling ... could you put the sling on for me? It ties at the back.'

She rose and forced a smile.

'Of course ...'

She tied the sling, then he turned and put both hands on her shoulders. Like himself, she was still in a dressing-gown. He looked with eyes growing suddenly dark and passionate at the filmy lace at her throat, then ran one hand gently down her back. She was so lovely, he thought, in that 'dusty pink' coloured satin thing she was wearing with a sash round the slender waist. Lovely and infinitely desirable and—*his*.

He said huskily:

'Fin ... darling ... last night was so heavenly. *You* were heavenly. Fin, do you love me?'

With all her soul she longed to raise her eyes to his and say 'Yes.' It would have been magical ... this ... the homecoming, the bridal and the future honeymoon ... were it not for those years of separation and ... for Gil. She hated herself because she still fretted for Gil ... hated herself for resenting Darley's mastership ... all that he had taken ... all that she had given ... a little because she had a nice woman's desire to give ... mostly because she owed it to him after all he had been through, and he had wanted her so much.

But the fact that he had come home and—so to speak—dragged her out of Gil's arms into his own—could not wipe out the last few months when she had been Gil's girl-friend—Gil's constant companion. He had looked after her well; understood her needs. Oh, what *was* there in Gil? Something a little harsh ... sardonic ... which had piqued and held her. She knew, for instance, that he was not to be controlled by her or by any other girl. He fascinated her because she was only a 'part of his life'. The rest of it ... his strength, his forceful character, his shrewd brain belonged to his job. To his ambitions to become a great director in the world of industry; and to enter Parliament like his father. Oh, they had talked ... how they had talked, every time they met ... arguing about world affairs ... and the aftermath of the war. More often than not Gil talked right above her head. About state control ... cartels ... Trades Unions ... a lot of things she only half understood. Sometimes her feeble little comments and ideas made him roar with laughter. He would say:

'Nella, you're so ignorant, you pretty thing! ... like most nicely brought-up, well-educated girls. You know a lot about Rembrandt or Beethoven, the great men of Art, and nothing about the giants of industry. That's what has made the world what it is today. The younger generation may be able to pick out a genuine painting or recognize a first-class composer ... but they put the wrong fellow into Parliament. Ah, but I adore you, Nella ... I want to teach you ... show you *my* way of living...'

She had listened for hours, fascinated ... well aware that he despised people like the Martingtons ... wanted to see the end of them and their autocracy ... yet perversely coveted their social status and their veneer. A queer, perverse creature altogether, Gil Bryte. Finella had been magnetized from the start by his individualism. Sure of him one moment ... afraid of losing him in another. And now that her husband had come home, ready to adore ...

she still could not bear to let Gil go out of her life.

Yet there was something quite determined about this new Darley which made it difficult for her to deal with *him*. This morning, indeed, she felt incapable of dealing with anybody.

She only knew that she did not want Darley to make love to her now ... the whole thing was too bitterly frustrating and unfair ... to them both.

Darley was pulling her gently towards him.

'Fin ... you haven't answered ... do you still love me this morning as much as you did last night?'

She gasped ... and nodded. Here was a way out ... she could answer *that* truthfully, now.

'Yes ... oh yes ... oh, darling ... mind my face ... my lipstick.'

Laughing, she pushed him away. He let her go reluctantly, worshipping her from the satin-red-brown head to the small, slender feet.

'All right ... I'll respect the make-up. Let's get cracking, shall we, darling, out into the fresh air. It's stuffy up here.'

Gladly she escaped to the bathroom to finish her dressing. Desperately she thought:

'I *must* speak to Gil ... 'phone him ... I must find out if he really is terribly annoyed about last night. But I couldn't help it. Oh, I wish we could be friends ... I don't want to lose him ... if only Darley won't be too possessive...'

But that was nonsense ... of *course* Gil and she could never be 'friends'. Darley wouldn't permit it, anyhow. He *was* possessive. He had a right to be. But she resented the right. And she despised her own weakness. She wished she were a harder character, less sympathetic; able to tell Darley outright that she had changed in her affections ... and that she was stifled by and afraid of this new, intimate life he wished to lead with her. But he was so sweet, and he had fought for her ... for his country all these years. She *couldn't* hit him a mortal blow right at the start. She must let him down lightly ... if she were to let him down at all. Meanwhile ... things might settle themselves.

Finella began to entertain the hope that all her problems would be solved for her by time. A forlorn, desperate hope.

Darley, on the other hand, believed that half his troubles were over; that he had been wrong to think, last night, that Finella had changed (except that she was older and less immature, of course).

But she had been adorable to him ... and if she seemed shy, uneasy ... it was understandable. Marriage was not easy ... a girl like Fin who had lived alone all these years had to get used to a husband ... adjust her emotions accordingly. He must be tolerant and make excuses if she made him feel at moments that she was not *utterly* his, in mind as well as body.

When she came back into the room, he admired her grey flannel suit and the grey 'floppy' felt hat on the tawny head.

'You look lovely! I love that get-up,' he said enthusiastically.

'Oh, it's very old,' she said, avoiding his admiring gaze. 'I . . . have nothing new. N-no coupons. I . . . ought to have a trousseau but . . . everything's so awkward. . . .'

'I don't care,' broke in Darley. 'It doesn't matter what you wear. You look pretty smooth to me, my Fin.'

She bit her lower lip nervously.

Her mind was on the time . . . on the thought that Gil Bryte would be in his office now . . . if only she could get away from Darley and make a telephone call. She didn't mean to be beastly . . . to waver in her resolution to give this marriage a chance . . . yet . . . she must make sure Gil wasn't angry.

Darley had not asked her what she wanted to do today. He had just taken it for granted she would wish him to go down to Godalming after lunch and see his mother and stay there for a few days. And of course that was the right thing. But in her present critical state of mind . . . to have to face up to her mother-in-law . . . and, possibly, Rachel Webb . . . and pretend to like it . . . that was asking almost too much.

64

In despair Finella watched Darley make an attempt to tidy his suitcase. The sight of him struggling with that one good hand of his roused all the intrinsic kindliness in her nature.

'Let me . . .' she said, and made the effort to create order out of disorder.

Darley watched her, full of tenderness. It was good to see her, his wife, doing little odd jobs for him like this . . . a real thrill. He said, gaily:

'Any good at darning Fin, my sweet? I've got a nice lot of holes in my socks.'

She coloured, feeling a trifle cross with herself because she was incompetent in the domestic sense.

'I'm hopeless at darning,' she muttered.

She had been driving an ambulance for five years . . . and before that she had been an artist . . . she had never really thought about settling down to cooking, housework, or *darning*. She wondered how many girls did think about marriage that way . . . or if they deliberately avoided the issue, hid the practical side under the glamour.

Darley laughed good-naturedly.

'I'll let you off, darling. I dare say Mother will oblige. She prides herself on her sewing.'

Finella's cheeks grew hotter still.

'No, of course not. It's my job, I suppose. I'll do it. I'd rather not ask your mother,' she said curtly.

He gave her a somewhat surprised look and

stuck his pipe in the corner of his mouth.

'How do you and mamma get on?' he asked reflectively.

'All right . . .' Finella forced the words.

'Of course you're different generations and won't always see eye to eye,' added Darley cheerfully. 'But I know she is very fond of you.'

'Is she?' This time Finella could not keep the bitterness out of her voice.

But Darley was deaf to it. He was in far too good a humour this golden spring morning to be aggressive or cantankerous about any subject on earth, and he was madly in love with this young wife of his . . . this warm, sweet creature who was still so much of a wonder and mystery to him. He felt almost humble before her; even *gauche*. He took the pipe from his mouth and drew nearer her.

'One kiss before we go out . . . yes?'

Obediently Finella raised her face. He drew her against him; gently at first but caught fire from her nearness. That embrace became prolonged and more than he had meant it to be. Blindly, dumbly, he urged response from her, but suddenly she broke away, breathless, trembling from head to foot.

'Oh, don't . . . let me *go* . . .'

At once Darley released her, once more master of himself. But he, too, was white and shaking now. He turned away.

'Sorry, darling . . . you're much too

66

attractive.'

'Oh, don't be so silly...' she stammered. But she knew that he was hurt. She thought:

'Is it always going to be like this? It'll drive us both ... quite crazy...'

Darley, kicking himself mentally for letting his long-repressed emotions run away with him, thought:

'It isn't quite the same for her ... as for me. I'm a tactless brute.'

Yet as he walked with her to the lift and she began to talk and laugh in a high-pitched voice that suggested more hysteria than humour, he felt some of his gaiety evaporate. Last night's suspicions returned.

This was not quite the blindly loving girl who had clung to him so broken-heartedly before he left England. What had happened to her meanwhile? Had there been another man in her life? *What did he really know about that life?*

And again there flashed into his mind the memory of her as he had first seen her last night ... dancing so gaily, eyes brilliant and happy. A Finella obviously confident of herself and her beauty and allure ... in the arms of that big, dark-haired civilian fellow ... Bryte. *What was there between Finella and Gil Bryte?*

CHAPTER SEVEN

Going down in the lift they were joined by two American officers. Finella was staring blindly ahead of her. But the Americans stared at her. Darley watched them. He saw the undisguised admiration in their eyes. He looked broodingly at the slender figure of his wife and began to realize how very attractive she was. He also thought, grimly:

'I'd better get wise to myself. No use coming home and starting to be madly jealous. *That* won't make for happiness.'

But jealous he was. Not of the Americans who would probably never see Finella again. But of this unknown man with whom she had gone out last night. The man who called her 'Nella'. Then as the lift stopped and Darley followed Finella out of it, he reproached himself.

'Ass ... don't become one of these punk husbands who can't bear their wives to have a platonic friendship with other chaps ...'

Back snapped the little devilish thought:

'*If* it's platonic ...'

They reached the ground floor.

Finella turned to her husband in the vestibule.

'Can you wait a moment, Darley ... I want to 'phone Barbie.'

'Surely, darling,' he smiled. 'Want some change?'

She gave him an almost timid, deprecating little smile in response which he did not understand, and said:

'No thanks . . . I have some.'

He stood waiting for her, thinking, frowning at his thoughts, wishing he knew more about her . . . her *real*, inner life. What was the use of holding her in his arms, sharing with her the loveliest intimacies of marriage . . . and knowing nothing of what was in her mind? That was what their long separation had done to them. He wondered, a trifle bitterly, how many other men were coming home to wives who had for five long years led their own lives, long weeks and months from one season to another . . . which were a closed book . . . For what could a man really divulge from all those airletters . . . mere words. *Last night I went out with a man called Bill So-and-So* . . . or *Last Sunday I was at a cocktail party* . . . or *Last night I dined and danced with a man I don't think you know . . . in the Irish Guards.* And so on. Parties, dinners, dances . . . moments shared with other men, most of whom the husband had not met. It was bound to be. A lovely young wife couldn't be expected to enter a convent while her husband fought for her . . . couldn't sit at home and knit every night . . . must have some outlet.

Husbands overseas had outlets, too . . . leaves

in a place like Cairo or Beirut ... exotic evenings on the Nile ... moments shared with girls out there ... in the Services ... in hospitals ... pretty wives of civilians living abroad ... nothing in it ... just reaction after the weary weeks of relentless advance ... or unforgettable retreat. A soldier's life. But he couldn't write about them to his wife at home. It would sound different from what it really was ... in a letter. That was the worst of letters ... of a separate existence. On both sides, it boiled down to the same hopeless inability to belong, body, heart and soul to each other. As they wanted to belong. Had *meant* to belong ... right at the start.

What if Finella *had* had her moments with other chaps. It didn't mean she didn't love him, her husband. It oughtn't to matter much now if she loved him completely and only, *now* that he was at home. (Yet it did matter ... frightfully ... damn it all ...)

Darley wiped little beads of perspiration from his forehead and fingered his uniform cap with a nervous hand. Yes, damn it all ... one felt a quite ridiculous jealousy when one was in love with one's wife. *And he hated those years Finella had spent without him;* resented every hour of them.

In one of the telephone boxes, Finella spoke to her sister a trifle shortly.

'Yes, it was Darley ... he came home

unexpectedly. We stayed at the Berkeley ... we're here now ... but going down to Lady M. after lunch. No, Barbie ... I don't know what our future plans are. I'll let you know. Must fly, darling ... good-bye.'

Barbara tried to keep her ... eager to know more of Darley's homecoming. But Finella wanted another number. Gil's number at the office ... she *had* to speak to him ... and yet she hated it ... with Darley outside there, waiting for her.

When at last she got through to the busy Mr. Bryte, her long slim body was trembling with nervous tension. She said:

'Yes, it's Nella ... Gil, I—'

'Why, *hello,* you're the last person I expected to speak to this morning,' interrupted Gil Bryte's voice ... curt, even acid. 'Don't tell me you've shed the conquering hero already.'

Finella blushed an angry red.

'Don't say those things ... I hate you when you're so ... so beastly, Gil ...'

'No, you don't, darling ... you like it—'

'Gil, if you're going to be a beast I shall ring off.'

'My sweet Nella ... if I'm a bit raw, it's not to be wondered at. My evening ... my dinner ... my dance ... and in walks a mere husband and carts you off ... a little rude, if I may say so, of the Major ... a little abrupt. No invitation to me to remain. Not the typical

71

Martington manners, surely?'

Finella said:

'You *are* being absolutely revolting, Gil. You have no understanding ... or you'd see that Darley couldn't want a third on his first night home. He'd cabled me to meet him here.'

'Did you know that?'

'Of course not, or would I have arranged to meet *you?*'

'Well, it was hardly an agreeable evening for me.'

'But you do understand, surely?'

'That the husband has returned and the boy-friend is "out" ... yes ... perfectly. Why have you rung me up?'

'Because you went off in a huff and you're still in one, Gil, and I ... I don't want it that way.'

'Which way *do* you want it, Nella?'

His voice was dangerously silky now. She knew him so well. She knew that he was in one of his black rages. She could see those cold, penetrating eyes of his half shut ... under black, lowered brows. Why did he dominate her so? Why was she fascinated by him even while she was infuriated? He could be so insolent, so overbearing ... yet she did not want to lose him altogether.

In a choked voice, she said:

'Oh, I don't know. I can't explain. I'm in a frightful muddle in my mind. You know how fond I am of you, Gil!'

72

'"Fond" was not what I labelled your feeling for me, my dear. Don't let's quibble. You *were* in love with me . . .'

She clenched her teeth.

'I know . . . I know . . . oh, you're driving me crazy. I can't help Darley coming home, can I?'

'I presume you . . . stayed together last night?'

'Yes.'

She was thankful he could not see the burning scarlet now of her face, her throat. But she could sense his primitive anger . . . surging at her . . . over the very wires. His voice came thickly:

'You can't do this to me, Nella. I won't be played with. Go and tell your heroic husband that you want your freedom and come to me at once, or . . . I'm through. Do you hear me? *Through.*'

She grew suddenly cold and very white. Misery flooded her very being, She said:

'I . . . asked you to let me . . . give Darley a chance. To be my friend . . . for a while. Oh, Gil . . . I need your friendship. We know each other so well. Gil, don't walk out on me. I'm absolutely wretched. Help me . . . to do what's right.'

Silence a moment. She called his name desperately.

'Gil . . . are you there?'

His voice came back to her as cold as her own now.

'Yes, I'm here. Though why I don't tell you to get out and finish this thing, lord knows. You ask me to help you to do what's right. Me, when I'm so crazy about you that last night I walked around London until morning ... trying to shut out the memory of you ... and him.' Bryte laughed. It was not a pleasant laugh to hear.

Finella whispered:

'Gil, forgive me ... I do care for you ... dreadfully. But I can't walk out on Darley now ... I want to do what's right ... and ...'

'And keep me, too ...' he finished for her. 'So what?'

'Oh, all right ... say good-bye ... let's end it ...' She caught her breath on a sob. 'I think that would be best. I can't bear any more.'

Silence a moment. She swallowed hard. Then came Gil's voice again ... this time very tender. (Oh, she knew how exquisitely gentle and patient Gil could be when he wanted to, and it was those moments that held her ... wiped out for her the rough brutality which at other times made her shy away from him.)

'Poor little Nella,' he said. 'Poor child ... trying to be good ... to uphold the honour and tradition of the family. Okay, so you shall. Far be it from me to play the villain of the piece. At least, not just now. Let Martington have his hour. Somehow I feel it will be short and sweet. You'll come to me in the end. I'll be waiting. Remember that. And ... darling ... are you there?'

'Yes...' she could scarcely say the word. The tears were running down her cheeks. (She was appalled to know that she was crying. Darley would see. She must control herself. She *must*. Oh, cruel Gil, who bound her to him with cords of steel ... she knew that she was going to have a desperate fight with herself ... as well as with him ... if she was to go on doing the 'right thing'.)

'Just remember that I love you,' said Gil. 'Good-bye.'

Biting her lips, Finella put down the receiver. Hastily she wiped her eyes and dabbed her face with her powder-puff, then ran a lipstick over her mouth. Whatever happened Darley mustn't see her upset like this ... It was mad and hopeless, anyhow, the whole affair, she told herself. She must not allow her feelings for Gil to assume such proportions and control her life. She must abide by her own resolve to 'give her marriage a chance.'

But one thing she had, at least, discovered from that 'phone call. Gil was not going to let her go; no matter how angry he was.

She went back to Darley, doing her best to smile and be gay.

'Okay,' she said. 'Barbie sends her love.'

'I hardly remember that sister of yours, you know,' said Darley, his eyes brightening as he saw the friendly warmth in his wife's brilliant eyes. 'Later on we must take her out. And I'd like to see my nephew-by-marriage ... young Mark, isn't it?'

Finella nodded. She was having a struggle to go on smiling and to make that heart of hers settle down ... it had beaten with such foolish passion in that telephone booth.

They started to walk out of the hotel. The April sunshine was golden and inviting. There was all the freshness of spring in the air. Darley felt good to be alive; to be home; in London, with his wife again. It was indeed the beginning of his long-delayed honeymoon, he thought happily.

A uniformed hotel employee came running after them.

'Excuse me, sir ...'

Darley and Finella turned their heads.

'The lady hasn't paid for her calls...' the man said apologetically.

'Oh, bother...' muttered Finella.

'Here you are, darling ... I've got it...' Darley held out some coppers.

The man said:

'Eightpence, please, sir. Two calls.'

Darley paid. Finella blushed a bright angry pink. She had been in such a turmoil of spirit ... she had forgotten to pay ... Now, of course, Darley knew she had not telephoned only to Barbara.

Darley linked arms with her and walked with

her into Piccadilly. Without undue suspicion he said:

'Who else did you 'phone darling?'

She hesitated and was lost. Darley then noticed the hesitation—and the bright flush. She wanted very much in that moment to tell him the truth! To say: *'I' phoned Gil Bryte . . . but I said I wanted to be friends with him . . . and I meant it . . .'* Instead, frightened of such a truth and its possible effect upon Darley, she stumbled into a falsehood.

'I . . . oh, only a friend I had to get on to . . . someone you wouldn't know.'

Darley was silent. He had made up his mind not to be jealous of Finella's past nor indeed of her present. But he knew somehow, instinctively, that she had spoken to the man of last night and the happiness faded out of his eyes again.

The girl glanced almost timidly at Darley's clean-cut profile. What was he thinking? He was a reserved man, this husband whom she knew so little. She was beginning to feel how little she did, indeed, know about him and his innermost thoughts. She made a big effort to be very charming to him, to make his first day home a good one. She said:

'Let's go shopping. Or would that bore you, d-darling?' She stammered a little over the unaccustomed endearment. Day after day she had written that word 'darling' . . . and it had become stale and ordinary from much use. Now, face to face with him, it meant so much more.

He turned to her, struggling against his inclination to question her further about that second telephone call.

'I was going to suggest a shopping expedition myself,' he said. 'I haven't brought you much home. Only some odd bits of silk and Italian leather-work. But I want you to have a real present. I have been waiting for this chance. Wouldn't you like a brooch ... a clip ... or some good ear-rings?'

'Oh no ... really, Darley ... nothing extravagant.'

He loved her for that ... he always had liked Finella for her absolute lack of the mercenary streak. He abhorred the 'gold-digging' type of woman.

'I want to give you something really lovely,' he said. 'Come on, let's go and look at the jewellers in Bond Street.'

She felt that she did not deserve a handsome present. She shook her head, but he pressed her on. Then she said:

'I want to give *you* something too ... I ... I haven't spent nearly all my allowance ... you must choose a lovely present, too, Darley.'

'You darling,' he murmured. Then a sudden thought struck him. He added: 'And by the way, has Mother ever discussed the family

78

fortunes with you? Finances are a bit bad, I believe. Her last letter worried me a bit. Mother's a funny person—always had a bit of a passion for investment and I haven't always seen eye to eye with her. Don't much fancy her broker-fellow. But I'm a soldier ... never dabble on the Stock Exchange. I left that to my father. Now Mother has control of most of his capital. A life interest, of course. Has she told you things were a bit rocky?'

'No. She never talked about finances to me,' said Finella, and wondered a little wryly what Darley would have thought of his mother's real attitude towards her. She had been treated by Lady Martington all these years with the utmost courtesy and correctness, but made to feel a stranger. As for the question of money—it had never interested Finella, anyhow. She would far rather have had a lovely picture or book than a jewel.

'Oh, well,' said Darley, 'I'm home now to help see to things. Darling, we won't stay too long at the Manor. I want to get cracking on a little place of our own. Don't you agree?'

That encouraged Finella.

'Oh, Darley, I'd much prefer that ... I mean I ... I love the Manor ... but your mother manages it so much better than I could.'

'Darling. I sympathize. Besides, I wouldn't really want to turn Mother out, although Father left me the place ... she's been there all her life.

She'd loathe going, and if I stay in the Army I'll be pushed around the countryside, anyhow. But we might try and find a tiny flat in town for the moment.'

'I'd love that,' said Finella.

Anything, she thought, rather than live at the Manor with Lady Martington.

A little more heartened, she walked with Darley through the pleasant sunshine and into Bond Street.

CHAPTER EIGHT

Dinner at the Manor was over.

Finella sat rather silent, listening to an animated conversation between her husband and Rachel Webb. It had been a foregone conclusion in her mind that her mother-in-law would have Rachel here to dinner tonight. Old General Webb had come with her. 'So that dear Darley shouldn't be the only man...' Lady Martington had announced. (Mrs. Webb was an invalid with arthritis of the hip and never went out nowadays.) But Finella knew that it was merely an excuse on Lady Martington's part to have her beloved god-daughter in the house. It was obvious to the girl, who was acutely sensitive, that Darley's mother wished to throw Rachel into his lap as much as possible.

80

To outward appearances, Lady Martington had been charming ever since Finella and Darley had arrived. The biggest and best bedroom facing South had been prepared for the pair—a handsome room full of Queen Anne furniture and with soft powder-blue carpet and curtains. The house was gay and golden with great bowls of daffodils. A special dinner had been cooked ... Darley's favourite meal ... pheasant ... (supplied by General Webb, who at the age of seventy-four was still a fine shot).

Finella looked around her. Darley sat at the head of the table, in his father's place ... it was the first time she had ever seen him in a dinner-jacket. He had wanted to change. It was so good to be in 'civvies' again after years of uniform. He wore a soft pleated white shirt. He looked handsome and debonair, but a bit tired. His arm was throbbing again tonight ... but he was in excellent form, enjoying being back in his old home ... chatting vivaciously with all of them.

His gaze travelled more often than not to the young wife who sat beside him, and she was well aware of the deep passionate love behind that gaze, and conscious, too, of the fact that it worried rather than flattered her. Yet he was so essentially *nice;* he had been so delightful to her all day. He had insisted on spending a lot of money, and the result was the beautiful ice-blue aquamarine clip which she wore tonight with her severely cut black dress which made her look so dazzlingly fair and slim.

Lady Martington, too, wore black. Critically, Finella regarded her mother-in-law. Smiling as usual (there was something so hateful about that smile, she always felt), yet Margaret Martington was a handsome woman with the straight classic features Darley had inherited and with a hard mouth and shrewd pair of short-sighted eyes which had none of his warmth. From what Finella had gathered, talking to people in the village, it was Sir George who had been the popular member of this family and Darley's nature was more like his.

Rachel Webb . . . at her best tonight, wore a long black evening skirt with red and gold brocade tunic. She was 'all over' Darley, thought Finella a trifle cynically. Smiling at him laughing at his jokes, interesting him with all the sporting news of the district. They seemed to get on very well. Finella could see that it must have been a bitter blow to Rachel when Darley married an entire stranger, like herself, Finella.

The Old General was a nice old man, if a bit too hearty and garrulous. He talked a lot to Finella, eyeing her admiringly with the bloodshot eye of an old hound. She listened to him patiently. But she knew that all the time she was haunted by the ghost of Gil Bryte . . . wondering what *he* was doing tonight . . . and if his thoughts were of *her*.

Lady Martington looked with pride and

pleasure at her son. But it was a pleasure diminished by two salient facts. One, that he was married and so obviously in love with this wife of his and Lady Martington could never forgive him marrying Finella; the other, the knowledge that she must sooner or later tell him what atrocious luck she had had lately with her investments. She was aware that Darley knew little or nothing about 'the City', but he wouldn't be too pleased to find that she had sold out some of his father's investments which were 'gilt-edged' in order to take a gamble. And she had lost. This gambling was Margaret Martington's one vice, and it had got the better of her. Of course she did not blame herself. She blamed her stockbroker. *He* had advised the buying and the selling. *He* was responsible for the fact that the Martington's capital was considerably reduced at present, and that Darley's allowance would have to be cut.

Uneasily she glanced at her son ... then with a deeper regret at Rachel. Dear Rachel. If only *she* were Mrs. Darley instead of that little outsider with her pretty face and penniless relations. *She* was only a liability to Darley. Whereas Rachel's father was a man of means, and Rachel, an heiress ... could have done so much for Darley.

Margaret Martington had arranged this dinner-party to amuse her son ... as a sort of welcome home ... and also because she wished to put off the evil moment when she must tell him about their reduced means. But she had had to bite hard on her lips when this afternoon Darley had so gaily shown her the clip he had bought for Finella. That must have cost a pretty penny. Wasted on that stupid girl. Well ... Darley would soon get tired of her. Lady Martington sincerely hoped so. One didn't, naturally, wish one's son to be involved in any scandal ... but it would be better for *all* of them if one day he had to get rid of that girl whom he had married in such a hurry five years ago.

Finella at that moment met her mother-in-law's gaze. Lady Martington was smiling. But there was such dislike in the cold eyes behind the rimless pince-nez she wore, that the girl shuddered. She was glad when Lady Martington rose and the dinner was over.

Of course, once they were in the beautiful Queen Anne drawing-room, softly lit by electric candelabra against the panelled walls, and warmed by a big log fire ... Lady Martington suggested bridge. Rachel Webb eagerly endorsed it. The General did not play, so Finella was called upon to make a fourth. But suddenly a little spirit of revolt entered her at the sight of the sneer she saw on Rachel Webb's smooth face. No, she would not play bridge and play badly, and be 'shown up' in front of Darley by that girl ... or by his mother. She said:

'I'm so sorry, I'd rather not play.'

Darley looked surprised. His mother's eyes narrowed.

'Why, my *dear* . . . if we want a game—'

'I'm sorry . . . I'd much rather not. I'm not good enough and I hate playing with good players,' broke in Finella with flung-back head.

Again Darley looked surprised. His young wife's attitude was peculiar, he thought . . . so unreasonably defiant. He was mildly amused, and strolled up to her.

'Didn't know you hated bridge so much, darling—'

'I . . . don't. I want to learn . . . but not tonight,' she said breathlessly. Then added humbly: 'Please forgive me, Darley. Am I . . . spoiling your evening?'

'Not at all,' he laughed. 'We'll play rummy if you like.'

Lady Martington sniffed. Rachel Webb looked scornful. The General saved the situation by saying:

'By gad . . . five to nine already. How about the news? War with Germany may be over . . . but we've got a lot to cope with yet.'

Grateful for the interruption, Finella rushed to put on the wireless.

Before the evening ended, Rachel Webb managed to get a few words alone with Finella by the fireplace, whilst Darley and his mother chatted to the General.

'Bit awkward for you, wasn't it ... being with your admirer at the Berkeley when Darley turned up last night? How did it go off?'

Hot, pink, the younger girl faced Rachel.

'Quite all right, thank you.'

'Oh, no doubt you're very tactful on such occasions, but I would find it *very* difficult,' drawled Miss Webb, throwing her cigarette end into the fire. 'Darley didn't mind then?'

'Why should he?' demanded Finella. 'I ... I didn't get his cable. He understood.'

'That's good,' said Rachel with a pretence of amiability which Finella suspected had more than a touch of venom behind it. 'Perhaps we'll see your Mr. Bryte down here again one day when he visits his factories. Good night, my dear.'

Finella looked after Rachel's thin, straight figure.

'How that woman hates me,' she thought.

She, too, hated Rachel. She hated her for having met and talked to Gil and guessed what was between them. She hated having Gil's name mentioned in this room tonight. Back came the ghosts crowding down upon her, disturbing the serenity of Darley's gracious old home.

She did not want to remember Gil tonight. She did not know how she was going to recapture the old, lost happiness with Darley ... unless she could cast out even the memory of him.

Lady Martington came back into the

drawing-room. Finella was putting away the cards. The older woman looked at the girl without friendliness.

'It was very selfish of you, refusing to play bridge,' she said. 'On Darley's first night home, surely—'

'I'm sorry. I said I was sorry at the time,' broke in Finella, her nerves already on edge. 'But I won't play ... when ... when Rachel Webb plays so well and makes me look so *stupid*. It isn't fair.'

Lady Martington raised her brows.

'Really, Finella ... don't raise your voice ... *please*.'

'Oh, leave me alone,' said Finella in a choked voice and rushed out of the room.

Darley having seen the Webbs off, came back.

'All alone, Mamma?'

She beamed at him.

'Yes, my darling. It would be nice to have a little chat by ourselves.'

'Where's Fin?' he glanced around.

'Gone up, dear. Tired, I think.'

'Poor pet. We've had rather a hectic day.'

Lady Martington put her tongue in her cheek.

'Finella is just a little ... shall we say ... neurotic, isn't she?'

'Is she?' said Darley, knitting his brows. 'I hadn't thought so.' Then added cheerfully: 'It's a bit of a business getting back to a normal married life again after the years we've been parted.'

'Yes, dear. I ... imagine very *much* of a business,' said Lady Martington pointedly. 'You don't really know Finella at *all*...'

'She's very sweet, Mother.'

Lady Martington cleared her throat. Then she said in a bright voice:

'Didn't darling Rachel look handsome tonight? She *is* a dear person. Been such a comfort to me all through this war ... like my own flesh and blood.'

Darley—lighting his pipe—could not begin to fathom what lay behind this sudden switch over from the subject of Finella to Rachel, but a vague uneasiness gripped him; the first intimation that perhaps Finella and his mother did not altogether 'hit it off'. He said:

'Rachel's a fine girl ... I'm very fond of her.'

Upstairs, Finella was fighting her own secret battle. She wanted to lock herself in her bedroom and howl like a child. A thwarted, defeated child. But it wasn't altogether 'her' bedroom, and she knew Darley would be up at any moment. She was never, presumably, to have a room to herself again. Darley had the right always to be with her. *Like last night.* It was what she had once longed for, blissfully ignorant of the snares and delusions which life had in waiting for her all through the war period. And now . . . she didn't honestly know *what* she wanted. She was only sure of one thing . . . that she was out of tune with herself and the world in general.

She looked almost with panic around the beautiful spacious room. The room—so she had been told—in which Darley had been born. She felt the four walls closing in upon her as though she had claustrophobia. She wanted to rush blindly out into the starlit April night . . . and be alone. Quite alone. She could not bear another twenty-four hours down here . . . with Lady Martington resenting her . . . Rachel despising her . . . and Darley following her around, expecting her to be all that she *ought* to be and felt incapable of being.

In despair she began to undress.

She had had her bath and was in bed when Darley came in. He looked at her and she gave him a little smile then hurriedly buried her nose in the book she had chosen at random (she didn't even know the title).

She felt horribly nervous . . . yes, her nerves were at concert pitch.

Darley sat on the edge of the bed. He thought he had never seen anything so lovely as his young wife with her tawny satin hair pinned up in a pale blue chiffon scarf; a pale blue swansdown cape over her bare shoulders. The room was redolent with some perfume she had used. A scent he had brought back from abroad.

'Je Reviens' it was called.

His heart began to beat madly ... as it had beaten last night. He forgot his mother's rather strange attitude downstairs and the one or two worrying hints she had given about 'things being bad' and that she must 'talk to him tomorrow about money.'

He remembered only that this was his second day home and the second day of his real marriage with Finella.

'Sweetheart...' he said softly. 'What are you reading?'

Finella, her heart fluttering, pushed the book towards him. He glanced at the title and smiled, his uninjured hand lying on one of her beautiful bare arms.

'*Cloister And The Hearth* ... gracious me, what an old favourite. The first novel I was ever made to read at my public school. Do you like it?'

She avoided his gaze, hunching her knees and putting her arms around them.

'I ... oh, I haven't really read it.'

'What do you like to read? What sort of books?'

'Oh, good novels ... anything...' she stammered.

He laid down Charles Reade's novel and took a suddenly grave look at his wife. He remembered what his mother had said ... about Finella being 'neurotic'. Was she? He hoped not. Yet why was she so nervous when alone with him . . . so difficult to fathom?

She was speaking now . . . hurriedly . . . as though to avoid a too-intimate discussion.

'Isn't this a lovely room . . . I always had the small one down the corridor . . . *this* is the room where you were born, isn't it, Darley?'

'Yes . . . and where my papa was born before me. The Manor has been in the hands of the Martington family since the days of William and Mary.'

'It's a wonderful old place. You must love it.'

'I do,' he said. Then suddenly he leaned toward her and put his arm about her . . . shutting his eyes as he drew in the fragrance of her hair. His lips touched one smooth cheek . . . strayed toward her lips. He whispered:

'Oh, Fin . . . darling . . . *my darling* . . .'

She could feel the urgency in his voice: the slight tremble of his body. And, like last night . . . something warm and urgent within her responded . . . and pity was blent with desire. She returned his kiss . . . then, as though it terrified her, tried to turn her head away. Darley held her more tightly.

'Darling,' he said. 'I love you. I love you so much that it frightens me. I couldn't bear to lose you . . . go away from you again.'

She did not answer. He added:

'Fin, my darling . . . *our* child will be born in this room one day perhaps. Fin, I'd so love a son

. . . do you want one, too? I've never asked you before about children . . . tell me . . . tell me, sweetheart . . .'

Speechlessly, she lay back on the pillow looking up at him with a sense of utter frustration. She thought: '*A child . . . to bind me down . . . to send Gil right out of my life . . . to pin me here, perhaps . . . with Darley's mother . . . oh no, no, no . . .*'

CHAPTER NINE

Finella found it virtually impossible to give Darley a direct answer to his question. Deep in her heart she knew that it was her duty to bear this man children. She was his wife. He had, so far as she knew, money and estates. He wanted an heir. Besides, in every man is the deep-rooted desire for a son. She had always despised women who would not have children. She would despise *herself* if she refused. And fundamentally, like her sister Barbara, she loved children.

The crux of the situation was: *did she mean to remain with Darley?* Would she ever grow used to her position as his wife? *Would she be able to put Gil Bryte right out of her life?* For, if not, and this war marriage broke up, it would be better not to have children. Essential in fact; since, in

Finella's mind, a mother could never, *must never* leave her child.

Only one thing remained ... in fairness to them both. To temporize.

She lifted to Darley eyes so frankly miserable and troubled that he could not fail to see the expression and drew back from her. He said:

'I think I understand ... we've only just come together ... you are very young still, my darling. We ought to wait. Yes, of course. Don't worry ... plenty of time, Fin ... all our lives together yet, eh?'

Tears sprang into Finella's large eyes now. How good he was. There was a frankness and chivalry in him that touched her to the core of her being; brought out all that was best in her. No man could be more sweet, more sympathetic. She wanted to show her gratitude. Like this, surely the gulf which the long years had widened between them would be bridged?

Of her own accord she reached up and kissed him.

'I do think you're a dear,' she said huskily.

Her touch was electric and passion flamed in him. He held her closely against him, his lips urgent, hot against the creamy smoothness of her shoulder.

'Fin ... you drive me crazy,' he said thickly. 'Darling, darling, I'm more in love with you now than ever. Do you realize that? Much more than I was when we first married. *Much* more.'

Helpless in his passionate embrace she tried to smile, to nod acquiescence, do anything but remember the awful muddle in her mind about this man ... the other man ... everything connected with her marriage. Darley ruffled the silken hair and covered her face with kisses. She could feel the hard beating of his heart against hers. At moments like these, she realized the strength in him ... in that one muscular constraining arm of his; she was aware of all that his kisses demanded. Here was no feeble boy ... but a man, desperately in love with his wife. She had to admire the hidden strength in Darley ... even while it frightened her. She heard his voice low in her ear:

'You're not afraid of me, are you, Fin? You do like having your husband home, don't you, darling, *don't you?*'

A harder, more selfish character than Finella might have hesitated then ... and hurt him ... struck a blow at his very manhood ... at the long dream he had dreamed about this, his reunion with her.

But whatever the future portended, Finella could not do that to Darley. Otherwise, she might as well have run out on him last night, she thought, and followed Gil blindly ... But she was not sure enough of herself—or careless enough of Darley's feelings. She whispered, recklessly:

'Yes ... yes, of course I'm glad you're

back . . .'

He said no more. He let the waves of his utter longing for her engulf them both. That night, Darley was a happy, confident man. But Finella, lying awake in the darkness, pressed her fingertips against eyelids that burned and ached and thought: 'In a way I didn't lie to him. In a way I *am* glad he is home. But I've grown up . . . grown away from him . . . and Gil has made such a mark in my life. Oh, I want to do the right thing. God *God*, help me . . . show me the way . . .'

She was awake most of the night. She envied the man who slept so soundly beside her.

When he was up, it was she who lay sleeping with the April sunlight glinting on the tangled red-gold of her hair, and her face half buried in the clothes. Darley, fully dressed, looked down at his sleeping wife with tenderness and decided not to rouse her.

He went downstairs followed by the old spaniel Sue who slept outside the door on his mat and had scarcely left Darley's side since he came home. Lady Martington was already in the dining-room pouring out coffee. Darley kissed her, then asked if Rose, the maid, might take Finella's breakfast-tray up to her.

Lady Martington looked disapproving.

'These lazy young girls . . . tut-tut . . .' she said with her mirthless smile. But she did not wish to annoy her son so she gave Rose the order to take coffee and toast up to Mrs. Darley.

Darley said:

'I don't think Fin's really lazy, but she has had a couple of hectic days and I don't think she's too strong, do you?'

'I'm sure I don't know, dear. I *hope* she is,' said his mother raising her brows. 'A delicate wife is a great drawback.'

Darley, as happy this morning as he had been last night, gave a good-humoured laugh and opened *The Times.*

'Oh, well, she must be constitutionally sound or she couldn't have stood that tough job she did all through the war. She's just tired and nervy . . . it's been a long strain for us all. You women who've worked and stuck the raids and so on have been magnificent, I think.'

Lady Martington did not reply. She was not so concerned with her dislike of her daughter-in-law this morning as her financial problems. She knew that she could not postpone the evil day when she must confide in her son. They could none of them go on as they were, and the sooner that girl upstairs learned that she could no longer extract expensive clips from Darley, the better.

Since Finella was absent, she'd take Darley into the morning-room after breakfast and tell him the exact position. She had decided on what she would say. *All* the blame must be put on her broker; none on herself. That was certain!

Finella, grateful for the tray that had been

brought up to her, was sitting up in bed in her little blue swansdown cape, looking and feeling heavy-eyed, when Darley walked in a couple of hours later. She gave him an almost shy little smile.

'Was it you who sent up my brek? Thanks awfully, Darley.'

He did not reply but sat down on the edge of the bed, fingering his pipe.

She noticed that he looked changed and worried. He frowned and seemed half afraid to meet her gaze. She thought, with a sinking heart:

'That old cat of a mother of his has been making mischief . . .'

Then Darley looked up at her and said:

'Afraid I've got bad news for you, darling.'

Her cheeks burned a trifle guiltily.

'What, Darley?'

He gave a self-conscious laugh.

'I think I married you under false pretences, Fin.'

'What on earth do you mean?'

'No—it wasn't false pretences,' he corrected himself. 'I had plenty of money when we got married. And if I haven't any now, it isn't exactly my fault.'

'Darling, what *are* you talking about?'

He told her then. His mother had exploded the bomb at his feet after breakfast. She had told him that they were virtually 'broke'. Yes . . .

97

broke ... the Martingtons who, as far back as Darley remembered, had always had everything that they wanted. Before the war, three cars, stables, a retinue of servants, lavish entertainment at home and abroad. At the time when his father had been knighted for services to the Crown, Darley remembered how luxurious life had been at the Manor; he had been stinted nothing in his own happy childhood; had an expensive education; horses, a handsome allowance when he entered the Army. Now, the source of it all ... most of it was gone. Of course it had been going, gradually, for years, Darley knew that. He repeated to Finella the long story his mother had handed out to him—of dwindling capital; falling prices on the Stock Market; heavily increased taxation for the 'landed gentry'; the ravages of a war that had entered its sixth year before Hitler was overthrown.

Darley explained that in his absence his mother had tried to save the situation by gambling—leaving the main investments to her broker. It was this fellow who had played the fool and let her down. Darley excused his mother ... (Finella knew that he would, whatever he felt about it). She had done her best, he said. What use had he been, overseas all these years? Bravely Mother had struggled alone and kept all financial worries away from him.

'In any case, I'm not much good at high

finance ... I might have found a more reliable broker. That's about all.' Darley finished with a short laugh and got up and walked to the window. He stared blindly down at the beautiful smooth lawns, and the chestnut trees for which the Manor grounds were famous were still in tight bud. The grey wall with the little wrought-iron gate leading into the orchard; the tennis-courts were all so dear and familiar to him; part of his dream of home whilst he was engaged upon that grim struggle for freedom. 'I'm just a soldier,' he finished simply, 'that's all.'

Finella sat listening. She had lit a cigarette and was smoking it reflectively, keeping her gaze on her husband's face. It had been so gay and triumphant last night. This morning he looked wretched and the wretchedness gave her a pang. She hated his mother more than usual for this. That selfish old woman with her mad passion for gambling in some form, whether it was in Monte Carlo or at bridge or on the Stock Exchange, was responsible for the *débâcle*. Only Darley would never reproach her. Her kind were to be seen before the war all over Europe, in the Casinos, raking in winnings at the tables with greedy, claw-like hands ... squandering everything in the last effort to retrieve the lost fortunes. And Margaret Martington had done this to her son ... while he fought for her. She called *that* love. She who dared to criticize *her*, Finella thought. But she knew that Darley did not see through his mother. He had grown up to love and respect her. He was still blind to her real faults. She said, at length:

'Don't look so worried, Darley, dear, please.'

He turned to her, his thin face reddening.

'But I am. Don't you see . . . this means we'll have to cut down to lord knows what . . . and let the Manor go . . . and that's unfair to you . . . at the very start of our marriage.'

'Let the Manor go? Do you mean get rid of it?'

'Not altogether, of course. But let it . . . yes, Mother quite agrees. We can't possibly afford to keep it up. We must let it furnished for a biggish rent until things buck up again. Investments may improve. Mother has every hope, and of course we aren't entirely ruined . . .' He gave a short laugh. 'There's enough for Mother to live on in a flat in town, like ourselves. Thank God my father tied a bit of it up. But not enough for me. And you see I've always had private means . . . Father used to say a fellow in the Regulars couldn't get on without it. I'd do better as things are, and if my arm doesn't improve, to resign my commission and get a civilian job.'

Finella gasped.

'Oh, Darley but why—is it as bad as that?'

'Pretty well. You see, I'm only Acting-Major. I'll go down to a Captain if I start again. I can't keep you on *that*.'

'But Darley—lots of Captains marry on their

pay.'

He gave another quick, nervous laugh ... trying not to show her what a shock his mother's revelation had really been to him. It was not too pleasant, coming back to a tale of ruin. For a bachelor, not so bad. But for a married man ... hellish. And only last night he had wanted a child. Good heavens, he thought ironically, he couldn't now keep himself and Finella as he wished to do ... let alone bring up a family. He felt frustrated ... even humiliated ... because of Finella ... and all he had planned to do for her and with her. He could not be angry with his mother. She had done her utmost best. It was that damned stockbroker, Blackley ... selling out the gilt-edged securities his father had bought ... against his mother's scruples. She had given way in the end, she had told him, only because Mr. Blackley had assured her he could make a lot more money for her. Injudicious of Mother, of course. But she had meant well, and, poor dear, had to cope all alone while he was abroad. Darley said:

'Listen, Fin. I myself know fellows, Captains in the Regulars, who have married on their pay. Yes, they manage. But it's a struggle. I don't want you to have a make-do-and-mend existence with me. I want you to have everything. This arm is not right. The best thing now is for me to get invalided out. If I am ... I can take a job. I shall look for a lucrative one ... yes, I'm sure I

101

can make more as a civilian than I ever shall as a soldier. I've got to, Fin ... to get back the family fortune. I can't let the old Manor go right out of our hands. It would do something to me ... it was my great grandfather's home and his father's before that. I've *got* to find a way of making money.'

Finella did not speak for a moment. Her heart was beating uneasily. She was thinking: *'Oh, lord, here's another obstacle for me to overcome ... I don't mind a hang about the money ... I wouldn't love Darley or any man for what he gave me ... but if Darley has this to face ... it will be all the more difficult to walk out on him.'*

He came up to her. His young bronzed face was suddenly haggard and older.

'Fin, I'm damned sorry. I realize what it'll mean ... to you ... till I'm on my feet again.'

Quickly she said:

'Oh, Darley, don't be too upset. *I'm* not. Money isn't so very important to me, honestly.'

He sat on the edge of the bed again and took her hand and kissed it, his eyes wistfully regarding her small earnest face in its frame of bright hair.

'Isn't it, darling?' he said. 'Well, it is to me ... because of what I want to do for you ... and, of course, for my mother.'

'We'll manage,' she said hurriedly. And added, with a laugh: 'Dear me ... we'd better sell my lovely new clip. You ought never to have

102

bought it.'

'Rot. Things aren't as bad as that. Only we—the Martingtons in general—will have to revise our way of living. Keep your clip, my darling Finella.'

But he was remembering, uneasily, something his mother had said in a plaintive voice, downstairs.

'I'm afraid you won't be able to go buying jewellery for Finella. Poor boy. You'll find that these modern girls want so much. And Finella has no money of her own. I don't know how *she* will take this. If only she had a little to help . . . money of her own, I mean . . . like our dear Rachel . . .'

That was all nonsense, of course. No man worth his salt would take money from a woman. He didn't care a hoot whether Fin had money of her own or not. But he had come upstairs wondering inevitably exactly how Fin *would* react to this bad news. He knew so little about her; had known her and her family for such a short time before his marriage. She was lovely and vital and young. A girl like that must want beautiful clothes and a good time . . . especially after the years she had worn uniform and worked in this war. He wouldn't blame Finella if she were sadly disappointed in him and the future he was offering her now. Yet now that she knew, she seemed to be taking it in a most generous and sporting manner, he thought. He was relieved and grateful and told her so.

'I don't mind if we haven't a bean so long as you love me, Fin,' he said huskily and drew her slender hand against his cheek, then dropped a kiss on the fragrant pink palm.

She looked almost in dismay down at the brown boyish head of her husband. She thought:

'Oh, why does he make things so hard for me . . . by being so nice.'

Aloud she said with pretended mischief:

'And supposing I hated the sight of you, you idiot . . . what then?'

He looked down at her, his eyes darkening.

'It wouldn't be funny, darling . . . losing you *plus* my old home . . . *plus* the cash. I could stick the last two . . . but losing *you* would kick the bottom right out of my world. Heavens Fin . . . If I thought another fellow . . .' He stopped abruptly, remembering his resolution not to be jealous of other men. Men like Gil Bryte who could afford orchids, no doubt.

Her heart knocked.

'Well . . . what?'

He flushed and laughed.

'Oh . . . just if I thought another fellow could get you away from me . . . I believe I'd want to murder him.'

She swallowed hard and her lashes fluttered. Those words . . . that tense, almost primitive look in Darley's eyes . . . terrified her. It was in

104

such contradiction to the chivalrous boy. She was beginning to discover with a vengeance how little any woman knew about a man until she lived with him ... and what strange dark passions, passions as old, as primeval as the earth itself, lay in all human beings ... under the veneer of civilization.

One could not play fast and loose with such a man as this ... or Gil Bryte, for instance.

She felt herself floundering in a sea of troubled reflections ... up against such complexities in life as she had never before dreamed of.

She felt her husband's lips touch her hand again.

'Don't look like that darling. It'll be okay. I'll find a job. I tell you what ... we'll have a day today in the country and run up to London tomorrow and I'll see a chap I know at the War Office and find out if I can get discharged with this arm, and if so ... it's Darley for a bowler hat and the city gent's suiting. Will you like me coming home every night at six to hang up my hat, darling?'

He laughed. She laughed with him, shaking her head. But both of them sat holding hands staring at each other uneasily, even timidly like children, scared of the unknown and uncertain of each other.

CHAPTER TEN

During the weeks that followed some of the first rapture Darley Martington had experienced at the commencement of his homecoming faded a little—half lost in the host of mundane, trivial annoyances and disappointments which gradually crept into his existence. He hated to see his old home put on the market as 'let furnished'. He was depressed because his mother, to whom he was devoted, seemed so down and unlike herself—also depressed no doubt because she had to part with her lovely home. He hated having to cut down expenses almost as soon as his much-needed leave had commenced. He knew it was essential he should do so, and he set about it doggedly, determined not to be extravagant. But it irritated him not only because he could not spend the money on his wife, but because he was a man used to throwing money about in a generous, cheerful fashion. Always the first to pay for any outing; to stand the drinks, to settle the taxis. A man used to a good club, to hunting, shooting and fishing. Such things must now go by the board. As anticipated, he was reduced to the rank of Captain, and it was a big drop from the pay of a field officer.

He lost some of his spontaneous gaiety and

boyishness during those difficult days that followed the breaking of his mother's calamitous news. He grew more silent and preoccupied. His attitude in its turn reacted on Finella. She was young and vivacious and wanted to be happy. She soon discovered that it would be difficult with Darley in his present mood. She was sorry for him ... knowing what the financial disaster meant to him. But she was not at all sorry for Lady Martington and secretly blamed her for the whole affair. Lady Martington remained hostile toward her ... sometimes openly so ... and so Darley could not fail, after a week with his mother and his wife, to see that they were not getting on as well as he had believed when he was away from them. He thought it only just to blame them both a little. Finella knew that and felt it bitterly. Darley did not know how *beastly* her mother-in-law had been to her, she thought. Lady Martington was a clever woman in her own way, if a fool about money, and she managed to keep her son very much on her side. It almost infuriated Finella at times to see how she 'managed' him; and how Darley 'fell for it'.

Those were not good days ... for any of them. Finella chafed to get away from the Manor. Darley wanted to go too, in order to be alone with the young wife who attracted him so vitally. He had fully meant to spend only a day or two down there. But now that this 'crash' had occurred, it was necessary for him to remain with his mother and settle affairs. There were two horses in the stables. The whole estate to see to. The family lawyer and accountant to be interviewed ... the future finances to be settled. It was the type of work Darley loathed. It irked him. He had hoped for complete relaxation alone with his Finella during this leave.

And Finella, left alone most of the day, had too much time in which to think and brood and remember the carefree magical weeks of her association with Gil Bryte. To recall everything connected with Gil that she missed more and more as time went on. It was bad for her, this brooding ... bad for her to be thrown too much with her mother-in-law. Their mutual antipathy was growing apace, and Rachel Webb was a constant visitor; ready for that game of bridge when Darley wanted one; always friendly and companionable to him; deeply concerned about the fallen family fortunes and anxious to sympathize and help.

She was outwardly friendly and pleasant to Finella, too, these days. But Finella distrusted her ... half resented her overtures of friendship. There was a mocking, almost sneering expression in her eyes which Finella saw and disliked. And Lady Martington deliberately sang Rachel's praises until Finella could have screamed.

Finella's honest wish to do her utmost to persevere with this marriage, was shaken sometimes at the end of a frustrating day at the Manor. And still the place did not let. Lady Martington was asking a huge rent ... anxious to make a profit and add to her now slender resources. The place was big and cost a deal to keep up. It needed a wealthy tenant. So far none had come forward.

Finella, who had hoped by now to be in her own flat in London, able to see her sister and friends, wondered how much longer she would be able to go on without showing Darley her true state of mind. When he made love to her now she resented it. And she was afraid that she might show *that*, too. Her nerves were badly on edge. Yet there were moments in his embrace when she wanted to break down and cry like a defeated child and cling to him with tenderness. She was still torn in two by emotions that she found hard to explain even to herself; something she could not calmly rationalize, any more than she could stamp out her longing to see Gil again.

Three weeks from the day Darley had returned home—and the position at the Manor was still unchanged. He, personally, had moved only a few steps further forward. He knew now, after various visits to a local hospital, that his arm would not be right for a long while yet, and that he must go on with treatment, also that in the not too distant future he might have to have another operation. He had discovered from discussion in the War Office that he could extend this sick leave for a few months more, then get right out of the Army if he chose. Therein lay his most secret and vital problem. Whether to quit his once-loved Army career and find a more remunerative job . . . or stay on . . . perhaps as a Captain, struggling on Army pay and allowances, and with a wife, for years.

It was a choice Darley had no real wish to make. He felt at times bitter toward life for doing this thing to him. The one compensation was Finella . . . her beauty and sweetness . . . all that was his. Yet even that seemed under a cloud now. He was growing less sure of her. He was distressed because she did not get on with his mother.

He began to realize in earnest that married life was not such a simple matter and that women were incalculable, inconsistent creatures.

There was an open clash one night after Rachel Webb and her father had dined with them. When the Webbs had gone Lady Martington remarked that she was deeply touched because General Webb had offered actual monetary help to the family.

'Of course I told him we couldn't *dream* of accepting it, but I thought it so good of him,' she said, addressing her son. (More often than not she ignored Finella when she discussed family affairs . . . one of the many barbed arrows shot in the unfortunate Finella's direction). 'But there you are . . . the Webbs are true friends. Dear Rachel is the same.'

Darley agreed.

'Damned decent of the old boy. Isn't it darling?'—he turned to his wife who sat silent. She had been struggling the whole evening against the inclination to run out of the room and leave Darley and his mother alone with the Webbs. Somehow that foursome always made her feel an outsider. Although, of course, Darley was sweet and attentive to her . . . and she knew how *he* felt. Lady Martington glanced over the rim of her glasses at her daughter-in-law's downcast face and with her freezing smile murmured:

'Better not ask Finella what she thinks. *She* has no love for Rachel.'

Finella's head shot up. An angry flush stained her cheeks.

'We were discussing the General—not Rachel,' she said.

Darley—unaware that he was treading on the edge of a volcano—looked at his wife in surprise.

'You like Rachel, don't you, Fin?'

Lady Martington intervened.

'I'm sure she doesn't, dear . . . and never did. She doesn't understand Rachel . . . of course, we must remember that Finella has led a very different sort of life . . . the artistic life . . . and

111

Rachel is a country-lover—'

She broke off. Finella had sprung to her feet. She stood there with blazing eyes ... shaking with anger.

'All right!' she said in a choked voice. 'Leave it at that. I don't understand your wonderful Rachel. I'm just nothing and nobody but a twopenny-halfpenny artist in your eyes. But I drove an ambulance for four years and I don't know what Rachel Webb did. Reserved occupation looking after her invalid mother and father, wasn't it? Very cushy. Oh, I admit that I don't like your precious Rachel..I don't ... I *don't!*'

'My dear!' protested Lady Martington in a voice of ice. 'Please control yourself...'

'Fin!' began Darley. He had gone quite white ... unprepared for the explosion that had followed his simple question to his wife.

Finella rushed out of the room. Lady Martington picked up her bag and switched off a table-lamp. With a sidelong glance at her son she murmured:

'Poor child ... I'm afraid she has an ungovernable temper. You'll have to learn to deal with it, Darley dear.'

Darley looked dumbfounded. He had never dreamed that Finella had a temper. She was highly strung, of course ... excitable ... that was the artistic strain ... he had always known that. But to fly into such a rage and be so

112

unpleasant about poor Rachel ... that flabbergasted him.

He said nothing but a brief 'good night' to his mother. He was too upset and dead tired. He had been up to London that morning interviewing a friend of his father's ... Sir Henry Wychless, who was a director of several important companies ... about a possible job. He had come home dispirited ... realizing how little suited he was, really, to any civilian job, trained from his boyhood for the Army. He had wanted to go up to Fin tonight and lay his tired head on her breast and be spoiled and petted. But it looked to him as though something quite different awaited him.

In their bedroom he found his wife laying face downward on her bed, sobbing as though her heart would break. At once his own irritation faded. He felt nothing but grief because she was miserable. He did not want his lovely Finella to be miserable. Why, good lord, he thought they had only had three weeks of married life ... after those five damnable years of separation. It couldn't come to *this* ... a family wrangle ... for no real reason at all.

But there was every reason ... and perhaps if Finella had been frank with him in this hour ... told him the whole long history of the petty differences between his mother and Rachel Webb and herself, and how Rachel had been thrust down her throat until it had become insupportable, Darley might have understood a little. As it was, Finella offered no reasonable explanation of her outburst. She felt that she could not ... must not tell Darley that she disliked both his mother, and Rachel Webb. How could she? Besides, now that the heat of the moment was over, she regretted her loss of control. It had only humiliated her in front of Lady Martington.

She wept and shook her head dumbly when Darley plied her with questions. Why was she unhappy? Why didn't she like Rachel? What was wrong? And so on ... until Finella felt fresh hysteria rise in her.

Darley looked sadly at the prostrate young figure, the tumbled beautiful hair which was molten gold in the lamplight. He caressed her, tried to kiss away the tears.

'I love you so much—and I can't bear you to be at loggerheads with Mother,' he said. 'She's so fond of you, darling. Do try and get on with her. I know she isn't artistic ... and you are ... but—'

'Oh, don't. Leave me alone!' broke in Finella, lifting a flushed wet face. 'I don't want to discuss it. It's nothing to *do* with my being artistic. I haven't had much chance to touch a paint-brush or play a piano or read a decent book since the war began. It's a bit silly for your mother to harp on this artistic business...' She gave a nervous little laugh and dragged her hand

114

away from Darley's. 'Oh, let's forget it. I'm sorry I was so stupid.'

Darley looked hurt. He said:

'Oh, all right ... if that's how you feel, darling.'

She made an effort to calm down and threw him a beseeching look.

'When are we going to have our own home together?'

'Soon now, I hope. This place is sure to let any moment. But I must just see to things for Mother until it is. Then we'll look for a flat and Mother is going to a hotel for a bit.'

Finella stared at the floor a trifle sullenly. So long as Lady Martington did not wish to share their flat with *them,* well and good, she thought. Darley added:

'I want our home together just as much as you do, Fin darling. Try to be patient and bear with the present situation. It isn't easy for any of us.'

She had no answer to that. How could she tell him of *her* personal difficulties ... the trapped feeling she had these days. That awful frightened feeling that things would never be right between her and Darley again.

Then she fell to remembering Gil ... Gil who had said he would be waiting for her. She could not remember him without a sensation of guilt ... of self-reproach ... knowing how much Darley cared for her. So in the end it was she who walked up to him and offered her lips.

'I've been awful . . . I know it. I'm just tired and silly. Forgive me,' she said.

He caught her close.

'Oh, my darling,' he said, and was happy again while he could hold her thus. She was so soft, so pliant, so adorable against his madly beating heart.

But his happiness was diminished . . . and his glorious illusions about marriage being such a facile thing . . . of 'roses and raptures' . . . were gradually diminishing too . . . spoiled by every little cloud that came between him and his Finella.

In the morning a fit of repentance seized Finella and a fresh desire to please Darley . . . poor darling Darley who had a bad arm and had faced so many disappointments since he returned to England. She even brought herself to apologize to his mother.

'I'm afraid I was very rude . . . do forgive me,' she said at the breakfast table.

Darley being present, Lady Martington had no option but to accept the overture graciously and say:

'Of course . . . of course, my dear child.'

But the glacier-like smile belied her words.

However, Lady Martington was in a good mood. She had had a letter from her agent. A handsome offer had been made at last for the Manor from a wealthy client who was willing to keep up the place just as they wanted it . . . and

116

to take on the horses and groom ... and in general be the type of client her ladyship desired.

'That sounds hopeful,' said Darley. 'What's the family consist of?'

'A bachelor, he says, dear ... but he entertains a good deal and needs a big place. He has a sister who has lost her husband in the war and she will run it for him.'

'And will pay what we ask?'

'So it seems.'

Darley turned to Finella. She had just finished breakfast and was on the floor beside Sue, stroking the old spaniel's silky coat. How young and attractive she looked this morning, he thought tenderly. The sunlight slanted upon her. She wore slacks and a pale-blue woolly jumper and had done her hair brushed up on top of her head in a bunch of curls. That was the *old* way ... just as he remembered her at Sandhurst when they had first met. Darling little Fin!

She smiled up at him—determined to be good-humoured and tolerant in this house today. And if the house was let, it meant that she could get away from her mother-in-law and have her own home.

'It all sounds fine,' she murmured.

'This man and his sister are both coming down at twelve to view the place,' Lady Martington observed. 'So please be here, Darley, to help me.'

117

Darley ruffled his wife's shining curls.

'We'll all be here,' he said.

And so they were ... gathered in the morning-room, ready and waiting for the only probable tenants they had had after the place. Lady Martington was relieved. And Darley had made a vow not to mind too much. But Finella thought only of getting away. The Manor had become to her a prison-house.

At a quarter to twelve a big American saloon car swept up the drive. The Martingtons, all three, looked out of the window curiously.

'Thank goodness it's such a lovely May morning—they'll see the Manor at its best,' remarked Lady Martington.

Finella, who, to please her mother-in-law, had changed from slacks into a crisp white blouse and grey flannel suit, glanced at the man and woman who were just stepping out of the car. The woman who came within view now looked youngish and quite attractive. She wore tweeds. The man was tall and ... suddenly Finella's heart gave a terrific jolt and every drop of colour drained from her face. At the same time Darley, too, saw the big loose-limbed fellow with the dark curly hair and strong jaw who was walking up to the portico. He turned round to Finella.

'Fin!' he said sharply. 'Am I dreaming, or isn't this *your* friend ... Gilfred Bryte?'

CHAPTER ELEVEN

There was no other course for Finella but to meet her husband's gaze squarely and reply:

'Yes. It is...' Then with a nervous little laugh: 'W-what a coincidence.'

Lady Martington pricked up her ears. Her quick, cold eyes behind the rimless glasses noted at once the changed expression on her son's face ... and the hot flush that had replaced her daughter-in-law's pallor. She said quickly:

'Gilfred Bryte? Is this the man who wants to rent our house? Do you know him, Finella?'

'Yes,' said the girl.

And her heart knocked against her ribs as she heard the front-door bell ring. Gil ... *Gil* the man who wanted to take over the Manor ... good heavens! It was more than a coincidence. She knew at once why Gil had done this. He must have wanted a country place and applied to Lady Martington's agents and been offered the Manor. And he was going to try and take it because it was a link ... a very definite link ... with *her*. Clever of Gil. Typical ... of the dominant male who so far had always had his own way in life.

She licked her lips ... they were dry ... and cast another nervous glance at Darley. He had walked away from the window and was standing by the fireplace, his brows knit. He looked curiously stern, she thought. But why? He couldn't *surely* be jealous of Gil ... just because of that night at the Berkeley. He knew nothing about Gil. Nothing. Of course Rachel Webb knew a little ... and if Gil came here to live ... the Webbs would call ... Gil would see more of Rachel. She might talk ... might talk to Lady Martington. Oh, Finella thought in dismay, what endless complications!

Rose came into the room.

'Your ladyship, there's a Mr. Bryte and Mrs. Lucas to see you. They have an appointment they say.'

'Show them in here, please Rose,' said Lady Martington with another curious glance at the young couple. For the moment she was perplexed by the seemingly awkward atmosphere between them.

Gilfred Bryte and his sister came into the room.

Finella's heart beat so fast that she could hardly breathe. She caught the back of a chair to steady herself. Her gaze was drawn ... as by a magnet ... to the big man who came with his quick determined step, just behind his sister, and who, in turn, looked straight at her.

Their gaze met ... held ... in hers, unspoken appeal and the old fascination ... in his, a grim humour ... as much as to say: '*Give*

120

me full marks for this, Nella, my poppet ... I've achieved a contact ... a most unquestionable one ... haven't I?'

But he did no more than bow to Finella and to the tall, well-dressed woman whom he presumed to be Lady Martington, then addressed Darley.

'How are you? We've already met, haven't we?'

'We have,' said Darley shortly. 'How are you ...?'

Gilfred, smiling, indicating the girl in tweeds who was with him.

'My sister, Mrs. Lucas.'

'How d'you do...' Darley and his mother chorused the words. Finella remained dumb ... incapable of more than a slight inclination of the head.

She had known, of course, that Gil had a sister. She had never been to his home. His father was an M.P. for a Midland town and his sister, Joanna (she must be nearing thirty), had been up in Scotland during most of the war. Her husband, a Major in a Scottish regiment, had been stationed there until "D" Day. And now Finella was remembering that Gil had told her that Harry, his brother-in-law, had been killed and poor Jo, as he called her, had gone back to her old home.

So this was Joanna ... she was not smart, but handsome in a big fashion ... rather after Gil's

121

build, thought Finella . . . dark curly hair; the same searching eyes under heavily marked brows.

She looked in Finella's direction and then came toward her. Seen nearer, Finella noted what a sweet mouth she had—quite different from her brother's; Gil's mouth was a hard line.

'You must be Nella . . . I've heard my brother speak of you,' said Joanna Lucas, with just the trace of a North-country accent.

Finella, not daring now to look at either her husband or her mother-in-law, for she was in an agony of nervousness, answered:

'Oh . . . y-yes. And I've heard of you, Mrs. Lucas.'

'Oh, do call me Jo. Everyone does,' said Joanna in a friendly manner.

Finella thanked her. Lady Martington froze at once.

North-country people . . . how she hated them . . . so lacking in 'finesse', in tact. Interesting, though . . . that the *brother* should know Finella so well and not the *sister*. Know her well enough to have a name of his own for her. As far as her ladyship knew, no one else called her daughter-in-law *'Nella'*.

Darley was harbouring more or less the same thoughts. But he fought against them. Pride was uppermost and an instinctive love for, and loyalty toward, his young wife. He was, at any rate, determined not to let this fellow see a trace

122

of jealousy, and with forced good humour now he addressed himself to Gilfred Bryte.

'Don't tell me *you're* the chap who is after the old ancestoral home,' he said. ''Pon my soul . . . how funny.'

'Yes, isn't it?' said Gilfred. He took his cue from Finella's husband, and was in his turn most amiable. 'Matter of fact I'm sick to death of London. Too many people, and I like country life. My father's house is too far from town for week-ends, so I thought this place sounded just the thing.'

Darley held out his cigarette-case. Under veiled lids he examined the face of this man who he presumed had been his wife's 'boyfriend' in his absence. Gilfred Bryte was not the type Darley would ever have chosen for a friend, yet he saw the attraction of the fellow; he had a virile and invigorating personality; something rugged and compelling about him.

The two men lit cigarettes, then Darley took Gilfred to the window and began to point out the tennis-courts and the orchards. The Manor was one of the biggest estates in the district, he said. But the house was modernized and comfortable and easily run with two servants, etc.

Finella's gaze followed them . . . the slimly built figure of her husband; the big man towering beside him . . . heard the vague murmur of their voices across the room . . . and

123

listened half-heartedly to what her mother-in-law and Jo Lucas were saying. Lady Martington was giving Jo a detailed account of how the house was run. She must go right over it in a moment. The cook might be induced to stay on. The gardener's wife, who occupied the little cottage by the drive gates, came in at week-ends to give a hand and did all their laundry. And so on.

But Finella was busy with her own conflicting thoughts and emotions; fascinated, she kept staring at Gil and Darley. Her heart hammered. Never had she expected those two to come in contact like this; never dreamed that the prospective tenant of the Manor would turn out to be *Gil* of all people in the world. She was terrifically thrilled to see him, yet half resented his being here. It was colossal nerve on his part; typical of the man who stepped in and took what he wanted at any price. It was that power in him, that ruthlessness that always probed the weakness in her own nature and held her spellbound.

After a while the two men came back to the fireplace and Lady Martington suggested that she should show Mrs. Lucas the house. Darley said to Gil:

'You'd like a walk round the grounds, wouldn't you, Bryte?'

'Thanks, I would,' nodded Gil.

'Hang on a moment . . . I'll just send Rose—

our maid—down to the cottage and get Wilkins our gardener. He'll be at his lunch, but you ought to have a word with him.'

Lady Martington moved out of the drawing-room with Jo, who, as she went, looked over her shoulder at her brother and said:

'Isn't it just the most heavenly old house you've ever seen, Gil?'

'It certainly is,' he agreed.

Finella was left alone then with the man whom she had been wanting to see so badly. He came quickly to her side and, with a rapid look at the door which had just closed on the others, seized her hand and kissed it.

'Nella ... sweetest ... it's good to see you again. Haven't I been clever ... fixing this?'

She looked up at him with mingled appeal and the old admiration in her large, luminous eyes.

'Oh, Gil, you ... you *devil* ...'

He laughed, showing his white, even teeth and shook back his head with its mass of thick curly hair. (She used to tell him he looked like a lion shaking his mane when he did that ... he refused to flatten down that mop of hair with brush or brilliantine).

'Well, a clever devil, you'll admit.'

Terrified, she dragged her hand from his strong fingers.

'You mustn't ... Darley will be back ... Oh, Gil, this is far too dangerous.'

125

'Rubbish, darling. I'll be careful, I had to see you again. You didn't ring me. I nearly went crazy. Have you been so engrossed with your husband? He's a nice chap ... but quietish ... too quiet and ineffectual for you, isn't he?'

She had to defend her husband.

'Not really. Darley has a big sense of humour ... but the war ... his arm ... a lot has been taken out of him.'

He gave her a penetrating look.

'Then you *have* been too engrossed ... you don't need me any more, Nella?'

Her cheeks flamed and her long lashes drooped.

'Oh no ... it isn't that ... it's all so difficult, I don't know where I am ... or what to think. But I ... *have* missed you most awfully, Gil, but—'

'But you're married and still struggling to be the loyal little wife,' he finished for her dryly.

'Yes,' she whispered.

He took her hand again and brushed it with his lips. She was half ashamed of the wild thrill that shot through her being at this proximity with Gil Bryte again. He had always moved her. She was Darley's now ... so much Darley's ... and yet ... could still feel that strong impulse toward Gil. What did it mean? Was she so mad and bad? She did not understand herself. She only knew that the main reason was that she had grown near to Gil these last six months ...

126

much too near ... and that Darley was the
stranger ... the outsider ... *not* Gil.

She said in a choked little voice:

'It isn't fair really ... coming here like this
... I know it was clever. You always get what
you want but ... I did ask you to let me give my
marriage a chance.'

He shrugged his shoulders and looked at her
with a touch of insolent humour in his
handsome eyes.

'Dear little Nella ... you haven't changed.
Still like a small captured bird, beating its wings
in a cage ... and then when the cage is opened
... too scared to fly out.'

She shook her head.

'Don't go on ... being clever. I can't take it
this morning, Gil. I'm too fussed and bothered.'

He softened and smiled down at her.

'You're very beautiful,' he said in a deep
voice. 'You always look your best in that grey
flannel suit with a little white bow at your
throat. I remember you wore that when I took
you down to Henley...'

'Don't remind me ... please...' Finella
begged.

He shrugged again. But he knew that she
needed no reminding. It had been in his car
down at Henley ... he had driven there on
business; she had forty-eight hours off from her
job ... and had gone with him ... and he had
stopped the car on a lonely by-road and kissed

her. It had been their first kiss . . . and she had been devastated . . . and he knew it . . . just as he had, himself, discovered that he was really and truly in love for the first time in his dynamic career. In love with a slender, dewy-eyed girl whose hair was like dark-red gold and whose eyes were smoke-grey under their silken lashes. In love with *another man's wife*. And that man overseas, in the fighting. Not a pretty thing . . . not a noble one. But Gil had no scruples when it came to breaking up this particular marriage. He considered it stupid if not criminal of Darley Martington to have married Nella when she was a mere child . . . then left her alone for five years to battle with life and her own loveliness.

He said softly:

'I'm never going to give you up . . . so don't waste time telling me to, my darling. Added to which . . . you don't really want me to step right out of the picture, do you?'

She had no time to answer. Darley opened the door and came in, followed by old Sue.

'Ready, Bryte?' he said.

Gil moved toward him.

'Okay.'

Darley came to his wife's side.

'Coming with us, darling?'

Her face was expressionless and she looked at neither man as she answered:

'No, I don't think so. I've got a bit to do upstairs. I'll leave you two alone to make the tour.'

'Oh, do come with us, Fin,' begged Darley.

'I'm busy, really,' she almost snapped, and added hastily: 'Please excuse me, Darley dear . . .'

Gil watched husband and wife, a satirical look in his eyes. Darley said:

'Oh, right-ho . . . see you later, then.'

They went their way. As the door closed upon them Finella moved slowly to the mantelpiece, put her arms against it and leaned her head on them.

She felt that her turbulent, difficult emotions were suffocating her so that she could scarcely breathe. For a long time she stayed like that . . . without moving . . . trying desperately to regain composure and collect her scattered thoughts.

And in the end . . . when she had pieced them together, one salient fact stood out: that Gil had been right when he had said that she did not really want him to 'step out of the picture'. Yet she dreaded him remaining in it. She was still so fond of Darley . . . so fond that she did not want to hurt him. Yet she knew if this kind of thing went on she might not be able to avoid doing so.

When she came down from her bedroom an hour later she found that Lady Martington had graciously arranged for Gil and his sister to stay to lunch, and that Gil had definitely taken the Manor for a year. What was more, her ladyship was in the best of humours, for Mr. Bryte

(North Country or not, he was really a very amusing and interesting man she had decided ... and after all, his father was an M.P.) had made her a very handsome offer. The Manor had twelve bedrooms and there was one wing, newer than the genuine Queen Anne part of the house, which was entirely separate from the rest and had its own bathrooms. Neither Gil nor Jo would need so many rooms. Just their own and one or two for week-end guests. They hoped to give tennis-parties in the summer, and so on. But they both felt, observed Gil, that it was absurd for Lady Martington to leave the home she loved so well and live in a small flat in town, when she might continue living down here and occupy the new wing.

Lady Martington told Darley and Finella with excitement of this offer.

'It really is very kind of Mr. Bryte and if he really means it, I can pay my share of expenses ... he suggests very little ... and be better off than I would be in London. And I do so dread the idea of leaving my old home, I admit.'

Darley was a bit dubious about the wisdom of such an arrangement and a little resentful since it seemed that Gilfred Bryte, paying for the upkeep of the place, would be in a position to patronize his mother ... yet Bryte, he had to admit, was certainly being very friendly and unpatronizing in his manner.

'What Jo really wants is someone like Lady

Martington to show her the ropes down here and keep the place as it is used to being kept. It would be a kindness to Jo,' he said smoothly.

The young widow, who seemd to have an abundance of good nature and the utmost simplicity, heartily endorsed this.

'I would love it if Lady Martington would occupy the new wing,' she said enthusiastically.

'And of course, any time Captain Martington and his wife wished to stay, there are plenty of spare rooms in the new wing, are there not?' added Gil with a brilliant smile.

'It's very generous of you, Bryte, I must say,' said Darley.

But Finella could not even say 'Thank you'. She stood by, listening to the discussion, while they drank cocktails, and feeling more than a little bewildered. Heavens, Gil was a fast worker. He had got Lady Martington on his side now ... and *in his house*. That meant Darley would be bound to come down here to see his mother ... and she, Finella, would come with him ... so the contact with Gil was yet more firmly established.

Her large eyes met his gaze and dumbly said: 'You *are* a devil...'

But he was gay and smiling ... if a little triumphantly.

Lady Martington was well pleased. Mr. Bryte seemed to have plenty of money; he had agreed without a murmur to pay a fantastic rent for the place and with herself virtually in control (for that Mrs. Lucas was obviously a stupid young woman and easily managed) things would not be bad at all. She said with her fixed smile:

'Well, well . . . fancy me living to become a paying guest in my own house! How amusing. This war has done very queer things to us all.'

'It certainly has,' murmured Gil and looked across the room at Finella. She looked back, her cheeks flaming.

Only Darley did not join in the light-hearted bantering talk of the moment. He sipped his drink in silence. For a good many reasons he was feeling considerably depressed. For with every day that passed, this homecoming of his was turning out to be less and less like the glorious return of his imagination.

And he wondered how many other soldiers were undergoing the same slow, insidious disillusionment.

CHAPTER TWELVE

A week later Rachel Webb cycled to the Manor about tea-time and found an unusual state of disorder. Wilkins and Johnny the boy were both in the house, helping to 'move things'. Lady Martington was transferring her personal belongings (and it had been agreed with Mrs.

Lucas, her own bed) to the new wing, which faced west. In order that the old part of the house should be spring-cleaned and ready for the tenants. Darley and Finella were also moving into her ladyship's new quarters.

Rachel had already heard from her godmother that Gilfred Bryte and his sister were renting the Manor and the arrangement that Aunt Margaret should stay on and 'supervise' as a paying guest. Rachel was vastly intrigued. Not only by the thought that she would keep her godmother in the district (which she wanted to do because it also kept her in touch with Darley) but because of the man who had taken the Manor. Finella's ex-'boyfriend'! That really was amusing. She could foresee quite a number of complications —and an entertaining time for herself. She had always loved Darley Martington and his marriage had been an embittering thing for her. Now that he was back and so much more the man than the boy, she was more than ever in love. And she hated Finella . . . frankly hated her. She saw none of the girl's good points; refused to make allowances for the fact that anyone so young and lovely and impressionable had been left at the altar, so to speak, to fight a world at war, alone.

If she could get Darley away from Finella, Rachel Webb would do it, and knew that she had his mother as a firm ally. She had been shocked by the revelation of the dwindling fortunes of the Martingtons, but that did not worry her for her own sake; she had all her parents' money coming to her and she would, she thought, be far more useful to Darley than that silly, penniless girl he had married.

She had a few words with her godmother who, wearing an overall over her dress, and with her immaculate grey hair tied up in a scarf, was carrying tray-loads of trinkets, ornaments, books and toilet requisites from one room to another. Rachel immediately took off her coat and hat and offered to help. As they worked, they conversed in their usual friendly manner. These two women, the young and the old, saw eye to eye in many ways.

'You must agree it is a good thing for me to go on making my home in the new wing,' Lady Martington told her god-daughter. 'I should have hated a cheap flat in town. My roots are here. And now I can have the same degree of comfort I have always had and at the same time make money. I can also keep an eye on my house. That Mrs. Lucas is easily managed. Such a raw young woman, my dear.'

Rachel was not interested in Joanna Lucas.

'What do you think of Finella's boy-friend?' she murmured.

Her ladyship paused in the act of pulling out a drawer from the tallboy in her old bedroom and looked sharply at Rachel's smiling face.

'Is Mr. Bryte an old "boy-friend", as you call

it ... (such a vulgarity, my dear ... that modern term ...) *Is* he a "boy-friend" of Finella's?'

'But of course. Don't you remember that day he came down here to see her when Darley was still away? I told you I'd met him here. It was he she was dancing with the night Darley came home, poor old pet.'

Lady Martington straightened her pince-nez behind which her eyes became like cold, hard gooseberries.

'Indeed, so *that* was the man. Yes, how silly of me. I do remember, now. Interesting, indeed.'

Rachel put a collection of clothes over her arm.

'Just as well Darley is so tolerant.'

'H'm. I wonder if he is ... if he *knows* ... and now I begin to wonder if I ought to be living under that man's roof,' said Lady Martington in a worried way.

'Oh, don't let us take it for granted there is anything really serious between Mr. Bryte and dear Finella,' broke in Rachel hastily. 'And if there is ... so much the better if you can keep an eye on the gentleman and watch Darley's interests.'

'Yes, perhaps you are right, my dear.'

But Lady Martington's eyes remained cold. She busied herself with her thoughts. Rachel smiled a little at her own as they passed down the corridor armed with their goods.

On their way to the new wing they ran into Finella. She, too, wore an overall and looked flushed and a little untidy. But with her tumbled tawny hair and pink cheeks, she was lovely enough to give Rachel Webb a pang of bitterest jealousy. However, she gave Finella a smile.

'Tremendous activity in the bee-hive,' she said with a show of jocularity.

Finella did not respond. She looked worried and upset and said to her mother-in-law:

'I'm terribly afraid Darley's arm is bad.'

'Why? What's the matter?'

'He has a temperature,' said Finella. 'I've just taken it. He was helping us move our things and we were just arranging, as a matter of fact, to go up to town tomorrow and look for a furnished flat as we thought we ought to be out of the Manor when . . . when Mr. Bryte and his sister come . . . and—'

'Well . . . what about his arm?' broke in Lady Martington with genuine anxiety.

'Well, he said he'd had a pain the whole morning, a throbbing in the old wound which he said always meant fresh trouble, and his head ached violently . . . that's why I took his temperature. It's over 101.'

'Good gracious . . . he must go to bed at once.'

'That's what I've said,' nodded Finella. 'Thank goodness we've moved our room. We're more or less straight in the chintz room, so shall I get Rose to fill a hot bottle?'

'No, leave it to me and I'll go alone and see him at once. Here, Finella . . . take this tray . . . and ring up Dr. Crawford.'

'Oh, he has got to see the M.O. from the hospital. If anything is wrong, he has to report there,' said Finella.

'I'll speak to Darley,' said Lady Martington with the cold hauteur she reserved for Finella and went her majestic way.

Rachel glanced at Finella as they carried the things across to the new wing.

'Most amusing, *your* pal taking over,' she murmured.

Finella, her head full of worried thoughts, looked puzzled, then, as she realized what Rachel meant, flushed brightly.

'Oh . . . I see . . . yes . . .' she stammered.

'Doesn't Darley mind . . . or is he going to be one of these complacent husbands?' went on Rachel who was out to jab at Finella today.

Finella's flush deepened.

'I don't know what you mean by "complacent husband", Rachel,' she said resentfully.

Rachel laughed.

'Of course I'm only chaffing you, but I mean . . . it must be a bit tough for Darley to have let his old home to one of your . . . er . . . admirers.'

Finella floundered for a suitable response, but

137

she never could cope with Rachel Webb's shafts and so, silently angry, said nothing.

But she was looking and feeling wretched when she deposited her mother-in-law's things in the room, then walked down the corridor to her new quarters. The so-called 'chintz room' was a big double room with its own bathroom, and faced the woods fringing the grounds. A rather lovely room, hung with old Jacobean chintzes, and polished oak furniture.

Finella, with her artistic eye, was quite conscious of the beauty and comfort of this place, but she had counted on getting away almost at once. She could not tolerate the idea of being here when Gil and his sister came. They were in some hurry to move in because Gil had had an offer for his own bachelor flat which necessitated him handing it over at once, and if he did not take up residence at once in his new 'country house' it meant his going to a hotel which he seemed disinclined to do. So Lady Martington had graciously consented for him to come down here on Sunday. And today was Wednesday.

Finella found her husband alone, sitting in a dressing-gown on the edge of his bed. He was fingering his injured arm, his brow puckered, and she could see him shivering slightly. Pity for him overcame all other emotions. Poor Darley ... it was tough luck ... that old wound troubling him again. He was so afraid it meant

138

another operation.

'Oh, Darley,' she said, 'get into bed . . . don't stay up a moment longer, my dear. You look so wretched.'

He looked at her. She was lovely even in that crumpled overall, and her eyes were soft with compassion as she approached him. But he felt dull and miserable . . . and not only because of his arm . . . but because of last night. Last night he had barely touched Finella's lips. He had had a sudden longing for the overture to come from her. All day he had been secretly gnawed by jealousy . . . by doubts about Gilfred Bryte. But he had said nothing. Done nothing. And Finella had been her usual sweet self. But he had *felt* that she was miles away from him. She had made no effort to come to his arms of her own accord. Long after she was asleep, he had lain awake smoking one cigarette after another . . . the pain in his heart almost as great a deterrent to sleep as the physical discomfort of his throbbing wound.

'Get into bed, dear,' repeated Finella.

'Mother's gone to fill a hot bottle for me and get aspirin and all the rest of it. A beastly fuss and a beastly nuisance the whole show,' he said shortly.

She sat down on the bed beside him, pushing a lock of silken hair back from her eyes.

'Poor Darley,' she murmured, then, looking at her hands: 'Gosh I'm dirty . . . must go and

139

wash. Moving is a grubby job.'

He stared at her moodily. She was like a pretty untidy child, he thought ... unconscious of her charm ... seemingly unaware of the power she wielded over men ... of the lure of those long slender limbs and that exquisite face. *Was* she the same Finella that he had loved and left five years ago? *Were* all his suspicions about Bryte unfounded? *Was* he just a damned fool ... over-anxious because he was falling every day more madly in love with his wife?

The old doubts tore at Darley. He shut his eyes and bit fiercely at his lips.

Finella thought his arm was hurting and put one of hers in a friendly, kindly way, around his stooping shoulders.

'Foul luck ... that horrid old wound ... wish I could do something for you,' she said.

The gesture, the nearness of her, the fragrance of her hair could stir him, even with the pain and fever of his wound. He caught her close, almost savagely pulling her against him, and brought his lips down on hers.

'You drive me crazy, Fin...' he muttered.

She gasped and pushed him away.

'Darley ... *really*...'

He sat up, deathly white, and grinned at her without humour.

'Yes, damned silly of me, isn't it ... to be so much in love with my own wife. Afraid the same fires don't burn in you, my darling. But never

140

mind. If I'm a nuisance, you're likely to get rid of me. I'll soon be back in hospital, if I know anything about it.'

She went scarlet, at a loss, as usual, to know how to justify her own reluctance and yet to show him the loyalty and affection that was deep-rooted in her. She tried to laugh.

'You are an old idiot . . . you can't make love to me when you . . . you . . . ought to be quiet . . . doped . . . resting . . . Darley, *darling* . . .' she went on stammering and laughing. 'Do let me help you off with your dressing-gown.'

He did not answer. He seemed to have collapsed. He let her do as she chose and she helped him into bed. He was shivering violently now and there were hectic flushes on each cheek-bone. Finella forgot the momentary crisis that had flared up with his embrace, and did her utmost now to look after him. He lay there, eyes shut, and he, too, tried to forget that unhappy moment when he had *felt* the faint shrinking of her body away from his. Here she was, being the anxious, devoted little wife. What had he to complain about? To the devil with this nonsense about her change of feeling and her ex-boy-friends. Hadn't he told her, himself, that he didn't expect her to enter a convent while he was away all those desperate nerve-racking years?

Finella drew the blinds, put a cool wet handkerchief over Darley's aching forehead and went to telephone the hospital which he had

141

been attending for treatment. The sooner the M.O. got here the better.

Darley's mother appeared with hot bottle and aspirin. Rachel Webb, she said, had just gone home, realizing that she was really in the way at the moment.

Half an hour later, the M.O., a nice young Captain in the R.A.M.C., had been, made his examination and decided that he must send an Army ambulance at once for Captain Martington. The sooner he was operated on, the better.

Finella and her mother-in-law lunched alone in gloom and the usual atmosphere of hostility which existed between them. Now and again Lady Martington let fall a remark. It was a mercy, she said, that Mr. Bryte was allowing her to remain in the house. Now if poor dear Darley was to be in hospital for several weeks, she would be near and could visit him. Just as well, too, with Darley ill, that he should go to hospital ... especially as Mr. Bryte and his sister were coming down on Sunday to live here. Darley would not want to be bothered with strangers.

Finella—who had been worrying about the immediate future—looked anxiously at Darley's mother.

'I can't very well stay here ... w-without Darley ...' she stammered. 'I ... I'd better go up to town and find a flat, hadn't I?'

'Certainly not,' said her ladyship sharply.

'You can't live alone in London. Darley wouldn't hear of it. Besides, don't you wish to be here where you can visit him daily? I'm amazed at you, Finella.'

Red to the roots of her hair, the girl stared at her plate. Her brain whirled. What a hopeless position. She could not stay in this house ... with Gil as its new master ... *could not*.

'I ... I could go to Barbie, my sister,' she said desperately.

Lady Martington looked at her over the rim of her glasses. She was remembering uneasily a hint that Rachel had dropped about Finella and Mr. Bryte.

'My *dear* Finella ... may I ask why you are so anxious to leave me and your husband ... and go to London?'

No answer. Finella floundered. Lady Martington added:

'You are not showing much feeling for Darley. I am more than displeased with your attitude ... toward both him and myself. If Mr. Bryte and his sister do not mind you remaining in my wing as a paying guest, you must certainly stay here and not go gallivanting up in London with your sister.'

CHAPTER THIRTEEN

Finella lapsed in despairing silence.

Really! The situation might almost be called funny if it were not so serious, she thought. Here she was trying to do what was right and get away from Gil, and Darley's own mother was baulking her. Finella did not see how she could refuse to remain here without appearing rude. Already she was unpopular with her mother-in-law and for Darley's sake she ought not to further the ill-feeling between them. Secretly she decided to get Darley on her side about this, if she could, although heaven knew she could not explain the real facts to *him*.

It was a pity, thought Finella, wryly, as she crumbled a piece of bread between slim, nervous fingers, that one could not be honest in this world without upsetting somebody's feelings. She would so much rather have gone to her husband and said: *'I don't want to stay down here because I'm more than half in love with Gil Bryte and I'm trying to get over it . . .'*

No husband would appreciate a remark like that because he would immediately become hurt and distressed and lose whatever trust he had in his wife. He might be thankful for her honesty but would scarcely appreciate being told that she was no longer in love with *him*.

144

So dismayed was she at the prospect of living down here in close proximity with Gil, right under the eagle eye of her mother-in-law, that Finella felt she must make a further effort to avoid the complications.

As soon as lunch was over she went upstairs to see Darley. It was half past one and the ambulance was expected in about quarter of an hour.

Darley looked flushed and his brow was knit with the pain of his throbbing wound. He had left untouched the broth that his mother had insisted upon sending up to him. But he managed to grin in a cheerful boyish fashion at Finella. That grin touched her deeply. Nothing, really, is more touching than courage. And she knew that to smile in his present state must have been an effort to Darley.

She sat down beside him and impulsively took one of his hands between her slim fingers. It burned with fever.

'Poor Darley,' she said gently. 'It *is* tough luck.'

He drew her fingers up to his lips and kissed them.

'Might be worse, Sweetness . . .'

(That gave her a pang . . . *'Sweetness'*. He used to call her that in the first days of their engagement. The word had a forlorn echo like the faint dim fragrance of some forgotten perfume or the sad echo of a remembered song

... and she wished with all her heart that that young subaltern whom she loved so madly had never been taken away from her by the ruthlessness of war and that she need never have changed, and that *Gil* had never been.)

Darley's eyes, bright with fever, scanned her face. He did not really know this young wife of his very well yet but he fancied he could recognize that troubled expression.

'What's worrying you, darling?' he asked.

She blurted out:

'Darley ... would you think it awful of me if I didn't fall in with your mother's suggestion about my staying down here, and if I went up to Barbie to live till you're better?'

He stared at her.

'What on earth do you want to go and live up in town for? Why, I'd never see you. Of course I know you and Mother don't always hit it off but it's only for a few weeks till I'm over this op ... then we'll have our flat together, darling. Why, I'd be lost if you couldn't come and see me. Will it be such a frightful bore?'

Silence followed this question. Finella looked and felt hopeless. Her cheeks were scarlet and her heart pounding. She could see that it was quite useless trying to get out of the invidious situation confronting her. Lady Martington didn't understand ... Darley didn't understand ... (Perhaps it was just as well they didn't ...) But it was all very difficult.

146

She mumbled:

'Of course it's not a bore ... I just thought it might be b-better for me to get away ... the house won't really belong to us ... er ... M-Mrs. Lucas might get fed up ... but I don't suppose she will ... I ... I'll stay, of course...'

Darley lay still. He was a little bemused with fever and pain and his thoughts were not quite clear in this moment, but he could not quite get away from the unpleasant suspicions that Finella's attitude roused in him. Suspicions about her friendship with that fellow Bryte. They had really been lying dormant in him ever since the night of his return when he found Finella with Bryte at the Berkeley. *What sort of friendship had theirs been?* Why didn't Fin want to stay down here? It wasn't only because of his mother, he was sure, although he knew that they got on each other's nerves. Did she want to keep out of the Manor because she *disliked* Bryte ... or liked him too much? He couldn't answer those questions neither could he ask them of Finella. His were dark, insidious thoughts that a man must keep to himself, unless he were sure of being on the right path. And it wasn't a path Darley wanted to tread. The last thing in the world he wished was to suspect his wife. But as he lay there brooding, an almost unconquerable jealousy gripped him. Suddenly he said in a rough, queer voice:

'Look here, Fin, do what you want . . . If you want to go up to your sister, go. It doesn't really matter.'

That frightened her a little and she bit nervously at her lower lip.

'No, darling, of course I won't . . . if you want me to hang on down here and be near you, I will.'

For the first time in their life together, he snapped at her:

'Well, for heaven's sake make up your mind and don't suggest first one thing and then another. It's so irritating.'

She drew her fingers away from his, her cheeks still crimson and her thoughts whirling.

'I'm so sorry. I didn't mean to annoy you.'

'It always annoys me when women can't make up their minds,' muttered Darley, who felt raw and ill. That wasn't in the least what he meant to say. He wanted to call her back to his bedside and get an assurance from her that she loved him, and that all this was nonsense . . . this worry about Bryte, and that he was just a jealous fool.

But he did not call her back and at that moment the ambulance arrived and there was no further time for conversation between them.

Just as the ambulance orderlies prepared to slide Captain Martington's stretcher into the ambulance he said:

'Hang on a moment . . .'

They stood waiting respectfully. Lady Martington was in the doorway, her eyes screwed up a little behind the pince-nez. Whatever else was unpleasant in Margaret Martington, her love for her one and only son was genuine. She did not like to see him lying on that stretcher, a blanket wrapped around him, his young face drawn and tanned cheeks livid except for the fever flush high on the cheekbones. She squirmed a little inside, remembering that her reckless selfishness in dealing with the family funds had lost so much for him. When he came out of hospital he should be able to go away for a long holiday, in luxury. Instead, he must either come back here as a paying guest in his own house . . . or go to a cheap flat in London.

Her reddened eyes turned to the slim girl who was now bending over the stretcher. She bridled. She thought, angrily:

'If *she* were not his wife, it would be better . . . I cordially dislike that girl . . .'

Darley held on to Finella's hand for a moment.

'So long, Sweetness . . . don't worry . . . I'll be all right,' he said.

But his eyes yearned at her. She bent quickly and kissed him on the lips.

'Good luck, darling,' she said.

Then he was gone. The ambulance moved slowly and smoothly down the drive. Finella

149

and her mother-in-law watched it out of sight. Finella's eyes were strangely wet, blurred with tears which welled from a heart aching for all kinds of reasons. She, too, had hated to see Darley on that stretcher. He had always been so gallant, so gay and so strong. She hated herself, too, because she knew that she had disappointed him. And she dreaded the future.

It was such a lovely May morning. The very first of May, thought Finella. Pale-blue sky, fluffy white clouds; green buds opening to the sun; slim green arrows of the new tulips pushing through the brown earth. All the sweetness and goldenness of spring.

She had wanted it to be a wonderful spring when Darley came home. And instead, they were both unhappy.

Lady Martington's acid voice brought her back to reality.

'Well, my dear Finella, no use standing here staring. We had better continue with our jobs.'

Finella followed her mother-in-law into the house. The elder woman added:

'I have my room to finish. Rose is going to help me as soon as lunch is washed up. You will have your room to see to. Then I think I shall lie down. I am a little tired.'

Finella, walking up the staircase, was thinking many things. She was thinking how handsome the old Manor looked—filled with the primrose glow of sunshine. This was a fine staircase with an exquisitely carved rosewood rail. It curved up to a broad landing. On the cream-painted walls were hung several oil paintings . . . the Martingtons of the past.

One always struck Finella in particular; the portrait of a young man in Georgian dress and peruke, one slender hand, half hidden by lace ruffles, on his waist. The face was Darley's; but the expression was not his. There was no kindness in this likeness of Darley's ancestor. The lips were bitter, the smile mocking. Yet it was Darley. And this morning in particular it was Darley. Just for a moment upstairs, before the ambulance came, when he had told her that he disliked women who could not make up their minds, he had looked bitter, like this young Georgian. It gave her a sensation almost of uneasiness. She did not want to make Darley either feel or look bitter. She mused that a Darley so changed would not be an easy person to deal with. Yet what could she do . . . how blot out the months that had belonged to Gil . . . and give to Darley all that he wanted of her, mind and body?

'We'll meet, maybe, for a cup of tea,' Lady Martington's sharp voice cut in on Finella's reflections. 'Are you listening, my dear? You haven't answered me.'

Then Finella, with a sudden dread of this woman and of being isolated here with her for the rest of the day and night, suddenly made up her mind what she would do.

'If you don't mind, I shall pop up to town on the 3.15,' she said breathlessly. 'I must see Barbie. It's rather important. She wants to see me. I can't go to the hospital today, in any case, and I'll be back in the morning in time to see Darley.'

Lady Martington turned and glanced over her shoulder at her daughter-in-law. She thought the girl looked rather flushed and queer. She also thought it peculiar that she should wish to rush away the moment Darley had left the house. However, let her go to her sister. If she *was* going to her ...

'I'll ring Barbara's place this evening and let you know if they have any news. I presume you'd like to know the result of the operation,' she said spitefully and with her iciest smile.

'Thanks ... yes, of *course* ...' mumbled Finella. 'Very kind of you. Shall I ... I ring you?'

'No, *I'll* ring,' said the other woman, and thought: 'I'll make sure you have gone up to your sister, my girl ...'

Finella fled to her room to complete the 'move'. She felt a trifle less hemmed in and stifled now that she could anticipate an evening with Barbie. That hateful old woman ... with her cold disapproval and malicious eyes. She didn't trust her. Finella knew it.

'Maybe she's right and I'm not to be trusted,'

thought Finella bitterly. 'Yet I want to be ... I want to be all that Darley thinks me. I don't want to hurt him or *anybody* ...'

If only she need not come back here this week-end and face Gil. But she must. She must be down here to see Darley ... She wanted to. Poor brave Darley who had got that beastly wound in defence of his country ... in defence of her, his wife. Of *Gil*, too.

Finella caught the 3.15 train from Godalming. She found time, too, to stop at a florist's and order a big bunch of sweet-smelling lilac to be sent to the hospital. On a card she wrote:

I am thinking of you. Get quite well, darling. Fin.

She meant it. She didn't feel a hypocrite. She loved Darley ... only not as she wanted to love him ... or as he wanted to be loved.

Finella was in a high state of nervous tension when at length she rang the bell of Barbara's little house in Bedford Gardens. Barbara herself opened the door. She wore an overall and held by the hand a small boy in a scarlet jersey and a diminutive pair of woollen pants. He had a grubby, chubby face and a mass of fair curls. Barbara stared at her sister.

'Fin—I didn't expect *you*, ducky. How lovely!'

153

'Hello, Barbie darling. Hello, my Mark...'
Finella bent down and lifted the small boy, who
squealed with delight.

Barbara closed the front door.

'I was just giving Mark his supper. Come
along up. How long can you stay?'

'Till tomorrow morning, early,' said Finella.

Barbara looked at her sister more closely and
saw the shadowed eyes and worried expression.

'Something wrong, Finny?'

'Everything,' said Finella with a hollow
laugh. She was carrying her small nephew, who
had already dragged off the little Juliet cap she
had worn, and with small sticky fingers was
threatening the clean frilled lawn collar on her
dark tailored dress.

'Careful of Aunty's dress, poppet,' warned his
mother.

But Finella hugged the tiny boy.

'Aunty Fin loves him to death ... bless
him...'

Barbara thought, as always when she saw her
sister with little Mark, how sweet Finella was
with children. She ought to have one of her
own. Perhaps now that her husband was home,
she would settle down to a proper married life
and have a family. It was what she needed,
Barbara was sure.

'Come and tell me all about yourself, ducky,'
she said, and led the way into Mark's nursery. A
delicious room with blue and white check

154

curtains, fairy-tale frieze and painted wooden furniture. Mark's father had made most of that furniture, he loved carpentering, and Barbara had painted it.

Finella sat on the edge of the table and lit a cigarette while Barbara put Mark back in his chair and tried to cajole him into finishing his bread and milk.

This room faced west. The last rays of the sun warmed it and touched Mark's curls to living gold. On the mantelpiece there were two photographs in a double frame. Barbara in evening dress. Jack in his naval uniform.

Finella looked at those photographs, symbol of happy parenthood, and at her small nephew's charming laughing face, while he munched a great mouthful of bread and milk, his big blue eyes grinning first at his mother, then at his aunt. Finella envied Barbara, as always, this happy home; this enchanting small son. It was what she had always meant should be *her* portion in life. She had wanted to be as happy with Darley as Barbara was with Jack; and to have a 'Mark'.

Barbara looked up at the sister who was two years younger than herself but had always seemed so very much a child.

Barbara was a different type, physically and mentally. She was much taller and of stronger build than Finella; they had little in common except perhaps the vivid bronze of their hair, the short nose and creamy skin. But Barbara's eyes were round and blue and she had a heavier jaw. She had never had Finella's air of fragility; or her elusiveness. She was a solid, dependable person. In the old days, when they had lived at home with their mother, it had always been Barbara who helped with the housework and cooking; Fin who was the artist; clever with a paint-brush in her slender, sensitive fingers; hopeless about mending or household 'chores'. When their mother was dying she had worried about Finella . . . left her in Barbara's care. And the elder girl, adoring her lovely and fascinating young sister, had done all that she could to help, to protect Finella. Somehow one always felt Finella must be 'protected'. Yet during the hard years of war, no girl had stood more physical discomforts, hardships of all kinds, in that tough ambulance job, than Finella. Her endurance had amazed Barbara. She knew now that there was strength and courage behind all that fragility.

But she had feared for the child the moment her marriage ended so abruptly on the very wedding day. She had wondered and so often worried over her . . . the consequences of those lonely years apart from Darley. And when Gil Bryte had come into Finella's life it was only what Barbara had dreaded all the way along. Now Darley was home . . . and all was not well. Barbara guessed it. And later, when Finella blurted out the whole troubled story, she knew that her fears for Fin had been founded. How best to help and advise her now was the problem.

Mark was in his cot, sleeping. The sisters sat in the small drawing-room—so full of the treasures Barbara and Jack had collected when they first married. Both loved old things. There were some charming pieces of Queen Anne in here; a tapestry fire-screen in a walnut frame; soft greeny-blue satin curtains which Barbara had cut and made herself, out of a big second-hand pair. She was clever with her needle. Clever with her life, Finella contemplated. She had got what she most desired out of it. But she *had* been lucky ... Jack had never left her for long.

'As far as I can see, you're just dithering between the two men, ducky,' Barbara said to Finella, looking at her with her round, kindly blue eyes. 'Why can't you chuck Gil Bryte and stick to Darley? He's worth it, surely.'

Finella swung round on her, her face passionate, rebellious.

'You don't understand, Barbie. I know Darley is worth while. I am still fond of him ... I swear I am. At times I ... I feel the old thrill. Then it fades ... I've seen so little of him ... he's so much of a stranger still. But I know Gil and he knows me. He fascinates me and I can't get away from him. Oh, you've never had to do

157

without your Jack for years and years. You don't know how lonely it was ... how empty ... one was starved for love and for someone to be nice to you and take you about and make you feel *wanted*. Gil provided all that for me and I can't suddenly put him out of my mind or heart ... just because Darley is home.'

Barbara sighed.

'Oh, dear! I see in a way what you feel. And I know I've been lucky with my Jack. But I don't *like* Gil Bryte ... I never did.'

'You don't really know him.'

'That's true. But he must be a swine ... to take the Manor like that ... keep it as a link with you ... Oh, Fin ... it was a clever move but a caddish one.'

Finella's lashes drooped and she gave a short laugh. She could see Gil's compelling eyes ... hear his masterful voice ... saying: *'You're like a small captured bird ... beating its wings in a cage ... and then when the cage is opened ... too scared to fly out ...'*

Clever, yes ... swine ... cad ... anything you like ... but she couldn't get away from him ... and couldn't get away from Darley, either.

With a half-sob she said:

'I don't want to go down to the Manor and be under Gil's roof. I promise you I don't. I tried to come up here to you. Lady Martington wouldn't hear of it. I think she half suspects me ... like Rachel Webb ... they'll both watch and spy on

158

me and life won't be worth living. But I've got to be there ... because poor Darley is in hospital. He looked so sad and in such pain this morning. Oh, Barbie ... I'm in a frightful muddle in my mind ... frightful ...'

Barbara moved across to the slender, quivering figure and put strong, comforting arms around it.

'My poor little Fin. It's a shame ... a shame things have turned out like this. I wish I could see a way out for you. ...'

Finella clung to her sister and burst into tears. But Gil's voice, half mocking, half tender, went on repeating in her brain:

'*Too scared to fly out ... too scared to fly out ... poor little Nella!*'

CHAPTER FOURTEEN

Finella spent the next three days at her husband's bedside in the officers' ward of the Military Hospital which was about a mile and a half from the Manor. It was a one-time asylum which had been converted into a war hospital. A big gaunt red-brick building standing on the brow of a hill with a lot of condemned labourers' cottages around it. Not the prettiest part of the countryside, and with a generally depressing atmosphere.

After four years of driving a Red Cross ambulance Finella had grown more or less used to the sight of hospitals, to the odour of disinfectants and even the grimness of death. But it had all left her with a slightly morbid strain which made her shrink now, in peacetime, from any connection with the old sights and smells. She did not like this hospital. She did not like entering Darley's ward, where there were several severe cases—men recently operated upon—limbless men, disfigured men ... many of them much worse than Darley. Some less so. All were amazingly gallant and cheerful in the face of their personal disasters. Darley was one of the most cheerful. And so, for his sake, Finella hid her own depression and morbidity and strove to be her most amusing, affectionate and attentive self when she was with him.

She used to sit by his bed, holding his hand, joking with him, telling him stories which she thought might interest him, connected with the Manor or their mutual friends. She brought him masses of flowers and books and what magazines she could collect. The other officers in the ward looked wistfully at the slender, beautiful girl who wore her well-cut suits so divinely and never had a hat on that tawny brilliant head. She always had a smile and charming word for those to whom she was introduced. They thought Martington's wife a 'dream'. They envied him. She was a wife worth coming home to. Lucky Martington.

But Darley Martington lay and wrestled with his own private problems and miseries and was not at all sure that he was so 'lucky'. How could it be lucky for a chap to be crazy about a wife who was not crazy about him. All these hours Fin put in at his bedside, her hand-holding, her little acts of tenderness and concern, puffing up his pillows, placing the bandaged arm in a more comfortable position, giving him his tea, bringing him presents. These things meant a lot. He hated it when she went away and left him with the maddening memory of rich, fragrant lips on his ... the lingering perfume of her hair ... He lived only to see her come back the next morning. With pride, with passion, with all the power of a man's love he would watch her walk into the ward, looking fresh and beautiful and infinitely desirable.

But he knew that everything she said or did was under a strain. He *knew that* now. Her laughter was a little too high-pitched and frequent, her attentions a little too forced. Something was wrong with this wife of his. Her thoughts wandered at times, her large smoke-grey eyes would turn from him suddenly and cloud with trouble. She seemed to him to be losing weight. Yet when he questioned her about herself, she 'pooh-poohed' any idea that she was not well or happy. She called him fanciful.

'You just hurry up and get well, Darley,' she would say. 'I don't like living at the Manor without you and I want our little flat together.'

He tried to believe her. He wanted with all the depths of his nature, all the wild desire that she roused in him, to think that this young wife of his wished to start her new life alone with him. But a shadow lay between them. Neither of them spoke or even hinted at that shadow. But it was there.

On this Sunday morning when she visited him she found Darley sitting up in bed looking and feeling stronger. When she bent to kiss him, he grinned up at her with the small-boy grin which used to captivate her when she first knew him. It caused her a little pang. He kissed her hard on the lips.

'Lord, you look lovely,' he said. 'Spring in your hair ... spring in your eyes ... and spring in my blood, darling ... damn it, I wish all these chaps would take up their beds and walk, and leave us alone.'

She laughed and drew back from him. He looked at her with bright, ardent eyes. She wore her grey suit and crisp, white blouse with a piece of white lilac pinned to the lapel of her jacket. She had brought him a lot of Sunday papers.

'Your mother is coming to see you this afternoon,' she said, 'so I won't come.'

His face fell.

'Oh, won't you, darling?'

'No—let her have you to herself. She likes it.'

'What are you going to do?'

'Take Sue for a walk, I expect. She sends you a wag, Darley. She misses you.'

'Good old Sue. I ought to get home in another ten days.'

Finella lapsed into silence. She was thinking: *'Ten days . . . with Gil . . .'*

Suddenly Darley asked:

'When does this chap Bryte and his sister turn up?'

'Today,' she said.

He frowned and ran his fingers through his roughened hair.

'Don't altogether like the idea of him or any other fellow taking possession of my home. My father would turn in his grave.'

'Never mind,' said Finella quickly. 'We must make some money and then we can all own the Manor again.'

'I don't want to think of money—it makes my spine creep,' said Darley with a wry smile. 'I've been a soldier all my life. To start contemplating an existence in a bowler hat as a city gentleman . . . phew!'

'You mustn't leave the Army—you love it!' she exclaimed.

'I shall have to, darling. I *must* make back what poor old mother has lost.'

'Poor, indeed,' thought Finella. 'Old ruffian.

163

Old gambler.'

'I think,' said Darley, 'I must have a chat with Bryte one day. He seems to own a lot of factories and so forth and be a man of substance. He might put me on to a good thing.'

Before she could restrain it, a hot flush stained Finella's face and she blurted out:

'Oh, don't . . . let's ask favours of *him*.'

'Why not?'

She dared not meet his gaze. Darley's eyes were so frank and inquisitive. . . . like a boy's . . . searching for the answer. The answer *she* could not give. She mumbled:

'Just *not* . . .'

'As you like. He's your friend,' said Darley, a trifle huffily.

They were silent then, slightly mistrustful of each other's thoughts and reactions. But Darley had noted her hot flush and wondered at it. If only he could get down to facts . . . about Bryte and Fin!

Finella changed the conversation and started to tell Darley that her brother-in-law had a new job, how he was going to be able to live in London in two months' time and be with Barbie and how happy they were. Darley only half listened. When Finella said at length that she must get back to lunch, they were both still guarded and the old barrier was between them. Darley looked at her slender loveliness, at the sun on her brilliant hair, and a wave of something approaching anger gripped him. It was too infuriating ... having to lie here chained to this damned hospital ward ... while Gilfred Bryte took possession of the Manor ... and was there to bask in Finella's smile; see her, hear her, talk to her. What would they talk about? What secrets in the past had they shared? What did *he*, her husband, know of these past five years she had spent without him?

He seized one of her hands so roughly that she winced.

'Darley ... you're hurting me ...'

Through his teeth he said:

'Don't go home and flirt with that jumped-up North countryman or I'll break his neck ... do you hear?'

She stared down at him, aghast. She had never heard Darley speak in such a voice ... or look like that. Of course, it was put on ... an exaggeration, she supposed, but there was an underlying bitterness and violence in him that reminded her again of that portrait of his Georgian ancestor ... and brought it home to her that this young man whom she had married was no weakling to be trifled with. She was between two strong men ... *two of them* ... God help her. She gave a strained laugh.

'Don't be so stupid. And what an old-fashioned word ... *flirt* ... you *are* silly, Darley!'

He glowered up at her, half in earnest,

half in fun.

'Don't you ever flirt? Eh, you beautiful thing?'

'Oh, I dare say,' she said, laughing oddly.

'I suppose you've only been on the most *platonic* terms with all your boy-friends while I've been abroad, eh?' He was being sarcastic now.

She bit hard on her lips.

'I don't know what all this is about. You're just—idiotic.'

'Possibly. Well—run along, darling. And ring up Rachel and tell her to come and amuse me since my wife refuses to come back today.'

So he had swung from Gil to Rachel. Finella's throat felt dry. She wanted to laugh the whole thing off . . . but something deep down within her was afraid. Yes, she was beginning to be afraid of Darley . . . he was so obviously jealous and possessive. As for Rachel Webb . . .

'I'll 'phone your girl-friend and give her your message,' said Finella coldly. 'So long till tomorrow, Darley.'

He caught her hand again and dragged her down to him.

'Kiss me . . .'

'Darley . . . be careful . . . the . . . the others will see—'

'See what . . . a chap kissing his very attractive wife as though he meant it?' mocked Darley. 'What a cruel sight!'

166

She tore herself away from him, crimson, upset.

'You're in a dreadful mood, Darley...' she said.

He did not detain her again. But his eyes, a little hot and heavy, watched the slender, graceful figure walk down the ward. And he was dismayed at himself ... at the turbulence of his own feelings. There were moments, he thought, when a chap could come near to hating a woman with whom he was madly in love ... just because he could not possess her utterly ... her mind as well as her body. It was altogether maddening, this feeling that Finella was not wholly his ... and that in some nebulous fashion which at the moment he could not define ... Gilfred Bryte meant something in her life.

Finella walked out of the hospital into the mild May sunshine and mounted the bicycle on which she had come from the Manor. She began to cycle slowly down the gravel drive through the gates of the hospital and out on to the main road.

She was still hot and angry ... not so much with Darley as herself. But she was thinking:

'If Darley and I go on like this ... with no real understanding ... things will come to a head and we shall be lost...'

She was feeling bewildered and hopeless when she got home. Rachel Webb was there, having a glass of sherry with Lady Martington. An impish spirit made Finella say to Rachel:

'Darley would like to see you. Do go along if you have time.'

Rachel Webb raised her brows.

'Thanks, I'd love to. But I thought you were there most of the time, Finella.'

'I'm not going this afternoon,' said Finella. 'I know Darley's mother would like to see him alone.'

'How thoughtful of you, my dear,' said Lady Martington with her most freezing smile. Then added with apparent innocence: 'That will suit me, really. You will be here to receive Mr. Bryte and his sister. It will be so nice for Mr. Bryte, since you two are old friends.'

Finella did not answer. But she saw Rachel's dark eyes sneering slightly. Trembling with anger, Finella turned and walked out of the room. Lady Martington and her god-daughter raised their sherry glasses and nodded to each other in perfect understanding.

For the rest of that afternoon Finella was in a 'state of nerves'. She did not want to be here alone when Gil and his sister arrived. But now she could not avoid it. But she decided that she could not and would not stand this sort of thing much longer. She must sooner or later break ... in which direction she honestly did not know.

She dreaded Gil's arrival ... and yet wanted

it. Wanted his particular understanding of her ... which at the moment her husband did not seem to possess.

She smoked one cigarette after another ... pacing up and down the drawing room, old Sue sitting in her accustomed place on the hearthrug, watching her. Up and down ... up and down, walked Finella ... the slim hand lifting the cigarette to her lips very slightly shaking.

It was about four o'clock when the sound of car wheels sent her running to the window. She saw Gil's big car coming up the drive. And a few moments later Rose showed him into the room, then went off to help the chauffeur, who was carrying in the luggage.

Gil, hat in hand, advanced towards Finella, his rugged face alight.

'Nella ... but how wonderful to find you alone!'

She stood rigid, her big eyes fixed upon him.

'Has ... your sister come?'

'No. Jo can't come down till Monday. You'll have the ugly pleasure of entertaining Gil by himself, my dear. Jo had to stay on with my father. He fell down and fractured a wrist the day before yesterday and she volunteered to remain with the old boy for the week-end.'

'I see,' said Finella.

Gil closed the door behind him and advanced toward her.

'Nella ... my poppet. It really is good to see

you again. You look entrancing. Where is mamma-in-law?'

'At the hospital ... with Darley ... you know ... he has had another operation on his arm?'

'Lady Martington mentioned it in a note she wrote me ... So we're all by ourselves. That sounds intriguing.'

He was beside her now ... very close. Too close. Her knees seemed to tremble under her as she read the old flaming ardour in his strange, keen eyes. She said:

'Oh, Gil ... be good ... *please* ... help *me* to be good...'

He laughed softly, caught her to him and set his lips to her mouth.

CHAPTER FIFTEEN

For a moment, weakly, Finella surrendered. That strange magnetism that was in this man always fired her blood, perhaps it was because he was so much stronger in every way than she was. So sure of himself.

It was a moment of abandon and forgetfulness, of everything but the close embrace in which he held her and the hard pressure of his lips against hers. Just for a moment her arms went round his neck and one

170

of her slim hands moved up and touched the dark roughness of his hair. But it was *only* for a moment and then the passion in her died down and she pushed him away almost violently.

'No,' she said through her teeth. '*No.*'

The man looked at her through narrowed lids, his breath quickened and his pulses on fire. But he did not attempt to touch her again.

There had been one or two women in Gilfred Bryte's life ... one girl in particular before the war, in his own home town, young and physically lovely and he had been her first lover ... and her *last*. He was a man of strong impulses and violent passion and Vera had for some time satisfied that side of him which was not taken up with his work. He had always put girls such as Vera into the background of his thoughts and actions once his gust of passion flickered out. With him, his job, his career, came first, and when he married he intended that it should be to a woman who could grace his home and be a companion to him. A woman of charm and culture who would also be the envy of other men.

Finella, in his mind, supplied all these qualities. She was enchanting to look at, and at the same time a girl with a flair for painting, for *décor*. She could supply all the artistic side which he, personally, lacked. He knew that his taste was none too good. He had sprung from humble parents and a humble home. But this place, for instance, and women like Lady Martington and Finella stood for the class which he outwardly despised but secretly admired. In Parliament, one day, he meant to stand for Labour ... but in his own personal life he wanted the glamour of the cultivated background, which he believed Finella could give him.

From the moment he had first met her he had been fascinated by her fragile and slender beauty, by her curious mixture of innocence and experience ... she, the tough ambulance driver, who was also a sensitive delicate creature, who shrank from hardship and suffering. That combination of spirit and helplessness in her was incredibly fascinating to him. He had never met any girl who intrigued him so; no one, indeed, whom he had wanted for his wife. But it was his ambition to get Finella away from Darley Martington and make her his own.

Why, he asked himself, angrily, at this precise moment must he remember Vera and her predecessors. Perhaps something in the way Finella's hand had just tried to smooth back her tumbled hair and wipe a smear of lipstick from the corner of the mouth he had kissed so madly. The way fear had shot into those large brilliant eyes when she had said 'No'.

Finella bore an uncanny resemblance in that instant to Vera, who had made the same gesture and murmured the same protest. (But Gil had been ruthless with Vera.) It was five years ago now and all over ... forgotten by everybody except, maybe, Vera's relations. But it had been a sordid business. For Vera had been unable to take care of herself; a little too simple and unworldly. She was a miner's daughter who had never left her native village. She had worshipped Gilfred Bryte and when he walked out on her she had killed herself. Poor, silly, tragic Vera ... She had thrown herself into the canal, and they had found her body and a pathetic note, in which she said she could not face life without the man who was the father of her unborn child.

Those who had known that that man was young Bryte were of no importance to Gilfred, and it had not mattered to him when they told him what they thought of him, then cut him dead. He had gone back to London and put the memory of Vera out of his busy life. But at times that frail, forlorn ghost haunted him and this afternoon, for some damnable reason, he thought grimly, the ghost came back to haunt him again ... incorporated into Finella. Absurd! He wanted to marry Finella. He would like his children to be hers.

But something made him leave her alone in this particular crisis. He drew a deep breath, smoothed back the hair which she had just touched with that half-frightened tenderness, which had fired him so, and smiled at her.

'Don't get fussed, my dear little Nella. Calm yourself. If you don't want me to make love to you, I won't.'

She flushed and tried to laugh.

'Really, Gil, we must be sensible. There's the maid and . . . and . . . anyone might see . . . and . . . oh, there are so many things against it . . . you know!' she added, stammering.

He walked to a table, took a cigarette from a shagreen box and tapped one on his thumb-nail.

'Just as you wish, my dear. But you can't expect me to keep my head for long. I haven't seen you alone since that night at the Berkeley, which was so rudely interrupted, I may say, and I still happen to be in love with you.'

She breathed fast and to cover her own confusion she, too, took a cigarette and let him light it for her. She wished she could control the trembling of her limbs, and the wild desire to throw herself back into his arms. But mingled with that desire was the memory of Darley with his bandaged arm, lying in hospital. If she betrayed him like this she would be unspeakable, she told herself. Of course, she had known the moment Gil took this house, and circumstances had forced her to stay in it, that this sort of thing would happen. She was bound to be exposed to temptation. She had not yet got away from the attraction of Gilfred Bryte. But she wished, miserably, that it wasn't so, and

174

that she could feel this way about Darley.

'Of course,' she heard Gilfred's voice, 'I may be making a fool of myself. You may not be in the least in love with me any more.'

Her nerves growing steadier, she dared to meet his gaze.

'Gil, I don't see what's to be gained by me telling you what I feel. I'm Darley's wife and he's home, and that's that.'

He shrugged his wide powerful shoulders.

'Sounds simple. But I think there's more to it than that, Nella. You're not happy. I know you too well. You used to laugh a lot with me. You had tremendously high spirits ... you were always like a delighted child about everything. Now you're sad and nervous. Don't deny it. The husband's homecoming hasn't been a success.'

Her lashes dropped. She did not speak for a moment. For some perverse unaccountable reason she did not like hearing Gil make that bald statement. It was altogether too frightening ... *if it was true.* She did not want to admit it in so many words, for in so doing she would be admitting her own failure in what she considered her duty towards the man she had married. It would also be defeat for Darley. A complete betrayal of his trust. She floundered for a suitable reply to Gil. She realized, vaguely that he was a menace to her and to Darley in no small measure, and that he was trying to shatter

175

her marriage ... blatantly hoping to do so, in fact. She could not, in the depths of her heart, admire him for it. For coming down here like this, deliberately to disturb her peace and seek to destroy her puny efforts at unity with her husband. She knew that if Gil had been what the world called a *good man* he would have gone out of her life that night at the Berkeley and stayed out of it. But one didn't love a man because he was good or cease to love him because he was bad. One just loved ... and in many cases madly, inconsequently, foolishly.

The trouble was, that, conscious though she was of her folly and of Gil's unworthy conduct in this matter, Finella had not sufficient strength to walk out on him and end this affair finally.

But that sense of decency and the echo of the love she had once felt so acutely for her young husband would not allow her to put Darley right away from her without a struggle. She was going to carry on with that struggle, she told herself grimly, even if it was to prove to Gil that she was not as painfully weak as he imagined. If he took it for granted that she was giving up the contest at once, he was wrong. His attitude did not make him the more victorious, and it made her less eager to give in. Here and now Gilfred met with that spirit in Finella which raised her so much above the level of girls like Vera.

Finella said:

'Let's try and play fair, Gil. After all, this is Darley's home and he's in hospital.'

Gil grimaced at her.

'Are you trying to appeal to my better nature, Nella, my sweet?'

'I don't believe you have one,' she said bluntly. 'You're an absolute fiend, Gil. You get what you want no matter whom you hurt in getting it.'

He opened his eyes wide in pretended astonishment.

'Darling, why the sudden lecture? Who am I hurting? You? If so, I'll quit right away. But I thought you cared about me as much as I did— and do—about you. At least, you gave me that impression before your husband came back.'

Finella knit her beautiful narrow brows in fierce perplexity.

'Don't you understand that *that's* the whole trouble. Things can't be the same because he *has* come home. But we've had this all out, Gil, I told you then, and I tell you now, I think it only fair to give my marriage a chance. I'm terribly fond of Darley and I ... I was more than that when I married him.'

Gilfred Bryte was encouraged by her words. His confidence that he had Finella within his grasp returned.

'Ah, Nella,' he said, 'I see it all from your point of view, but marriage isn't good enough when a woman's only *fond* of her husband.

You're more than fond of me, aren't you, Nella?'

'You've no right to ask me that now.'

'I had no right to ask you before, but I did, and I shall go on asking,' he said, with a flash of insolence, and then laughed and moved toward her. 'Nella, darling, what do you take me for? A half-wit? I assure you I understand the position fully and the law is all against one fellow taking away another chap's wife, but I'm out to do it this time if I can and that's honest.'

It was too honest for Finella. It floored her. She was caught helplessly in a trap between the lure Gil had for her and that other loyalty and affection which she genuinely felt toward Darley. She thought:

'I wonder how many other girls are going through this ... with husbands coming back whom they haven't seen for so long that they're strangers ... and with another man in their lives ... Oh, it's an absolutely *ghastly* position. There are moments when I'd like to run away from both of them. Yes *both of them*.'

Gil caught one of her hands and squeezed it.

'Poor little Nella. I'm badgering you. Sorry, sweet. I'll try to be good. I've so looked forward to coming down here and being near you, and it was such a delightful surprise to find you alone in the house. Give me credit for the fact that I didn't know this would happen when I took the Manor.'

178

'No, I suppose not.'

'Then smile at me, Nella. Let's try to enjoy ourselves since we're thrown together. I'll be awfully discreet and I won't kiss you again until you want me to. There! Will that do?'

With a returning sense of humour, Finella smiled and shook her head at him.

'I know you won't stick to it but I'll try to believe you.'

For an instant his dark compelling gaze held hers.

'I want you, Nella. I want you more than anything in the world. Remember that,' he said in a low voice. 'Remember the words of that old song ... "*Don't you know, little fool, you never can win. Use your mentality, wake up to reality* ... "'

But Finella, fancying that she heard a footstep outside the door, tore her hand away and gave a nervous laugh.

'It may be "reality", but I don't think it has much to do with my mentality,' she said. 'It's just the way things are. Now do go and unpack, Gil, and forget about me.'

'The first command I obey. The second one is impossible,' he said slickly.

But he went, giving her a quick ardent look over his shoulder before the door closed behind him.

Finella walked to the window and looked blindly out. The May sunshine was dappling the

179

lawn which, at the moment, old Watkins, who had been head gardener here for thirty years, was cutting as fast as his arthritis would allow him. Darley's spaniel, Sue, lay in a warm patch on the gravel path, licking her paws. Finella remembered that she had promised Darley to take Sue for a walk. She felt utterly miserable. Gil's presence in this house was going to bring her no happiness, and she knew it, but the challenge to her loyalty and her strength was still on. And she did not intend to relax her efforts to meet it.

CHAPTER SIXTEEN

When Darley told his wife that he expected to be out of hospital in ten days, he was over-optimistic. The operation was a success but the healing process slow. At the end of the fortnight he was still in the ward, and although allowed up during the day, they could not let him go home, because of the dressings.

During this fortnight Darley's mental state was not enviable. He saw Finella every day. More often than not twice a day. She was always gentle and charming to him. She never failed to bring him some little gift, whether it was a new book, a bunch of flowers or some cigarettes. But the shadow between them, which he had felt so sensitively of late, was still there and certainly not diminishing. Neither were matters helped by his knowledge that Gilfred Bryte had taken up residence at the Manor, and motored down every night from his job, and spent most of Sunday there. Darley—who had at the commencement of his return home made up his mind not to be jealous—became increasingly so. And it was mainly because of what he *did not know*, rather than of what he *knew*.

He asked Finella endless questions about Bryte and his sister and she appeared to answer them with nonchalance. The inference of her replies held nothing in the least suspicious. She said that Gil and Mrs. Lucas, his sister, had settled down in their new home and appeared to like it enormously; that they were easy-going and no trouble and that Joanna had endeared herself to Lady Martington from the outset, flattering her by begging her to continue running the place in her own way. She appeared to be a quiet, good-natured, rather indolent woman, who was willing to be 'managed'. And, as Finella said to Darley: 'Mother does like to do the managing.'

Financially the thing was working out beautifully from Lady Martington's point of view. She could go on being lavish as her own extravagant nature desired, and Bryte and his sister did the paying. Money, with them, seemed to flow like water. Darley's mother sniffed a bit and called them '*nouveau-riche*', but she liked Joanna Lucas and she had a certain admiration, she admitted for Gilfred. She had always admired success and he, obviously, was a prosperous man.

Darley, however, was not satisfied with the position. It rankled with him continually that his home should now be paid for by an outsider. He began to develop a fetish about making some money for himself, and being able to restore the Manor completely to its rightful owners.

He made up his mind to resign his commission. He also decided not to discuss the matter too fully with Finella ... or even with his mother. He grew a little bitter and introspective during that session in hospital. It was against his true principles, the fundamental qualities of his nature, to concentrate on the thought of money and the making of money. He despised the power that it was ... the pull it gave fellows like Bryte. But he was forced to recognize the fact that in the past he had not given money sufficient thought. He had been so used to all that he was given by his father and to his life as a Regular soldier which, in peace-time and before he took on the responsibility of a wife, had held no financial terrors.

He made up his mind to leave the Army as soon as they would release him. He would work for Henry Wychless. The baronet, a man in his early sixties, had been a lifelong friend of

Darley's father. He was a wealthy man, senior partner in a big firm of international stockbrokers. His only son and heir, Peter Wychless, had been killed in the war. He was not a Regular but had been on the Stock Exchange in his father's business. The war had robbed him of his chance to make good and done to him what it had done to many other promising young men: flung him into a uniform and after four years of fighting extracted the toll of his life. Peter Wychless had been one of the heroic band of Airborne troops who had died at Arnhem.

When Darley had seen Sir Henry up in London a few weeks ago, the old man, broken by his loss, had intimated that he was attached to the man who was one of Peter's best friends and had at the time hinted that it was 'a pity' Darley was a soldier.

'More future for you in my sort of life, my boy,' he had said. 'Wish I had a chap like you to take Peter's place.'

It would be, Darley had reflected many times since, a wonderful chance for him. If he cared to chuck the Army, Wychless would employ him ... and he might learn more than a bit about making money.

Sometimes Darley lay awake at night in that officers' ward picturing himself as a prosperous business man ... and all he would do to get back the money his mother had lost; and all that

183

he would do for *Finella*.

In his imagination he bought wonderful things for his wife. Gorgeous clothes which would grace that marvellous and alluring figure of hers, wonderful jewels, a luxury flat in town, holidays on the Continent, once the old gay haunts ... Monte Carlo, Biarritz, and the others, had revived again. Fin would be ten times more beautiful and attractive than she was now; and she would be grateful to him ... repay him with her kisses.

Exaggerated, ridiculous flights of imagination. Darley laughed grimly at himself and such fancies. He knew that Fin would never love him any more because he could buy her diamonds. She wasn't like that ... she never had been, nor could be, a gold-digger.

He knew, too that he only built up these extravagant pictures in his mind because he was secretly afraid of losing her altogether.

He grew moody and his temper took an irascible turn in these days. More often than not when Finella came to sit with him he was short with her, sometimes he tried to goad her into saying something positive about herself and her feelings toward him. He would feel a demon within him which needed some outward expression. He could not stand watching her grow quieter, more subdued, every time she saw him; and feeling her drift further and further from him. Why, even their conversations these days were strained; held little of the old gay *camaraderie*. He wanted to *force* her to disclose her secret heart to him. He could not bear her elusiveness. It drove him crazy. Yet he had nothing with which to accuse her, openly. But he would say:

'Suppose you spend the evenings looking lovely for your old boyfriend . . .'

Or:

'Do you and your boy-friend manage to get away from Mamma and the sister now and again, and have fun . . . ?'

Petty, unfounded . . . he knew it . . . and she was extraordinarily patient. She did not flare up or snap back at him. She just smiled . . . (the very quality of the unknown, the secretiveness of that smile of hers tormented him) and told him he was 'silly'. Only once he got her on the raw and she flashed:

'Do stop calling Gil my "boy-friend" like that . . . it annoys me, Darley. . . .'

Then he told her he was sorry and that he adored her and that he was a jealous fool. He lapsed into sullen silence and fancied he saw weariness and even despair in her large smoky eyes. And he cursed himself for a fool and felt that if his marriage failed . . . it would be his fault. That was one side of it; the mood of a moment. He decided to put all his trust in her. Then back he would lapse into a morbid craving to know what there had been between Gilfred

Bryte and his wife in the past.

Gradually he began to attach importance to anything and everything that his mother—or Rachel Webb—had to say about what was going on at the Manor. Lady Martington never came out into the open about Fin; did not let Darley know that she actually disliked her daughter-in-law. But she dropped clever little hints . . . and those hints tormented him when, after she had gone, he brooded over what she had said.

'Your pretty Fin is enjoying having people in the house,' Lady Martington said lightly, on one occasion. 'That Mr. Bryte is quite a gay dog. They rolled back the rugs last night and danced to the radio. Fin is such an exquisite dancer.'

Darley knew it. How often in the past he had held that slender, seductive body in his arms and told Fin how 'exquisitely' she danced. Those were the old Sandhurst days when she had eyes for no man but himself. He brooded darkly over the picture of her dancing with Bryte, at the Manor . . . he could not stop himself from a mental flash-back to the night at the Berkeley when he had surprised Fin . . . seen that look of rapture on her face as she moved round the dance-floor with the other man.

There were innumerable other little hints, all so innocent, all suggesting that Lady Martington was glad 'dear Fin' had some brightness in the house . . . and that she got on *so* well . . . with Gilfred. Such *old* friends, etc., etc.

Then Rachel Webb. Rachel—who relaxed from the rather hard person she was with others and became soft and sweetly sympathetic with Darley. She did not like Gil Bryte and bluntly said so. Once Darley asked her a question about him and Rachel replied:

'Don't ask me. I shall just be catty about him. I think he is rather sinister. I can't imagine why Finella bothers with him.'

'*Does* she bother with him much?' Darley asked, with a smile, trying to assume indifference. And Rachel, shrugging her shoulders, answered:

'Oh, of course, they were great friends while you were away. But I couldn't be bothered with him. He isn't my type.'

Bleakly, the young officer thought over those words. Did Rachel mean that Bryte was *Fin's type?*

Again he made an effort to control his feelings and laughed at Rachel.

'Oh, you women! And what sort of chap *is* your type may I ask, my dear old Rachel?'

She gave him a melting look from her bright dark eyes—a look Darley could not fail to understand—and said:

'I think you know that. You know *me.*'

He flushed and averted his gaze. It was the first time she had ever intimated openly that she cared for him this way. They had always been excellent friends. He admired her. But thinking of 'types', she had never been his. She was the antithesis of Fin ... there was nothing essentially sweet or gentle about Rachel! And she had none of Fin's languorous beauty. Yet when he looked at Rachel this moment he saw that she was undeniably an attractive young woman. Her figure had improved; she was well-dressed and she had a clear sun-browned skin, beautiful teeth, and intelligent, sparkling eyes. He had often wondered why Rachel didn't get married. His mother had at times suggested that it was because she was in love with him. He had never believed her. But today ... he had to half believe it. At least, if Rachel was not serious about him, she was being extremely nice. The natural masculine vanity which had been recently so bruised by Fin ... was flattered by the melting softness in those brown eyes of Rachel's. He found himself touching her hand and murmuring:

'My dear ... you're a grand girl ... it's nice having you around...'

At once her firm brown fingers closed convulsively about his. She said:

'Darley...'

Just his name ... nothing more ... but with a throb in her voice. After she had gone, he lay contemplating the fact that his mother was right. Rachel was in love with him. And Rachel was still to be wooed and won.

It was a distinctly pleasant and soothing thought for a man who was fast reaching the conclusion that his wife was no longer in love with him. But the honey of that thought was painfully mixed with gall ... his bitter, desperate love for Finella.

Darley's wife, herself, was not to be envied her state of mind. Since Gil came to the Manor, these days had been the most awkward and disturbing in her life. He had kept his promise not to make love to her or kiss her again. In front of Lady Martington he was tact itself. But there were always moments when they were alone ... when he made some quick-searching remark to bring the blood to her cheeks and the old half-fearful, half-ecstatic thrill to her heart.

'You must meet me alone ... either down here or up in town ... soon ... or I shall go mad,' he had said the last time he had the opportunity.

She had answered, breathlessly:

'No ... I can't ... leave me alone, Gil ...'

But he would not leave her alone and she knew it. She knew, too, that she was failing Darley and that he was unhappy. She felt that from day to day they were both living on the edge of a volcano. The tension was almost unbearable.

She went up to Barbara one night; she came back the next day more than ever restless and unhappy. Jack, her brother-in-law, was home on leave. Barbie looked so radiantly happy. She had watched them go off arm in arm to their room and thought:

'Oh, lord ... I wanted to be like that with Darley. I *wanted to* ...'

But it had all gone wrong. And one could not command love from any one source, nor give it, just because one *wanted* to. The mainsprings of love are more mysterious and unaccountable than that.

Before Finella left Bedford Gardens, Barbie had looked at her half in pity, half in reproach and begged her to 'try and be happy with Darley'.

She had tried. But it didn't seem to work. Yet neither was she happy any longer in the old, carefree way when she was with Gil.

Darley came home.

On the day he was due to arrive, Finella went down with a temperature due to a heavy cold. Her head ached so that she could barely lift it. She had fully intended to go to the hospital with a car to fetch Darley. But Lady Martington insisted upon her going to bed.

'Apart from giving that horrid cold to Darley just when he is still so unfit ... I don't like germs spread through the house,' she announced with her usual tartness. 'In fact I suggest Darley sleeps in the dressing-room tonight. I'll tell Rose to help me make up his bed there.'

Finella complied. She had no particular wish to share her room with Darley. The last thing she wanted was to cope with emotional problems tonight. And a streaming cold and thick head were not conducive to glamour, she told herself wryly. She was better shut away from the whole household.

Lady Martington took pleasure in informing Finella, with one of her cold smiles, that dear Rachel had gone to fetch Darley.

Finella looked indifferent. But as she lay in her darkened room—the curtains half drawn to shut out the sunshine, for it was a beautiful May Day—she thought about Darley and Rachel Webb. And her thoughts were not so indifferent. That girl thoroughly disliked her. And she seemed, these days, to impress Darley. He was always talking about Rachel. It was not that she was jealous, Finella told herself . . . far from it. But she was feminine enough to resent her husband's interest in any other woman—especially one who was an enemy.

It was three o'clock when Rachel drove Darley up to the front door of the Manor. Lady Martington was at a local committee meeting. Joanna Lucas was up in town for the day. Gilfred, as usual, was at work. In fact, for the last two days he had been staying in London, too busy to get down here.

Finella, nursing her aching head and blowing

her small nose forlornly, heard the front door shut . . . heard various sounds . . . Rachel's self-confident little laugh . . . Darley's voice . . . old Sue's hoarse delighted barking, welcoming her master home.

Finella supposed that Darley would come straight up to see her. She lay wretchedly thinking about everything, dreading the immediate future. Thank goodness she would not be downstairs tonight . . . having to face both Darley and Gil. How she hated this communal life! She wanted to get away; yet even more did she dread taking up life quite alone with Darley. He looked at her so strangely nowadays . . . sometimes almost suspiciously. He made her feel uncomfortable and guilty. Yet she had nothing, really, these days, she thought, to feel guilty about. She was doing her level best; and it was not her fault if she could not establish a close bond with Darley.

Darley did not come up to see her.

Finella felt suddenly stupidly annoyed; mainly because it was Rachel Webb who was downstairs with him. She waited for half an hour, then in a fit of childish pique, got up, put on a long blue house-coat, combed back her thick, red-gold hair, and powdered her nose. She wrinkled her small nose at her reflection in the mirror. (No girl looked her best with a bad cold, she thought.)

She went downstairs—meaning to make a

192

nice little speech of welcome to Darley. After all, he *was* the wounded hero . . . and she never forgot that . . . her share of the debt his country owed him.

She reached the library door and pushed it open. She looked in just in time to see the astonishing sight of her husband standing in front of the fire which Rose had been told to light in the Captain's honour . . . with Rachel in his arms. They both seemed lost to the world in that embrace.

CHAPTER SEVENTEEN

Finella's first inclination was to walk into the library and say: 'Don't mind *me*, Darley. How charmingly you kiss, Rachel!' But she reconsidered that decision and quietly withdrew before either of the two could see her. Slowly she walked upstairs. Her face was scarlet. She thought:

'It would be making myself cheap to walk in on them. I couldn't bear to watch them spring apart and stutter out excuses. All that sort of stuff. Much better not.'

Better to save her own dignity. Whatever Rachel might say in the matter, Finella disliked the idea that Rachel Webb might 'crow over her'—having proved herself so fascinating that she had managed to induce Darley to forget that he was a married man.

Once in her bedroom again, Finella took off her housecoat and climbed back into bed. She hid her face in the pillow. She was shivering. Her body felt hot and cold in turn. Her head was throbbing. Doubtless this little 'incident' had sent her temperature up again. What an idiot she had been to go downstairs. Her intention had been to welcome her husband home. She laughed—not a very gay laugh—at the thought. He was being very warmly welcomed by his old friend, Rachel. She could not forget the sight of those two ... Rachel's enraptured face ... Darley kissing her.

'As he has so often kissed me,' thought Finella. 'Really, men are peculiar. One woman does as well as another.'

Then she retracted that unpleasant theory. It wasn't really true in Darley's case. He was not by nature promiscuous. In fact she, who knew him fairly well, was convinced that he was fundamentally a faithful man. If he was out for 'fun and games' with Rachel, it was her— Finella's—fault. It would be absurd of her to adopt the 'injured wife' attitude. What about her own disloyalty ... and the feverish kisses Gil Bryte had taken from *her* lips?

Finella sat up with a jerk, pushed the heavy red-gold hair out of her eyes and pressed a handkerchief to her mouth. She felt *awful*. Not only with her cold ... but with her thoughts. They were not happy ones. By right she ought not to be at all upset what she had just seen. She ought to be mildly amused ... even glad that Rachel, or any other woman, was taking Darley off her hands. After all, wasn't that what she wanted? Queer, but she did not in this moment feel that it was. Dog in the manger, perhaps, she reflected bitterly. And she did *not* relish the thought that Darley was attracted by Rachel Webb. Darley was her husband. The impudence of Rachel ... Lady Martington's precious god-daughter ... trying to steal her *husband*.

Finella began to shake with helpless laughter. She laughed until the tears ran down her flushed cheeks. Tears that were more of anger than sorrow. There was a certain sardonic humour in the situation, she thought. She was still mad about Gil ... and yet hated to see another girl in Darley's arms. That was inconsistency if you like! She knew it. It frightened her a little ... to know herself capable of such feelings. Could it be that she loved *both* those men? That would be hateful and unfeminine. She and Barbie used to have debates on life and love and men and women, and once had agreed that the average man was capable of loving two women at the same time, and still being a nice person. But that no *nice woman* could do so. If she really believed that, then she, Finella, was not *nice*.

She flung herself back on her pillows full of cold and fever and misery. It was all too confusing. She didn't really love both Darley and Gil. Not in the same way. Darley was her first lover . . . her husband . . . the one to whom her loyalty was due. Gil had come between them in Darley's absence and was still here, an apparently insuperable barrier. He attracted her—so she thought—in every way. But was it only infatuation? Would her desire for him in the future suddenly vanish overnight and leave her to regret, bitterly, that she had, by her own conduct, driven Darley away from her?

She began to cry again, wretchedly . . . then realized that she was only making herself feel worse and doing no good . . . stopped crying and took two aspirin. She lay down again and tried to blot out the whole mental picture. But she found herself uncomfortably picturing those two downstairs—and still—whether inconsistently or not—resenting it.

Could she have seen into the library at this moment she would have found Darley and Rachel no longer kissing . . . but seated side by side on the chesterfield . . . Darley filling his pipe . . . Rachel smoking a cigarette. The man was the most disturbed of the two. Rachel was smiling, calmly, and if her pulse-beats were faster in this, her 'little hour of triumph', no one would have known it. The fingers holding her cigarette were quite steady. But Darley was flushed and upset.

'Don't know what made me do that, Rachel,' he was saying. 'But somehow, when you stood there looking so damned attractive, I just had to kiss you, somehow. You know, you've got the most provocative way with you these days. Why didn't you produce it for me in the past? Good lord, we've known each other years and never done anything like this before.'

Her dark eyes sparkled at him.

'Perhaps you never noticed that I was rather fond of you, Darley,' she said. 'But I always was.'

He looked and felt dismayed.

'Were you?'

'Of course. You blind old bat. Your mother knew . . . but you seemed so keen on your job in those days and then . . . Finella appeared on the horizon.'

He stuck the pipe in his mouth, scowling a little. It made him feel uneasy and guilty to think of his wife. Damn it all, a chap ought to have more control. He must be in a vulnerable state . . . to be led into kissing Rachel in that passionate fashion. But he had been so damned upset lately about Fin . . . shut out, somehow . . . lonely in his fashion . . . disappointed. Rachel was an old, tried friend, and she had been extremely attentive to him while he was in hospital. Just now she had come close to him, put her hands on his shoulders and told him how happy she was to see him back in the Manor. There had been a definite invitation in her eyes . . . her lips. And he had 'fallen for it'.

She looked at him covertly through her dark lashes and guessed what he was feeling. Softly, she said:

'Don't feel bad about it, Darley dear. I . . . liked it, you know . . .' She gave a little laugh.. 'I liked it very much.'

Darley's hazel eyes softened. He squeezed her hand then abruptly dropped it.

'You're rather a darling.'

'You aren't so bad yourself,' she murmured back.

'But—'

'But there is Finella,' she finished for him, nodding. 'Yes, I understand. You're very loyal.'

He lit his pipe, talking in between the puffs.

'You see . . . Fin means . . . so much. But things . . . haven't been . . . too easy since I . . . came home.'

Rachel listened, her heart leaping. That admission on Darley's part was more than agreeable to her hearing. But she was a clever woman and she knew that if she wanted to dig deeper into Darley's affections she must on no account run down Finella, nor make too obvious an effort to get him. She said:

'I do realize it. War marriages are like that and Fin is so . . . young and beautiful.'

'She is, isn't she?' said Darley, with an

eagerness that annoyed Rachel considerably.

'And these young pretty children—she seems so much younger than I am—don't realize the effect they have on men,' added Rachel. 'Fin attracts all men, vitally. Of course I'm not surprised.'

Darley fastened on that remark 'all men'.

'Do you think she attracts this fellow Bryte?'

Rachel did not reply for a moment. Then she looked at Darley with a bright, covering smile.

'I really don't want to discuss Fin and her attractions. It makes me far too jealous . . . ' She gave a little laugh.

His thoughts were distracted from his wife back to Rachel—to her rich sun-browned skin and agate-dark eyes. A real good-looker, Rachel. Superb on a horse—damned good at all sports. And very feminine when she wanted to be (as well he knew . . . had known just now when she kissed him). He could not help feeling flattered by her devotion. It was rather touching . . . and he felt sorry that she had always cared this way and he hadn't known . . . not that he would necessarily have proposed to her; he had never felt 'like that' about Rachel. He knew her so well. And from the moment he set eyes on Finella, he had fallen in love with her. He was still in love—that was the tragic part—and she wasn't. He was growing increasingly sure of that.

Man-like in this moment, he accepted

Rachel's devotion and could not altogether deny that he was sensuously stirred by her.

He touched her hand again in a kindly way.

'Dear old Rachel . . .'

She bit hard on her lip. This wasn't really what she wanted from him. It enraged her to know that his heart was with that girl upstairs. But she took what the gods offered and was content to wait for more.

'Darley,' she said. 'Dearest Darley . . . you can count on me always . . . always, my dear.'

'I've no right to do that, Rachel.'

'But it would give me such a thrill to know you did. That if you ever . . . wanted me . . . ' she lowered her lashes in a way calculated to disarm him or any man . . . 'you'd come to me, my dear.'

He was embarrassed yet still flattered. He raised her hand to his lips.

'I won't forget that, Rachel. Bless you.'

Rachel looked up at him. He was no longer looking at her. She supposed he was thinking about Finella again. Oh, damn, *damn*. She, Rachel, was so crazy about him. How handsome he was . . . and how much more attractive than the young, immature Darley used to be. He was every inch a man and that touch of bitterness . . . of hardness, which this war marriage of his seemed to have endowed him with, only served to increase his charm in Rachel's eyes. She had far more use for this man than for the gay boy of former days.

She managed to quell the tumult of her own passionate heart and smiled at him.

'Things have been getting you down lately, I know. It isn't much fun having strangers in the place and, as you know, I cordially dislike Gilfred Bryte.'

'I'm not sure I'm not beginning to dislike him,' muttered Darley.

'Fin assures me he's awfully nice,' said Rachel innocently.

'H'm,' said Darley, and narrowed his lids.

'Do you know,' added Rachel, 'I want your advice. I know a girl whose husband has just come back from the war ... and she's in an awful way because he has found someone else ... some nurse he met on active service. Poor Betty. It's awful for her. But that's the trouble—not having seen each other for all those years—and Ronnie has just been carried away. It's a question of propinquity. Don't you think it will come right and that Betty will get him back?'

Darley knit his brows and smoking hard at his pipe stared at the floor.

'I don't know at all,' he said at length. 'It depends on how much Betty and Ronnie really cared for each other at the start. If it wasn't the real thing—he may never go back to her. He may stick to this nurse.'

Rachel sighed.

'Oh, dear, that's what I'm afraid of. . . .'

She continued to watch Darley through the dark fringe of her lashes. She had made up the whole story on the spur of the moment. 'Betty' and 'Ronnie' did not exist except as figments of her imagination. But she saw how the story affected Darley; that his thoughts immediately leaped to his own case. She said to herself:

'*And Finella may never go back to Darley, either . . .*'

Darley suddenly put pipe in pocket and stood up.

'I ought to nip up and say a word to Fin,' he said abruptly.

Rachel also rose. She was well aware that Darley was worried again. It suited her that he should be so. She gave him a charming smile and held out her hand in friendliest fashion.

'Okay, Darley? You will—rely on me always?'

He took the hand, grateful for what he felt sure to be a sincere gesture.

'Always,' he said.

She watched the slim, graceful figure of the young man disappear from view. She had to stifle her longing to call him back and say: 'Let Finella go . . . let her go to Bryte. Take *me*, Darley. I'm yours for the taking . . .'

In the hall she met her godmother, who had just returned from her committee meeting. Something in Rachel's face made the older

202

woman stop and question her.

'Nothing wrong, is there, my dear?'

'No,' said Rachel sadly. 'Only I wish . . .'

'Wish what, my dear child?' Lady Martington smiled at Rachel affectionately.

'Oh, nothing . . . just that poor Darley were a little happier,' murmured Rachel, then added: 'I must go . . . I'm late now. I promised I'd be home for tea.'

'Where is Darley?' asked Lady Martington sharply.

'Catching a horrible cold from Finella's germs, I should imagine,' said Rachel with a malicious grin, and departed.

Lady Martington clicked her teeth with annoyance. How foolish of Darley to go *near* that girl with her heavy cold . . . she must get off her things and go in and get him out from Finella's room, *at once*.

Whilst her ladyship divested herself of hat and coat, the young Martingtons were indulging in a somewhat negative conversation.

'Sorry you've got this filthy cold, darling,' Darley said with forced brightness as he entered his wife's darkened room. He sat down beside her, adding: 'Bit of a change, *me* sitting beside *you*, eh?'

Finella had drawn the bedclothes up around her in a lump so that Darley could only see a flushed cheek and lock of satiny hair.

'Yes,' she said, and sniffed.

'Colds can make you feel blasted awful.'

'I know.'

'How did you catch it?'

'Can't think. May is a treacherous month, of course.'

Darley grunted a laugh.

'H'm. Isn't there something about not "casting a clout till May be out"?'

Finella weakly, hoarsely, echoed the laugh.

'I believe so. But I didn't cast any clouts.'

'No—you never wear anything but a handful of silk or chiffon,' he said, and wished darkly that he was not assailed by the disturbing memory of Finella standing, as he had often seen her lately, slim, smooth, exquisite in her gossamer lingerie.

She blew her nose and muttered:

'You ought to have seen me in woolly bloomers when I drove the ambulance.'

'You'd still have quickened the heartbeats, I'm sure, darling,' he said.

They both laughed. Neither of them enjoying themselves or the conversation in the least. Outwardly it was just the frothy type of talk they used to have and find pleasure in when they were first lovers . . . today, they were uncertain of each other and themselves but they hid their innermost doubts and fears. Darley was thinking: 'She isn't particularly pleased to see me. Hasn't even held out her hand. Nothing like poor Rachel's welcome for me, I must say.'

And Finella ruminated: 'I wonder what he'd say if I told him I'd seen him kissing Rachel. He's just double-faced, pretending *I* attract him.'

Yet she knew that it was not pretence that had she thrown herself into Darley's arms in the old impulsive way, Rachel would not have counted with him.

'You must hurry up and get well. There's our flat to find,' Darley was saying in the same, rather metallic voice. 'I heard from a chap in the hospital whose wife has been looking for one that they're almost impossible to get—furnished or unfurnished. It's this damned housing problem which we all expected when the war ended.'

'There are all kinds of post-war problems, it seems to me,' said Finella darkly.

Darley's hazel eyes, moody, worried, stared down at her. Her face was still only half visible. But he had an almost uncontrollable longing to lean down, ruffle that gorgeous hair of hers and then pull her, cold and all, into his embrace. How, he loved her and only her. He regretted that kiss downstairs! Regretted encouraging Rachel even for a moment. If only Fin loved him ... (what the hell did she mean by that remark just now ... 'other post-war problems' ... hers, of course ... the problem about not being in love with her husband any more. Of course she *wasn't* ... she hadn't actually told him she wasn't . . . but *he knew*.)

'I suppose we'll end up in a prefabricated house,' Finella added with a little giggle which ended in a cough.

Darley stood up.

'You ought to be quiet, darling. I'll leave you to sleep a bit, shall I? You don't want to get that cold on your chest.'

'No, I suppose not,' said Finella.

Lady Martington hastened into the room.

'Darley, my dear boy, I'm so sorry I was not here to welcome you home. I had to go to that committee meeting. And, Darley dear, *don't* catch Finella's cold . . . you aren't in a fit state . . .'

'I'm just coming out of the infected area, my dear Mamma,' he said with a gaiety he was far from feeling. 'And don't worry about me. I don't often catch colds . . . strong as a horse except for this damned arm.'

'I've had your bed made up in the dressing-room, dear, much wiser. . . .'

Their voices died away as they left Finella's room together and closed the door.

Finella lay still, finger-tips pressed against her aching eyes. She felt thoroughly miserable for a variety of reasons. And suddenly, most strangely alone. She half wished Darley had not gone. That they could have gone on sharing silly jokes. They used to have such fun . . . before the war . . . before Gil came into her life . . . and now, perhaps, she had lost Darley altogether. Not necessarily to Rachel, But in a measure, maybe, she *had* lost him. And she was not at all sure that she liked it.

CHAPTER EIGHTEEN

The week that followed Darley's return home was altogether a disturbing and disagreeable time for Finella.

The one bright spot was that Darley's arm appeared to be healing up properly this time. But it had done that so often in the past few months then broken out again, and they dared not pin too much on its permanency. He was still unable to use the arm and still unfit to take up military duties.

The time was drawing near when he would have to go before another medical board and unless he was found fit he might be invalided out of the Army whether he wished to stay in it or not. Aware of this fact, Darley got in touch with Sir Henry Wychless again and prepared the ground for his possible entrance into civilian life as an employee of the old baronet.

Lady Martington fussed a lot over her son, irritated him and nearly drove Finella frantic, since nothing that she personally did for Darley was right. Rachel Webb was a daily visitor at the

Manor and very often came at night to play bridge which Finella felt was deliberately arranged by Lady Martington so as to throw Darley and Rachel together and show up Finella's 'stupidity' at card games.

Meanwhile Gilfred too was very much on the scene. He managed to make himself perfectly charming to Lady Martington. He was careful to be equally charming to Captain Martington, and when with the family never allowed himself to betray the fact that he was madly in love with young Mrs. Martington. For that Finella gave him his due.

But on the occasions when he caught her alone for a moment or two, he left no room in her mind for doubt that he still wanted her.

Once, when bridge was in progress and Gil was 'dummy' he wandered into the hall and met Finella who had been making a cup of tea and was carrying the tray to the drawing-room. Rose had gone to bed. He stopped her, put both hands on her shoulders, looked up and down the slender figure in the black dress, and said:

'How thin you are getting, my Nella. Much too thin. I don't like it.'

She looked up at him with unhappy eyes.

'It's nothing. I've had a rotten cold and only just got over it. I . . . cough a lot at nights. . . .'

'Does it disturb the husband?' asked Gil softly.

She flushed.

'He . . . doesn't sleep in my room.'

'How can he keep away?' asked Gil dryly and with a short meaning laugh.

She swallowed hard.

'Don't be so . . . ridiculous, Gil. . . . He . . . doesn't want to catch my cold and he . . . thinks I get more rest if I'm alone.'

'Oh, my dear, don't bother to explain. These domestic details don't really interest me. All I know is that you are too thin, far from happy, and that it is time this farce ended.'

She looked at him under lowered lashes, then darted a swift worried look at the drawing-room door.

'*Ssh.*'

'Rubbish to that, Nella. I've got to be allowed to talk to you. When are you going to meet me in town for lunch? I may sleep under your roof, but as a method of keeping in touch with you, my dear, it is a failure. You drift through the house like a phantom . . . always out of my reach.'

'Gil, what's the *use* of us meeting?'

'We need a conference, my dear, on the situation.'

'It . . . hasn't changed.'

'Hasn't it? Aren't you even more out of sympathy with Darley than you were at first? Don't you loathe that old so-and-so Lady Martington and wish the double-faced Miss Webb to Hades? Don't you find the whole

209

layout is getting you down almost unbearably?'

She stood irresolute, heart hammering. *Damn
Gil* . . . as usual, he had the situation in a nut-
shell. But the one fact which he did not mention
(because he obviously did not realize it) was that
she had reached a pitch of uncertainty about her
own feelings . . . as divided between himself and
Darley. She stammered:

'Oh, I'll meet you sometime . . .'

'Name the day.'

'Oh, very well. Monday . . . I'll meet you for
lunch on Monday, Gil.'

'Very well. One o'clock, The Mirabelle,' he
said quickly.

She started to move away. He bent and kissed
her on the mouth. She gasped a little and looked
up at him in a hunted way. She didn't want that
. . . didn't want to be swayed by physical
contact . . . and something in this big, powerful
man, always drew her to him. Against her better
impulses, her better *self*, perhaps. But at least it
was comforting . . . to be loved so completely,
so consistently . . . as he appeared to love her. It
meant something . . . in this life of uncertainty;
of emotional instability in which she found
herself existing with Darley.

But as she carried the tea-tray into the
drawing-room she felt no happier for Gil's kiss;
nor for the prospect of their lunch *à deux* on
Monday.

She looked round the room. Joanna had gone

to her room. At the bridge table Lady Martington was examining her score block through her lorgnettes. Rachel was sharing a joke with Darley. Finella looked at her husband. Darley had put on a dinner-jacket tonight in honour of the little party. It suited him. His wounded arm was still in a sling. But he was looking better after a week of peace and plenty here, which he had spent mostly sitting out in the garden. They had had a generous quota of sunshine. He had recovered some of his tan. He looked very attractive, Finella thought, and regretted the wall that had risen between them; for their complete lack of knowledge of each other's innermost thoughts and feelings these days.

Then she thought she caught a secret look between Darley and Rachel. Her cheeks burned and she set the tray down with a little bang on the table. They all turned and looked at her. Lady Martington said:

'Do be careful, *please*, Finella.'

Darley got up and said:

'Want any help, Fin?'

'No thanks—get on with the game,' she muttered.

'It's rubber,' he said. 'Rachel and I have swiped Mamma and Mr. Bryte.'

'Good. That comes of having a first-rate bridge player like Rachel for a partner,' said Finella, with a brittle laugh.

Rachel looked out of the corners of her eyes, shuffled a pack of cards and thought:

'One might almost think she was jealous . . . if one didn't know she didn't care a row of pins about Darley . . .'

Rachel was enjoying herself. This week had been very delightful for her; she had spent a great deal of time in Darley's company with the exciting knowledge between them of their one long kiss. She fully intended that it should be repeated before long.

That night when Finella had gone to her room, she heard Darley call out good night to his mother, then go to his own room. She switched off her light and lay thinking restlessly about one thing and another. After a while the communicating door opened and Darley let in a shaft of light. He came in and through the dimness she saw the slim figure in the familiar dressing-gown. He came and sat on the edge of her bed.

'Well, darling,' he said cheerfully. 'I enjoyed my bridge. Won six bob from Mamma. Shall I spend it all on you?'

Finella sat up. She had not yet taken off her little pale-blue cape. She switched on the table-lamp beside her bed. Darley's heart yearned toward her. She looked lovely and rather sophisticated with her tawny hair tied up in a chiffon scarf, lips still red, eyes mysteriously shadowed under their exquisitely long lashes.

Suddenly, without waiting for her to answer his question, he leaned down and put his good arm about her, pulling her fragrant slenderness against him.

'Fin,' he said huskily. 'D'you know I haven't really kissed you for weeks. What with my going to hospital and your cold and one darned thing and another, we seem to have entered on a pretty platonic plane, sweetheart, and I'm not sure I like it.'

She tried to laugh though her heart fluttered. She had become used to that 'platonic plane' and she had never, really, grown accustomed to her intimate life with her 'returned soldier'. She said, stammering:

'I ... no ... I suppose you haven't k-kissed me much.'

His lips brushed the curl of hair visible on the white forehead, then the fringed eyelids.

'Fin, I'm still so much in love with you,' he said.

'Are you?' Her own voice was a mere whisper. She was thinking: 'So much that you can kiss that horrid Rachel Webb ...' and then, with all her feminine instincts aroused, she surrendered to Darley's embrace. She wasn't going to let Rachel get him so easily as all that. She was much more attractive than Rachel ... she would *show* him ...

Finella drew Darley's handsome head down to her.

213

'My cold's quite gone . . . you needn't stay in that other room if you don't want to, Darley,' she said in a breathless little voice.

'Fin!' he exclaimed, his pulses leaping. And he took her lips with a feverish passion that set fire to hers.

That night he did not leave her. And he thought that perhaps he had been making a mistake about Finella and that she was not so cold and reluctant to him after all, and that all that jealousy about Bryte was nonsensical and without foundation. He fancied that the wife he held so close to him was the woman he had dreamed of . . . hoped for . . . all through the damnable years of their separation. He was entirely happy when he thought about it all that next morning.

And Finella? Finella was neither so happy—nor so sure about anything. Perhaps she was a little shamefaced . . . wondering if she had had any right to encourage her husband just because she resented another girl's appropriation of him. On the other hand, it was not only that. She wanted, with all her soul, to make her marriage 'go', and put an end to the affair with Gil. More than ever she decided to finish *that* for good and all. To get away from here . . . from *him*. Until she had done so she could never hope to make a clean sweep and become all that Darley wanted. There was something so very dear and charming about Darley . . . she admitted it . . . and she liked to see him happy. She hated disappointing him as badly as she had been doing all these weeks.

She finished this week-end at the Manor full of good intentions. But the spell that Gil had put upon her was not yet broken . . . she knew it all that Sunday which she was forced to spend in his company. Every time his gaze met hers and she saw what was written in his eyes, she weakened in her resolve to break with him entirely.

What was it he had once quoted to her:

'Don't you know, little fool, you never can win . . .
Use your mentality,
Wake up to reality . . .'

But which *was* reality? Her feeling for Gil, or for Darley? Oh, lord, if only she knew!

She was deliberately sweet and charming to Darley that week-end. It gave her some satisfaction to see that he was so much better physically and mentally.

Then Monday came . . . and fresh complications.

They were due to go up to town on an early train. Finella announced as they were dressing that she was going to spend the morning with Barbara. Darley also was to be in town. He had a lunch date with old Wychless. They were to

215

meet in the early afternoon and house hunt. Finella was to get lists before then.

But a telephone call for Darley changed the plans, most uncomfortably for Finella. Wychless had been called out of town suddenly and cancelled his lunch.

'That's okay, darling,' Darley said after he told his wife about the call. 'I'll take you out to lunch. I'd like to celebrate . . .'

Finella coloured and did not look at him.

'Celebrate what?' she said. She was powdering her nose.

He came up behind her and dropped a kiss on her neck. He liked her in that black suit and white shirt, he thought. It made her look incredibly slender and *soignée*. He said:

'You being such a darling to me . . .'

She felt her heart hammering. What was she going to do now? Blast old Wychless and his change of plans. She was due to lunch with Gil . . . and Gil had already gone. She couldn't warn him. He wouldn't be in the office this morning, either. He was at some factory. Besides, she wanted to have this lunch with him. She really and truly did want to ask him to put an end to it all.

'Where'd you like to lunch, Sweetness?' Darley asked. 'I'm broke, but you can choose any place you like between an A.B.C. and the Ritz.'

She tried to laugh.

216

'Oh, I'll let you off, darling. Meet you after.'

'Not at all. The lunch is on me, my dear Mrs. Martington,' he said, and kissed her neck again.

In desperation, Finella thought:

'Oh, what's the use of all this lying and dissembling. It's so stupid. Better be honest. *Tell him.*'

And suddenly she stood up and faced Darley, her head thrown back.

'To be quite candid, my dear, I've got a lunch date and I rather want to keep it if you don't mind,' she said.

He stared at her. He had just slipped into the coat of the grey tailored suit with the white pin-stripe which he was wearing, and was readjusting his tie. He looked at Finella, some of his high spirits and humour evaporating.

'Who is the date with, darling? You mean Barbie?'

'No.'

'Then who?'

She could see that he was disappointed and perplexed. She plunged into it now, head first.

'As a matter of fact, Gil asked me to lunch and I . . . I'd like to go if you don't mind, Darley.'

He flushed and his brows drew together. All his old dislike and mistrust of Bryte returned, wiping out the lovely memory of Finella in his arms these last two nights. He said coldly:

'Oh, I see.'

Finella, heart racing, said,

'We're quite old friends, you know. I didn't think you'd mind.'

Darley gave a short laugh.

'Of course not. But you see quite enough of your old friend down here these days, surely.'

She felt cornered against her will, and exasperated.

'For heaven's sake don't become a possessive husband!' she blurted out. 'It's such a bore.'

She hadn't meant to say that at all. It was to cover up her own confusion. She couldn't exactly explain to Darley that she wanted to end what had been an affair between herself and Gil. And she disliked being 'put on the spot'. She added:

'After all, I'm not trying to meet him secretly, am I?'

Then Darley, very white said:

'No—thanks for telling me about it. But I still think you see enough of Bryte down here and that it's quite unnecessary of him to ask you out to lunch. As for being the possessive husband, my dear girl, I'd hate to be that and bore you. Carry on, do. I'll find someone to lunch with.'

Then Finella—on the raw—lost her head.

'I'm sure Rachel would lunch with you,' she said.

'Why Rachel?'

Finella shrugged her shoulders. She was trembling with nerves now.

'Oh, perhaps I'd be called a possessive wife if

218

I suggested I might prefer you to take her out to lunch than to *kiss her*.'

Darley's eyes widened with astonishment. He flushed crimson. Then he said,

'I see. And how do you know that I have kissed Rachel?'

'I happened to come down and see you . . . the day you came home.'

'I see,' he repeated. 'And you've been letting it rankle and holding it up against me all this time?'

'Not at all,' said Finella with a wild little laugh. 'Kiss anyone you want. I couldn't care less.'

(That wasn't what she had meant to say, either. She was plunging now into deeper waters than she had ever intended to swim. Things were all going wrong . . . all her good intentions.)

Darley, hands doubled at his sides, said:

'I owe you an apology for kissing Rachel. That is, if you really object. But as you appear to be on the friendliest possible terms with our Mr. Bryte, I don't see that you have much right to complain of what I do.'

'I didn't complain . . . until you forced it out of me.'

'Oh, my dear girl, don't let's continue this brawl,' he said, his eyes hot with anger. 'We're obviously at cross purposes and I don't really know why you have been so nice to me all the week-end. Unless it was because you had your lunch with Mr. Bryte today to look forward to.'

She gasped.

'Oh, that's a mean, *hateful* thing to say.'

She stood there, trembling from head to foot. They glared at each other with something that was akin to *hatred*. These two who had been such passionate lovers.

It was their first real quarrel. And they both of them knew that they were treading on thin ice; saying things which they might bitterly regret.

CHAPTER NINETEEN

Darley was the first to recover himself. He smoothed back his hair with a nervous gesture, then moved away from Finella.

'I think,' he said, 'we've said enough—if not too much—to each other already.'

But Finella was scarlet and shaking with anger. Womanlike she was not so ready to abandon the quarrel. Darley might wish to shirk the issue, she thought. She refused to. She said:

'I—don't agree. There is still a lot to be said.'

His own anger died down. Bitterness remained and a sense of emptiness. He had been so much in love with this lovely wife of his these last two nights ... this morning ... when in the first pale light of dawn he had wakened to see the rich satin of her tumbled hair and the sweet unconscious grace of her lying sleeping beside him, he had thought, with a sense of pride and contentment, that the long difficult years of war and separation had been worth while ... to find in the end a wife so sweet and adorable and to have little to worry about beyond a 'gammy' arm and a dwindling income. Those things did not matter in comparison with the happiness of possessing and being possessed by his Finella.

Now this ... the hateful truth had leaped at him from behind the shadows ... the truth which for some time now he had subconsciously felt to be lurking there, waiting to spring. She did not love him. She was bored by him and she would not give up a lunch date with Gilfred Bryte in order to lunch with him, her husband.

In a cold, distant voice, Darley said:

'What else is there? You obviously don't care a damn for me. You've only been pretending. That's that.'

'Oh, don't be so childish!' she flashed. 'Of course I care ... and I ... I haven't been pretending.'

He raised his brows with a smile of incredulity.

'Really?'

Still shaking, she tried to beat down her own futile anger. What right, asked her small inner voice, had she to be so angry . . . when she had, really, brought the whole thing down on herself . . . she and Gil . . . between them . . . they had ruined this marriage. She said:

'There's no question about my not caring for you, Darley.'

He shrugged his shoulders, walked to the windows and stared, without seeing, down at the garden. The sun was coming out, breaking through the early mist. The grass was glittering, as though hung with a cobweb net of diamond-dew. It was going to be a warm day. Darley felt suddenly immensely sad.

'Oh, hell!' he said. 'What's it matter? I haven't much to offer you these days . . . I see that. Bryte's a rich man. Maybe you and he—'

'Oh, be quiet . . . don't say such things!' broke in Finella in a horrified voice. 'You *mustn't* say them. Gil's money is no attraction. I . . . I—Oh, you're crazy to suggest such a thing!' she finished lamely.

He turned to her. He looked haggard, older.

'Fin, if you care for this man—'

'Don't!' she broke in again, breathing fast. 'I . . . refuse to listen. I don't want to discuss it. I—Oh, please stop it, Darley. It's madness. You're making a mountain out of a molehill.'

'Am I?' He gave a short laugh, kicked his toe against one of her satin mules and sent it spinning across the carpet with more force than he had intended. It caught Finella on the ankle

222

and she bent down with a little cry. At once he apologized, his face red. 'Sorry ... I didn't mean to do that.'

She echoed his nervous laugh.

'It didn't hurt.'

'Fin,' he said, 'maybe *you've* made a mountain out of a molehill, too. I ... mean ... my kissing Rachel ... meant nothing either.'

From under lowered lashes she gave him a look which he found difficult to fathom. She said:

'Okay ... then don't let either of us ... say any more or think any more about such nonsense. We're a modern couple, aren't we? We ... don't have to lock one another up and brandish the key *à la* reign of Queen Victoria ...' (another unhappy laugh) 'I certainly don't mind about *you* kissing Rachel. You've known her long enough ... and if she amuses you—'

'She doesn't,' Darley broke in, his anger rising again. 'But she's fond of me and I am of her and I must admit she had—or seemed to have—more interest in me for the moment than you had. But you were very sweet to me all the week-end and I thought—'

'Well, go on thinking it,' Finella put in hastily. 'Don't jump to conclusions.'

He frowned and stared at her. He did not understand her this morning. She appeared to him to be hedging ... getting right away from the subject of Gilfred Bryte and harping on that of Rachel. Certainly she did not seem to want to come out into the open and tell him precisely and candidly what she felt about Bryte. He, Darley, was now no less in the dark about Finella's relationship with Bryte than he had been before. And he knew that he was still fundamentally, primitively jealous—or at least suspicious. But he had no great desire to prolong the argument. It was leading them nowhere—unless to disaster. She maintained that he was making a mountain out of a molehill and he had to agree that they were a modern couple and he should not behave like a possessive Victorian husband. Well—the only thing to do was to let the whole thing slide. . . . The more that was said the worse it might become. He could not really tolerate the idea of a really bitter, lasting quarrel with Fin.

Suddenly he moved to her side and caught her in his arms. With a sound like a groan he buried his face against her warm white neck, then kissed her hotly on the lips.

'Oh, darling,' he said. 'We mustn't fight. I never imagined we ever would, you and I. Fin, we love each other, we're happy together . . . we can't be so mad as to accuse each other of fooling around with anyone else. Not seriously.'

She could not wholly surrender to that embrace . . . she was still too tied to her memories of Gil . . . and their past association.

Yet she wanted almost desperately to respond to that boyish, rather touching appeal of Darley's. She covered her confusion with an attempt at flippancy.

'My dear old Victorian lord and master...' she touched his cheek with her lips. 'Really ... you are absurd. Where's our sense of humour gone, Darley darling? I remember we used to say when we were engaged that no marriage could survive without one.'

'Quite,' said Darley, echoed her laugh and let her go although he had an almost overpowering desire to keep her in his arms, to cover that lovely, mocking face with kisses and to say: 'I *feel* possessive about you, damn it ... and I won't let you lunch with Bryte ... *damn him!*'

Instead he said with a casualness which cost him an effort:

'Okay. You win. Carry on and keep your date with this fellow. And I'll take your advice. I'll ring up Rachel and ask her to lunch with me.'

'Why not?' Finella turned to her dressing-table to repair the make-up which Darley's kiss had smudged. 'We've both been idiotic ... about nothing. We'll meet and flat-hunt afterwards.'

'Okay,' repeated Darley. 'I'll nip down to the study and 'phone.'

He did not know why he was doing it ... except to prove to himself as well as to Finella that there was nothing at all serious between

225

Rachel and himself . . . and also to get back his sense of proportion. If Fin wanted to be 'modern' and keep lunch dates with other fellows . . . he must let her do so. He would show her that he did not mind. But deep down inside him he knew that he did mind; and only because it was Gilfred Bryte. For no other reason. Had she been lunching with any other chap, he wouldn't have bothered his head. But Bryte . . . that fellow kept looming in front of him as a menace . . . yes, a menace was what Darley called him and how he thought of him . . . as connected with Fin. And he wished this morning, not for the first time, that he had never allowed his mother to accept Bryte's hospitality at the Manor. The less Fin or any of them in the family saw of him . . . the better.

Finella completed her make-up, brushed her skirt and then took a tiny black felt hat, with the new high crown, down from the wardrobe and stuck it at a becoming angle on her lovely head. Black kid gloves, black bag, and she was ready for the day in town. But she felt inordinately miserable as she went downstairs. The 'flare-up' with her husband had not ended very satisfactorily. And it had not helped the tension between them. Once again she was conscious, guiltily, that she had disappointed him and that she and she alone was to blame. But at least she had made this date with Gil in order to put an end to the affair. She did want to establish a better understanding with Darley . . . just as she had wanted, right from the start, to make her marriage succeed.

She heard the telephone bell tinkle. Her lips twisted. So Darley had 'phoned Rachel. She was none too happy about *that*. She was only too sure at the moment that Darley would forsake Rachel Webb at any moment in order to come to *her* side . . . but she was not really anxious to share him in the slightest degree with Rachel. She did not know what had possessed her even to suggest that Darley should take Rachel out. It was dangerous. . . . Married couples who started 'dates' with other people and led their own lives, courted danger . . . were always skating on thin ice. It wasn't the sort of marriage Finella had ever wished for or approved.

She *must* let Gil go altogether . . . or smash up things between herself and Darley for ever. She saw that with painful clarity this morning.

At the breakfast table the young couple talked, laughed and joked as though that ugly moment had never occurred upstairs. In fact, they looked and seemed so devoted and happy that Lady Martington felt a bit depressed. It was no wish of hers that her son's marriage should last. Neither did she want them to get a flat and get away from her influence. A trifle sourly she said:

'Well, I expect you'll have plenty of difficulty finding a suitable place at your price. And if you

227

can't find a nice modern flat, I suggest you stay here. You're not fit, Darley dear, to rough it, and Finella is *not* an experienced housewife.'

Darley smiled.

'I won't mind "roughing it", Mamma, and I'm sure Fin will soon learn how to run a place of her own.'

'H'm,' said Lady Martington in a sceptical voice.

Finella felt challenged.

'I'm *sure* I shall,' she said in an aggrieved voice.

Joanna Lucas, who was present, threw Finella a look that might almost be called envious.

'You're lucky, my dear,' she said. 'I remember what a grand time my husband and I had getting our first home together.'

Finella looked back at Gilfred's sister and remembered her tragedy ... poor Jo ... who had been widowed in the war and had no job in life now but to run a home for her brother. And what an uncertain, thankless job ... for Gil who might change his mind about living down here and go his own way in his selfish, ruthless fashion at any moment.

Finella was conscious of a slight sensation of shame. When one thought of Joanna ... and all the other women who had dreamed in vain of getting a little home together with the men of their hearts ... men who had never come back

228

... it was positively wicked to be restless and discontented ... and to imperil, even for an instant, that happiness which Darley had hoped to come home to.

She looked across the table at her husband and for an instant their gaze met. Her cheeks burned and her lashes drooped. Darley did not understand the blush or the expression. He was none too happy in his own mind about the whole situation. But he determined not to show his feelings any more. So he said in a jocular voice:

'Well, Mamma, one day in the near future, no doubt you will hear that your blue-eyed boy has perished, not by the sword, but through the cooking of his exquisite bride. But he is willing to risk it.'

Lady Martington gave an acid smile. Joanna laughed. And Finella thought, humbly:

'I will try ... I *am* fond of him ... terribly fond ... that's the trouble. I must just try to get to know him better.

'Like I got to know Gil. One doesn't necessarily know the man one lives with intimately as I've lived with Darley. That's the awful part of marriage. You can live together and remain mentally strangers.'

And, indeed, she felt on no very close or binding terms with Darley when they were in town together that morning. She went with him to Lloyds Bank in Pall Mall where he changed a cheque. He went with her to her sister's home to pick up a dress which she had left there, and wanted. Barbie and Jack were out. Young Mark was there with the daily girl who was minding him for an hour. Darley had not made much acquaintance in the past with Mark, but this morning he stopped to admire and play with the small boy. He was a great success with Mark, who screwed up his face and threatened to cry when his new, nice uncle departed. As they drove away from Bedford Gardens in a taxi, Darley looked at Finella and said:

'Barbara's done jolly well, producing a kid like that. I like young Mark.'

'Yes, he's a darling,' nodded Finella.

Darley's fingers reached for and twined about hers.

'Wouldn't you like a son . . . of your own, Fin?'

She did not reply at once and he felt the almost instinctive shrinking of her slender hand in his, and, disappointed, withdrew his own and added with forced cheerfulness:

'Oh, well, no use wanting. We can't afford a child just now, I fear. Not until our fortunes revive a bit, anyhow.'

'No . . . I agree,' said Finella.

Then silence fell between them. And they both felt very far apart.

CHAPTER TWENTY

That lunch with Gilfred was destined not to take place after all. When Finella entered the foyer of The Mirabelle, the receptionist, who had seen the tall, beautiful girl with the tawny hair and languorous, graceful figure many times in the Club with Mr. Bryte, handed her a telephone message. Finella read it and felt a ridiculous desire to laugh hysterically. It said:

Mr. Bryte rang up to offer a thousand apologies but he cannot get back to London in time for lunch. He would like you to 'phone him at Emberbrook at 3.30.

Finella crumpled the message up and walked out into the street again. The sun was shining. The spring morning was warm and golden. London looked its best. Finella walked into Berkeley Street and across to the Buttery where she found a stool and ordered a snack for herself.

So the whole of this morning's unhappy misunderstanding and tension with Darley had been for nothing. Gil hadn't kept his date. Of course, she knew full well that it was not of his choosing. He was a busy man and still working for the Government, continually pressed for time. She knew the Emberbrook number. She had often called him there. It was one of his factories in Thames Ditton. Of course he would be full of apologies and suggest another date. And she would have to make one. Or tell him over the 'phone that she was 'finished'. But he wouldn't let her do that. She knew her Gil. He would laugh and ring off. No, she would have to see him and assure him this time that she was really 'through'. She could not go on like this ... with Darley.

But she regretted this cancellation of the lunch today. First of all, she could have lunched with Darley and saved all the unpleasantness this morning. Secondly, she had wanted to get the 'showdown' with Gil over. Now, she thought miserably, it was still hanging over her head.

Meanwhile, no doubt, Darley and Rachel were having a very nice lunch together while she, Finella, munched a sandwich all alone.

Again she felt an hysterical desire to giggle.

When she met Darley at Harrods Estate Office at half past two, she was bound to admit that she felt sheepish as Darley asked, politely, if she had enjoyed her lunch and she replied that she had had it alone.

Darley raised his brows and pushed the green felt hat he was wearing a little back from his head. (He had put on a grey civilian suit this morning. It made him look younger, Finella

thought, more like the young subaltern she had
first loved so madly before the war. She hated
khaki . . . the mere remembrance of it and all it
stood for . . . she would have it all her life. The
uniform of war. That beastly war that had done
so much harm to men and women like herself
and Darley.)

He said:

'Dear me. Fancy old Bryte letting down the
girl-friend. Poor show . . . what?'

Finella coloured and snapped:

'Don't be so silly. He couldn't help it.
Anyhow, I hope *you* enjoyed *yourself.*'

'*Very* much, thanks, darling,' said Darley
with enthusiasm.

Finella looked at him through her lashes
gloomily.

'Where did you go?'

'L'Ecu de France.'

Finella sniffed. One of the best restaurants in
town . . . and one of her favourites. Of course
Darley *would* go there. Sheer perversity of spirit
combined with feminine jealousy made her add:

'What was Rachel wearing?'

Darley considered this.

'Oh, a green thing . . . I can't describe
women's clothes. But she looked damned
smart.'

Finella sniffed again. She knew that 'green
thing'. She had seen Rachel in it, down in
Godalming. Smart enough. Rachel had a good

233

figure for a tailor-made and green suited her dark eyes and tanned skin. Finella felt suddenly absurdly cross because she had not gone to L'Ecu de France with Darley instead of Rachel. Then she derided her own sentiments. What did she care? But it was aggravating that Gil had had to put her off ... and that Darley should know it. Her vanity suffered.

She spent the next hour or two with her husband, flat-hunting. It was a thankless job. London was crammed. Flats were hideously expensive and with Darley's falling income they could not pay the exorbitant rents that were being demanded.

At the last moment, just when they were both feeling hopeless about the situation, they were offered a tiny unfurnished house in South Kensington at a more moderate rent. The agent apologized for it. It was really in a 'slum', he said. Captain Martington might not care for it. But Captain Martington was only too eager to see it.

'Slumming is about our mark just now,' he said to Finella, as they took a taxi to the address they had been given.

She agreed.

'I couldn't care less,' she said. 'I'm tired and sick of house-hunting. If it's possible, let's take it.'

It was only just possible. It was a new, small, labour-saving house with two sitting-rooms and two bedrooms. Everything was 'electric'. Darley peered at the kitchenette. It seemed to him impossibly small.

'You couldn't manage with this, could you, Fin? I mean ... after the Manor ... having Rose and everything—'

Finella said quickly:

'I'll manage. It's not too much and I'll get Barbie to teach me cooking and if I could find a woman to 'do for us' in the mornings, it'd be quite all right.'

He eyed her dubiously. She was so very chic and lovely in her black tailor-made; her new clip on the lapel of the coat; the silly little hat perched over her brow. His heart sank a little. Finella—who looked like a 'million dollars'—to have to come here and 'manage' in this small cheap house. It wasn't much fun for her. Damn that fellow Bryte who had made a fortune. *He* could give her anything she wanted. . . .

Finella's beautiful eyes looked at him wearily.

'Oh, let's take it and be done, Darley. I'll manage,' she repeated. And she was thinking: 'I've never used an electric cooker. Ours was gas in the old home ... and I'm a poor hand at anything of this sort ... I can paint ... I can drive an ambulance through a blitz ... but can I run a house for a man like Darley? Oh, well, I'm not going to let his mother think I can't ... or let Gil think I'd rather be with him. I *will* manage...'

The beautiful tawny head was flung back. Finella gave her husband a glittering smile.

'I'll get along fine here,' she said. 'Let's take it, and furnishing it will be a lot of fun.'

So Darley told the agent he would take the little house for six months. They all stood outside it a moment, looking up and down the funny narrow street which was a 'blind alley', and quiet, although it led out of one of the busiest thoroughfares in South Kensington. Rows of small flat-roofed houses each with their window-box—long casement windows with filmy net curtains; coloured doors. Finella looked at No. 18 John Place. At the turquoise blue paint; two small trees in gay blue tubs; the quaintly Continental atmosphere of the street. A couple of small boys ran down it, yelling. A tabby-cat leapt gracefully on to the windowsill to bask in the sun. An old woman came down the road, shouting raucously to another at the bottom of the road. This was John Place and her future home. It would be hot and dusty in the summer and cold in the winter, and not very convenient. But if one were in love, thought Finella, it could be paradise.

There was a tragic look in her large eyes as they drove away, looking back at the pathetic yet gay little house.

If only she loved Darley as she used to, and could forget Gil. If *only* . . .

'What are you thinking of, Treasure?' asked

Darley.

She swallowed hard. He hadn't called her 'Treasure' for a long time. That name, too, belonged to their days when they had first been in love.

She did not answer, only shook her head soundlessly. He leaned across the taxi and was surprised and dismayed to see two large tears trembling on her lashes.

'Why Fin!' he exclaimed. 'What is it? Don't you want to take the place? Is it too cheap, too much of a comedown for you? Darling, I'm sorry I've lost so much money. I meant you to have a luxury flat. Oh, Fin . . . if you don't want to start life in John Place with me—'

'Shut up,' she broke in, choking, trying desperately not to cry. 'Oh, *shut up* . . . of course I want the house I . . . why, I rather—I like it. I'm only tired.'

He fell back, uncertain of her and himself, accepting her explanation, uncomprehending her mood, and remembering a little uneasily Rachel Webb's last words to him; standing outside L'Ecu de France, her agate bright eyes shining like Finella's, with the glint of unshed tears.

'You don't know how much it meant to me . . . coming up here . . . lunching with you today . . . it's such fun, you and I being alone . . . for once. *Dear* Darley!'

Rachel was in love with him. Finella wasn't.

And they both so nearly cried and were both so incomprehensible to a mere man.

All the way from John Place to Waterloo Darley pondered on the strangeness of the opposite sex in general, and of his wife in particular and felt his old wound throbbing as it always did when he was over-tired.

He supposed that he ought to feel fairly satisfied about the position. He had taken a house and Fin wanted to run it for him; he would become a civilian soon and with any luck Wychless would help him get back some of the money poor Mamma had lost. As for Rachel . . . well, he wouldn't be a man if he were not flattered by her devotion. But he didn't strictly want it; neither, he told himself, ought he to encourage her. It wasn't fair. Neither did he approve of this whole business of himself and Fin not being possessive, and leading a modern couple's life.

Where was it all going to lead them? He didn't know. But he did care—inordinately.

Finella was quiet and preoccupied with her own secret thoughts and problems for the rest of that evening. Lady Martington, hearing that her son had found and taken a tiny house and that she would be saying good-bye to him and the influence she exerted over him, felt personally injured, and sulked.

Gilfred Bryte came home late; too late to find Finella in the drawing room although his sister,

Lady Martington and Darley were still downstairs.

He heard about the house in John Place, for his sister told him as soon as she saw him.

'Weren't they lucky, Gil . . . it's a dear, wee house, Captain Martington says, if in a rather slummy place.'

Darley put in with a laugh:

'Oh, Fin and I feel we shall rather enjoy slumming.'

Gilfred smiled, but it was a smile that stretched his mouth and escaped his eyes. Those penetrating eyes became steely points. He left the party with the excuse that he must fetch a box of cigars from his room; boldly walked straight upstairs and stopped outside the room which he knew to be the young Martingtons'.

He tapped softly on the door.

'Nella . . . are you there, Nella?'

Finella was sitting on the edge of her bed in her dressing-gown, brushing the rich satin of her hair with slow, rhythmic strokes. As she heard Gil's voice, she looked up sharply, the brush suspended in her hand.

'Who is it?' she asked.

'Gil. I want to speak to you, Nella.'

'Oh, Gil, you can't possibly now'—she walked to the door, opened it and spoke to him through a crack. 'Go away, Gil, please.'

'I want to explain about our lunch.'

'I understand. Business kept you. I wasn't

cross. I knew you couldn't help it.'

He tried to force the door open further.

'I must speak to you ... for a moment. The husband is downstairs with the others ... it's quite safe.'

She gave a shocked exclamation.

'Gil, are you crazy? Go away at once. It's neither the time nor the place for a talk.'

But he pushed against the door a little harder and now they faced each other. He looked with appraising eyes at the slim figure in the pale-blue satin dressing-gown. He said in a low voice:

'Nella ... *angel* ...'

The quick nervous colour flooded her face. It was a wild delight to see him and hear him and know that she could, if she wished, be caught in his arms, her lips crushed with kisses. She had always felt like that about Gil ... strong, powerful, clever Gil. There was something so devilishly attractive about him. *Devilish*, perhaps, was the word, she told herself wryly. Yet she did not want to give way to this temptation. There was Darley downstairs ... Darley to whom her loyalty was due because he trusted her and with whom she was going to share that funny little house in the 'slums'.

She said:

'I can't possibly talk to you like this now, Gil. But I do want to see you. I've got so much to say. We'll meet in London, shall we?'

He controlled his own longing to snatch her

240

into his arms. He could hear voices. Certainly he must not risk the old lady coming up and witnessing this *tête-à-tête*. on the other hand he was so crazy about Nella, he half wished the Martingtons would find out the whole affair. Then there would be a showdown and Nella would be forced to come to him for good and all.

He said:

'When and where can we meet?'

'In town . . . the Caprice . . . Wednesday?' she whispered hurriedly. 'Be quick, Gil.'

'Very well. I won't break the date this time, business or no business. We've got to settle our account, Nella, finally.'

'How do you mean?' she asked uneasily, opening the door a crack wider.

He caught one of her hands and brushed it with lips that burned against her palm.

'I mean that I'm fed up with this situation, Nella, and you're going to quit Darley and come to me,' he said. 'Good night, my dear.'

'But, Gil . . .' she began in a shocked voice.

But he had gone. He turned at the end of the corridor, blew a kiss toward her, half mockingly, and disappeared into his own wing of the house.

Finella went back into her room. Her heart pounding and her excitement at seeing Gil had given place to a queer uneasiness. *Settle their account*. Rather a sinister way of putting things. What exactly did he mean? And could he possibly take it for granted that she would 'quit Darley' and go to him.

She sat down on the edge of the bed and stared at the floor. Her lips felt dry. She felt suddenly afraid . . . ashamed of the whole affair. It was clandestine—wrong—it had been wrong right from the start. She had been drawn into it through loneliness—through all the feverish circumstances of the war which had caught so many lonely young people into its toils; and flung them together, often with disastrous results. But since Darley's return home she ought to have been strong—either put Gil right out of her reckoning . . . or told Darley that she wished to leave him.

Did she wish to leave Darley?

Gilfred's ultimatum, flung so suddenly and sharply at her, devastated Finella's consciousness. She put her hands up to her forehead. Her brain was whirling. She scarcely knew what to think. She tried to picture life completely without Gil . . . in that tiny house at John Place, with Darley. Well, that was simple. She knew what that would mean. But now, for the other picture . . . of telling Darley she was in love with Gil . . . flinging herself into a divorce . . . and eventually marrying Gil. Not so simple. *How would she like it?*

Facing herself with the two alternatives tonight, Finella knew almost without hesitation that she could never choose the latter course.

242

She could not hurt Darley so badly ... could not bring down on him the dishonour and misery of a divorce. Not Darley, who loved her and had come back to her with such faith and happiness. Deep down in her heart *she did not want to leave him*. It had been exciting, the affair with Gil ... it had filled a gap while Darley was abroad ... but she had never meant it to be anything more; certainly not wished it to break up her marriage.

Finella stood up, her face grown suddenly white. She was trembling a little. She thought:

'I must tell Gil quite definitely on Wednesday that the whole show is over *completely*.'

When Darley came up to his room he found his young wife in bed and presumed her to be asleep; she lay so still, the long lashes sweeping her cheeks. He did not wake her. But he picked up her hand and touched it with his lips.

Finella was far from sleeping. She was merely evading a conversation with Darley. She felt so miserable. That kiss made her much more so. It was the same gesture that Gil had made a few moments ago ... a caress on the same hand ... yet such a different kiss. Darley's was so much more tender, more kindly. Gil was a fascinating man but he was not, could never be, as worth while as Darley. *She knew it*. She knew, too, that there was a tie between her young husband and herself which would never really be broken. *They belonged to each other*.

Long after Darley had turned out the light and gone to sleep, Finella lay awake brooding, thinking of the two men ... of those two kisses which were so symbolic ... and her heart and mind were sadly confused. But she did at least know her own mind. Whether she would ever really love him again or not, she could never, *never,* leave Darley for Gil. But there remained at the back of her mind, a queer uneasy suspicion that Gil would not be willing to leave it at that. He would not let her go so easily.

CHAPTER TWENTY-ONE

Finella was strangely relieved when Gilfred's sister informed them at breakfast time the next morning that her brother had gone down to Bristol for a couple of days. He would not get back, she said, until Wednesday night.

Lady Martington said with her humourless smile:

'Dear me! The poor man works so hard and is away so often I wonder he bothered to take this house!'

Joanna smiled and shook her head.

'Oh, we never know in the family why Gil does things,' she said. 'But he just must always have his own way.'

Finella looked at her plate. Perhaps she alone

244

of them all knew the real reason why Gilfred Bryte had taken the Manor and sometimes she fancied that Joanna knew and gave her curious, if not reproachful, glances, now and again. But Joanna was not one to say anything nor criticize the brother whom she obviously adored. But Finella knew in that moment that she no longer loved Gilfred Bryte as she had once loved him before Darley came home. As is the case with all infatuations, this one came to a sudden and unexpected end. She realized at that breakfast table when Joanna announced that Gil had gone away for forty-eight hours that she was extremely glad, and she did not want him to come back. She did not want to keep that lunch date on Wednesday. She would only do so because it was going to be the last clandestine meeting she would ever have with him. She had tried to put him out of her life because of Darley's home-coming. Now she was going to put him out of her heart and her mind. She was not going to let that powerful and fascinating personality of his sway her any more. She was going to devote herself entirely to her husband and to that little home they had found in John Place.

Suddenly she gave a quick, shy, upward look at Darley. He was reading *The Times*. She noticed two things about him in that moment; first that he was looking so much more mature; he had aged even during these few weeks he had been back. Secondly, how much better his arm was. He could use it a very little ... stiffly ... but a little. She looked at his slim tanned fingers holding the paper and thought, with a new warm rush of feeling, with what desperate tenderness those hands of his could caress and how crazy she had been ever to allow herself to grow away from him. She had loved him once very much. She *must* love him again. She *would* ... it was all there ... but Gil had tried to stem the tide of her love and had, in a measure, succeeded. But she would end that success.

She began to think of the funny little house in London and all the things she would do ... how she would make Barbie show her the way to cook simple dishes ... how she would show Darley what a good wife she could be and prove to that hateful mother of his that she had been wrong in all her assertions that she, Finella, was no kind of a wife. She would start now to be a real wife to Darley in every sense of the word.

Finella's heart began to swell with these good intentions. It was as though the confusion in her mind and heart had been cleared away by a magic hand. Consequently she felt enormously relieved and light-hearted. On an impulse she leaned across the table and said to her husband:

'Darley darling, it's a glorious morning—you could do with some sun and air. Why don't we go out for a picnic?'

He looked up from his *Times*, blinking with

some astonishment. It seemed to be the old impulsive Fin speaking to him and not the rather baffling, subdued young woman whom he had found on his return to England. His eyes sparkled at her.

'That sounds very tempting, Treasure.'

Lady Martington clicked her tongue.

'I never heard of such a thing! It's not nearly warm enough for a picnic ... just the very beginning of the summer ... most treacherous.'

'Oh, I dare say we'll survive it, Mamma,' said Darley, with his boyish grin. He was used to his mother's fussing and always good-tempered about it.

Her face softened as she looked at him. She added:

'I thought we might drive in to Godalming and do a little shopping and have tea. Rachel seems to have a little petrol to spare and she said she'd take us in the General's car. It would be a pity to miss the chance.'

Darley looked doubtfully from his mother to his wife. Finella's eager expression changed. Her cheeks coloured.

'Oh, of course, if you've arranged a tea party with Rachel, don't bother,' she said stiffly.

For an instant Darley hesitated. Then told himself delightedly that Fin was jealous. Yes, *jealous*. It was written all over her. Nothing could have pleased him more. In a spirit of mischief he said:

247

'Rachel's a jolly good driver.'

'Excellent,' said Finella in a freezing voice, folded her table napkin and rose. She was not going to invite Darley to a picnic with her a second time. Some of her good resolutions wavered. Always Rachel ... Rachel ... it was enough to irritate anybody.

As she walked out of the dining-room she heard her mother-in-law's voice trying as usual to add fuel to the fire.

'Our Finella seems a little out of sorts this morning.'

In a childish fit of anger Finella swung round at the door.

'I'm not at all out of sorts, thank you, but I have no wish to spend a lovely day like this in teashops at Godalming. Darley naturally can do just as he wishes. *I* am going to have a day in the country and on my feet.'

With this she walked out. She walked out into the garden and turned left through the wrought-iron gateway which led into an old walled-in fruit garden. The blossom was coming out. The air was rich with the scent of it in the sunlight. The birds were carolling madly and the sky was a clear delicious blue. It was one of the loveliest of the late spring days which Finella had always loved in Darley's old home. She was quite well aware that it wouldn't be so lovely up in John Place and yet she had entertained a sudden crazy idea that she might be happy up there with

Darley. That was, if he still loved her as much as she believed. And if the shadow of Gil could be wiped out. But she had forgotten, curiously enough, about Rachel. She hated that girl's very name and of course such a feeling could only have one explanation . . . she wanted Darley for herself . . . she, his wife. Nothing would induce her to give him up to Rachel, which was, she knew, Lady Martington's dearest wish.

Then she heard Darley's step on the gravel path behind her. She turned to see him approaching. He was grinning, hands in his pockets. He wore grey flannels, a blue pullover and an old silk scarf with his regimental colours round his neck. He came closer to her and looked down into her eyes.

'Fin, darling, why did you run off like that in such a huff? You little idiot, didn't you think I wanted to have a picnic with you?'

Her eyes gleamed up at him resentfully and her cheeks were hot peony red.

'Your mother does nothing but push Rachel down my throat. By all means go into Godalming with her if you want to.'

He caught hold of her by both arms.

'Darling idiot, I don't want to go into Godalming one little bit. I loathe teashops, you ought to know that. It seems to me you don't know much about me at all these days, Fin.'

'Nor you about me,' she said in a choked voice.

'Darling,' he said. 'There's no reason why we shouldn't learn to understand each other a little better, is there?'

She shook her head with an embarrassed laugh but he fancied the laughter was perilously near to tears. Her under lip was quivering. All his deep love for her rushed to the surface. He pulled her close to him, so close that she could feel the hard beating of his heart.

'Fin,' he said huskily. 'Darling angel, I'm crazy about you, you ought to know that. The idea of a whole day in the country picnicing with you ... and it being *your* idea ... is just wonderful ... too wonderful for words.'

Her spirits rose again. She felt nearer to him in that moment than she had done for long months. Suddenly she flung both arms around his neck and pressed her cheek against his.

'Oh, Darley, let's have fun today ... real fun like we used to,' she said in a choked voice.

He kissed her hard on the lips and when he released her he was shaking a little.

'You always were a bit of a witch, darling,' he said with a laugh.

They started to stroll back to the house. She tucked her arm through his.

'Will your mother be very cross?'

'Can't help it if she is.'

'And will Rachel be very disappointed?'

'I can't help that either,' he said abruptly. 'And now let's stop worrying about other people and concentrate on ourselves and be one hundred per cent selfish today, shall we?'

'Yes, definitely.'

When they were back in the house they were laughing and talking, both on top of their form. Darley tackled his mother straight away by demanding a thermos flask and a bag with some sandwiches.

'Tell Rose to get cracking. Anything for me except spam. I've had too much of that in my career as a soldier. Fin and Sue and I are going to walk *and* walk. It'll do us all the world of good. And I promise you, dear Mamma, that we won't sit on the damp ground without a ground-sheet. We can take mine.'

Lady Martington shrugged her shoulders. She was annoyed because Finella had won, but she had to give in with as good a grace as possible.

And so, for Finella and Darley, there began a new and lovely day spent in each other's company and with nobody else ... save Sue, the faithful old spaniel who capered madly after the rabbits in the hedges or followed at their heels, worn out, tongue lolling, golden eyes full of content. A day of sunshine and fresh air ... Finella and Darley walked with linked arms down white roadways flanked by hawthorn hedges that smelled exceedingly sweet, skirted woodlands that were still delicately green with first budding leaves, through tiny hamlets, over the Surrey hills and down into the valley where the river ran. Always with the sun on their faces and the wind lifting their hair. They walked and they talked until their legs ached and they could think of nothing more to chatter about. It was, as Darley reminded Finella, like days they used to have when they were at Camberley ... the sort of days he had dreamed of in the heat and discomfort of the desert, and in the snow and ice of the bitter Italian campaign, and, later, during that last terrible drive into Germany itself.

He had dreamed of an English day like this with Finella beside him, laughing at him with her great shining eyes and lifting her cherry-red mouth for his kisses. Whilst she, savouring it all with him, wondered why she had ever been so crazy as to think about Gil Bryte or contemplate even for an instant a break-up of this marriage which was really so near and dear to her heart.

There was one poignant and unforgettable moment between them. They had come to the brow of a green hill right away from any dwelling and spread their picnic lunch under an oak tree in a field where the grass was dry and they could sit without fear of the chills or lumbago prophesied by Darley's mother.

They had finished the meal and Darley was lying on his back smoking a cigarette. Finella sat beside him; she, too, was smoking. Sue stretched out, panting and completely exhausted, snapped at the flies which worried her. Finella looked at the old spaniel and laughed.

'Poor old Sue. She isn't as young as we are, Darley, and I think we have tired her out.'

Darley rolled over on his side and looked up at her.

'Sure *you* haven't done too much, Precious?'

'I'm a bit tired,' she admitted. 'But I'll be fit for miles more after this rest. I'm not really a fragile flower, you know.'

He threw away his cigarette and put a warm hand on her knee. She was stockingless. Her legs were brown and smooth and cool to touch.

'But you are a flower, darling,' he said. 'And a very lovely one, if I may say so.'

'My lord and master may say what he wishes,' she said, and put out a slim forefinger and brushed his lips.

He caught the finger and then the whole hand, crushing it in his own.

'*Darling* . . .' he said.

She gave a little uneven laugh. She did not know what madness possessed her, but ever since she had got up this morning she had been fired with a new warm emotion toward this young husband of hers. An emotion that had been growing apace all through this sunny day. She shook back her hair. He thought how wonderful it looked in the sunlight, rich and gleaming like gold with the glow of a fire on it. She was wearing a short grey flannel skirt and a little pale-blue jumper with short puffed sleeves. He suddenly reached up and caught her hand.

'Fin,' he said, 'I don't know what you're doing to me today, but one might almost suppose that you were trying to put temptation in my way.'

She gave a little giggle.

'What kind of temptation?'

'Well, you're much too attractive, damn it.'

'*Well*, I'm your wife, am I not?'

'My love, you are,' said Darley, and pulled her down to him and put his lips against her throat. 'Fin, darling, darling ... don't go on being a temptation unless you want to be kissed,' he added thickly. 'What's come over you? What's made you so adorable all of a sudden?'

'Oh, I don't know!' she said. But her arms went round him and held him fast. 'Darley, I don't understand myself always. But I ... of *course* I want to be kissed!'

'Then you shall be,' he said. 'I adore you, you know that. Only lately I haven't felt very sure about *you*. I ...'

She put the palm of her hand over his mouth.

'Don't let's talk about it. Don't let's spoil this moment.'

'Nothing could spoil it,' said Darley, and took her mouth with a passion that was as blinding as it was sweet.

Finella shut her eyes. She could no longer see

the blue sky or the lovely green of the oak or the cattle grazing at the end of the field. She knew suddenly and definitely that she was in love with Darley again and that, God willing, they could start again up in that little house in John Place and she would make a perfect home for him and theirs would be a perfect marriage.

She found herself murmuring incoherently against his lips:

'You asked me once if I wanted a son ... we both thought it would be unwise ... no money ... all that ... but what would it matter? I'd like to have a son ... like Mark ... I'd *like* to be everything to you, Darley. . . .'

She broke off, silenced by the pressure of his lips and the hard clasp of his good arm. It seemed to Darley in that moment that she was, indeed, everything that he had ever wanted and that money or no money, the world was his and this young lovely wife in his arms was the world.

CHAPTER TWENTY-TWO

It was a remarkably radiant Finella whom Gilfred Bryte watched while she walked down the street from the Berkeley toward the Restaurant Caprice. He sat there at the wheel and watched from his long, black, expensive-looking car, one hand in a chamois leather glove holding the stump of a finished cigar. His pulses thrilled. Lord, but the child knew how to walk, he thought. She was as graceful as a gazelle and very smart in her black and white outfit. He recognized it. He had seen her in it many times, although the Nella who had figured most prominently in his existence used to be seen, more often than not, in the uniform of an ambulance driver, a forage cap sitting jauntily on that glorious tawny head.

Gilfred Bryte threw away the cigar. He leaned out of the car. He felt pleased with life and looked it.

'Nella,' he called softly.

She stopped beside the car, a look of surprise on her face. She recognized the car, of course. Gil used it for his job and it often stood outside the door down at the Manor. But she had not expected to see Gil in it today.

She gave him a grave little look.

'Hello,' she said.

He opened the door.

'Jump in, my sweet.'

Her eyes widened.

'Aren't we eating here, then?'

'Nope. I have a better idea.'

She shrugged her shoulders and sank into the luxurious padded seat. Gil slammed the door and let in the clutch. The big car moved smoothly down the road glittering in the spring sunlight. Gil turned into Piccadilly and cast an admiring glance at the girl's profile.

'Nice hat, Nella.'

'Glad you like it, Gil.'

'You're very formal today.'

She did not answer but sat staring at the traffic ahead of them. She felt distinctly uncomfortable. She knew that this could not possibly be a pleasant hour ahead of her. She had but one thought in her head today: to make Gil understand that their 'affair' was over for good and all. She knew he would be difficult and she shrank from the thought of a scene. Yesterday, with Darley, had been so heavenly: yesterday and last night they had re-established their old love. They had been lovers, walking on air, gazing at the stars—foolish, absurd, ridiculously happy. She had, as it were, emerged from the old clouds of folly, of discontent, of doubt, into the clear certainty of her love for Darley. Theirs was a world which neither Gil nor any other man must enter or spoil now. She looked at Gil's strong rugged face and marvelled that she had ever allowed him to possess her imagination or warp her judgement. She knew that her love for him was dead—like cold ashes—and that nothing could revive it. She felt, too, a sense of shame because human emotions could be so transient, so shallow. But she could at least believe and thank God that her love for Darley and his for her was lasting and sincere and deep.

She was ashamed because she had once encouraged Gil. She hated herself for every kiss she had given or received. She thought how awful it was that one could want to kiss a man one day and hate the thought of it the next. Yes, *awful*. But it was human nature. Things like that happened. Things resulting from the madness, the depression, of war. She regretted, bitterly, now, that she had ever allowed such weakness to overcome her, and ever been disloyal, even in the smallest measure, to her husband.

Gilfred's deep voice broke in on her somewhat feverish reflections.

'Really, Nella, you are very odd. Aren't you pleased to see me again? Come, come my poppet, you're not going to tell me you've cooled off your old favourite, are you?'

She winced.

'I—Oh, there's a lot to explain and talk about, Gil. Let's go somewhere quieter when we *can* talk.'

'That's what I'm aiming for. And does the—er—lawful wedded spouse know you are meeting me today?'

Finella bit her lip. Strange, how she resented this kind of flippancy from Gil today. But during the last forty-eight hours she had changed completely. Body and soul, she belonged to Darley now. She found it irritating to hear Gil speak of him with a veiled sneer. And

258

equally irritating to know that she had not told Darley that she was meeting Gil. Perhaps it had been a mistake; it was always a mistake to prevaricate ... especially when one loved someone very much. On the other hand when she had announced to Darley that she was coming up to town today, he had taken it for granted that it was to see Barbie and Jack. He had offered at once to come up with her.

'Can't be parted from you, my dearest love,' he had said. 'But I've got to see old Wychless about some stocks and shares I'm dabbling in, and also take a dekka at the War House. I want to know how I stand about my Army job. You stay with Barbie till I'm through with all the stuff, then I'll pick you up, angel.'

She had not denied, then, that she was going to Barbie. (She could get along to Church Street directly she left Gil.) She was so happy and Darley was so happy ... she could not bear to upset him by telling him that she was meeting Gil yet again. He would begin to suspect ... to wonder why she should bother to fix up all these private lunches ... especially when Gil was expected back at the Manor tonight. So she had let the thing slide ... foolishly perhaps ... but Darley did *not* know where she was.

She felt almost resentful as she answered Gil.

'Nobody knows where I am lunching.'

'Good, my sweet. Then it won't matter where we go. You're in no hurry, are you?'

'I'd like to be at Barbie's soon after half past two, Gil.'

He frowned, then laughed.

'Oh, rubbish, darling. It's quarter past one now. I want a little time with you. You've neglected me shamefully lately.'

Finella's cheeks burned. She gave him a quick, nervous look.

'I ... I'm sorry, But I ... I'm meeting Darley.'

Gilfred's lips tightened. He swung the car round a corner and said,

'I'm sorry, too, but the lord and master must wait. He's had a lot of you since he got back. I want you this afternoon to myself. And I want to clear the air between us once and for all, my dear.'

'I'm only too anxious to do *that*,' she said.

He gave her a swift look.

'Humph. You sound sinister. Not going to tell me you're backing out altogether, are you, Nella?'

She felt her heart race and her cheeks paled a little with her intensity of feeling.

'Yes, if you want the truth, Gil. I *am* going to tell you that ... I ... want to end our show for good and all.'

'And why?'

She hesitated a moment, then said simply:

'Because ... forgive me if this upsets you ... I've fallen in love with my husband all over again.'

Silence a moment. Gilfred Bryte drove on, accelerating a little. His own face had whitened. An ugly look of resentment came into his eyes.

'Not so good, Nella. A bit ... shall we say ... too sudden. A few weeks ago you were more or less mine, weren't you?'

'No ... never, Gil. I ... admit I ... had a very strong feeling for you and you were good to me when I was lonely and the days were so difficult. You were a grand friend I ... I'll always appreciate it. But I told you I wanted to give my marriage a chance once my husband came back ... I was always honest with you about that, wasn't I, Gil?'

He was deaf to the sincerity of her appeal. He said sullenly:

'Maybe, but you gave me a damned good idea that you wouldn't find it a success and that you'd leave him for me.'

Her face grew scarlet.

'I never meant to. I'm sorry, Gil. I know I'm half to blame. But please try to understand. I *have* found my marriage a success and I ... want to keep it so.'

'It's a very sudden discovery.'

'Maybe. Things in life happen that way.'

'And a nice break for me,' he added bitterly.

'Oh, please forgive me if I've hurt you,' she said with distress. He set his teeth.

'Well, I'm not a weakling, my dear, and I'm

261

damned if I'm going to give you up without a fight.'

Her heart sank. It was what she feared. She began to see just what sort of man she was up against; what a bad type in which to put her trust. His strength was of the egotistical ruthless kind. He was selfish to the core. Any decent man would be sorry he had lost, but give a woman up with good grace . . . to her husband. Finella despised Gil for his exhibition of his so-called 'power'. She said:

'You *must* let me go, Gil. Darley and I are quite happy together. We are moving into a new little house in town as soon as we can get it ready. You . . . needn't see me any more. I can make an excuse not to come to the Manor when you are there.'

He pulled the car up with a jerk as a lorry stopped unexpectedly in front of him. His mouth was savage.

'You little fool—why do you think I took the Manor? Because I enjoyed playing bridge with that old battle-axe of a mother-in-law of yours . . . or just wanted to smell the roses?'

She bit her lip . . . loathing his brutality. She began to wonder why she had ever been attracted by him (such is the course of a burned-out passion) and to compare him more than unfavourably with Darley . . . Darley who had strength of character too, but was so tender, so chivalrous with it.

Gilfred put his foot down on the accelerator again. Words began to pour in a torrent from his lips. Ugly, abusive words. He abused her . . . and Darley . . . and Lady Martington. He accused her of 'using' him only when she wanted him . . . and her husband and mother-in-law of taking his money . . . also of 'using' him. He wasn't going to stand for it, he said. She wasn't going to get away so easily.

And she listened, shame for him and herself pouring over her like a hot flame. She thought: 'Oh, Darley . . . my darling . . . I hate myself for ever shutting you out . . . for *this* man . . . my darling, forgive me . . .'

At length she pulled herself together and, sitting upright, became aware that they had reached the Embankment and the Albert Bridge. For a second she stared at the dusky gold of the river in the sunlight and a grey barge drifting under the bridge, at the big handsome buildings on the other bank. Then she said:

'We're going much too far out, Gil. I've got to be back at Barbie's at half past two. I told you.'

Gilfred gave an unpleasant smile and turned the car on the bridge.

'Sorry if you're going to keep the lawful-wedded waiting a bit, my poppet, but this is to be *my* afternoon. As a matter of fact I've brought a nice picnic basket with some cold lobster and a half bottle of fizz for you. We'll find a warm spot in some meadow once we get out of the suburbs, and have a happy hour or two together, shall we?'

He could not have struck a note less agreeable to Finella ... when she thought of that *other* picnic ... the other man. Once again a feeling of hot shame and regret swamped her. She said:

'Turn back at once, please, Gil. I don't wish to lunch with you at all under these circumstances. You're being much too horrid.'

He laughed but made no attempt to slow down. And now Finella began to feel frightened. She pulled at Gilfred's arm.

'Don't be a fool, Gil,' she said. 'Turn back ... please.'

'Sorry, I've no intention of doing so. You can stop at a call box if you want and let Darley know you can't make it.'

She sat still a moment, dismayed, the red blood staining her face. So *this* was the real Gil, this man whose sense of power had intoxicated him to such a pitch that he could use it without real feeling, without pity. He was none of the things she had once thought him. His charm, his fascination, had cloaked a mean, utterly selfish disposition.

She looked dismayed at the streets through which they were now swiftly moving. Clapham Common, Streatham, Croydon ... miles away from Barbie's house. She would never get back in time to meet Darley. He would go there to fetch her so gaily, so full of good spirits. Last night he had held her close and said:

'Now I do truly believe you love me, my Fin. I don't ask anything else of life . . . and I've been a silly ass to doubt you or worry about your boy-friends. You belong to me. Darling, you are absolutely mine now.'

She had clung to him with all her strength and with sincerity she had answered:

'Yes, absolutely . . . *darling* Darley.'

She couldn't let him down after that . . . she *couldn't*.

She pulled Gilfred's arm again.

'Please stop the car, Gil. If you don't—I shall jump out.'

'What . . . and kill yourself?' He gave her a quick, sardonic look, then shook his head and laughed. 'Don't be fantastic, darling.'

Helplessly she stared ahead of her. She felt ready to cry with mingled exasperation and rage. In her imagination she pictured Darley arriving at Barbie's house . . . Barbie telling him she was not there . . . Darley's disappointment which would rapidly be followed by worry and suspicion. Then, if he found out that she had broken her appointment with him because she was driving out of town with Gil . . . Gil of all men whom he disliked and whom, she was sure, he had always suspected . . . he would never trust her again.

She hated Gil now . . . *hated* him. He was behaving like a cad. She knew now why even when she had been most attracted by him *something* had always prevented her from wanting to leave Darley for him.

She turned suddenly and flamed at him.

'Gil, you're all kinds of a beast. I want to get out of this car and go back. Stop ... *stop,* I tell you. ...'

He flashed back.

'Let go of my arm, you little idiot, unless you want to turn the car over.'

She was past caring. She tried to wrench the steering-wheel out of his hands and guide it, herself, to the side of the road. It was at that moment that an American lorry came round a corner. The driver was badly exceeding his speed limit and on the wrong side of the road. The big black Lagonda which Gilfred was driving swerved violently and the two vehicles met.

Finella was never afterwards clear about what happened or where they were ... it was somewhere on the London-Brighton road in an open space leading toward Reigate Hill ... but she heard her own voice screaming ... Gil hoarsely shouting ... felt the Lagonda spin round ... then a smashing sound of breaking glass and splintering wood. After that it was as though someone beat her on the head. The sunlit world revolved and blacked out.

It was not long after this that Darley stood in his sister-in-law's drawing-room in the little

266

house in Bedford Gardens, trying to solve the mystery of Finella's absence. Barbara, the moment she opened the door to Darley and he said he had come to 'fetch Fin', knew that something was wrong. She had not been warned that Fin was supposed to be lunching with her, and she felt cross with her sister for behaving like this. But, loyal to Fin, she played up as best she could.

'She isn't here yet, Darley,' she had said. 'But I expect she'll turn up at any moment.'

Darley was not worried then. If Fin had changed her mind and lunched elsewhere, he did not mind. He was sure she would be here by half past two, as promised. He had a cigarette with Barbara and laughed and joked with the small boy. He was in excellent spirits; happier about his young wife than he had been for a long time and pleased at the news he had received this morning. The Army was not going to release him just yet. He was to give the arm a chance to heal up and have a further Medical Board. But old Wychless was being a great boy, had promised him a niche in the firm and was already putting him in the way of making some money. Poor old Mamma had messed up the family funds ... but Darley could pull them together, and Wychless was the ideal fellow ... clever broker and financier that he was ... to help.

He grew restive, however, when at three

o'clock Finella had not put in an appearance. He began to walk up and down the pretty Regency drawing-room, his smile replaced by a puzzled frown.

'What the devil can have happened to her, Barbara? She said first of all she would be lunching with you and quite ready for me to pick her up at two-thirty.'

Barbara hesitated before she answered. She was secretly worried. Darley was such a dear ... Fin had been such an idiot about Gil Bryte ... and her marriage in general. She did *hope* Fin wasn't playing a stupid game with Darley ... letting him down openly now.

At length she said:

'Have another cigarette, Darley. She's sure to turn up any moment. I expect she decided to do some shopping. She said there were one or two things she wanted for your new house. And you know the business of getting taxis these days and buses are always so packed. . . .'

Darley nodded. He began, mechanically, to build a house of bricks for young Mark. But by half past three he was annoyed as well as worried.

'Fin might have 'phoned me ... it's just chucking away the afternoon,' he said.

It was at that moment that the telephone bell rang. Barbara answered it.

'Perhaps that is Fin . . .' she said.

But it was not Finella. It was a call from

Godalming from Lady Martington. And now Barbara turned a white, frightened face to her brother-in-law.

'Oh, heavens!' she said under her breath.

Darley's heart missed a beat. He flung away his cigarette end and went across to the telephone.

'What is it? Is it Fin? Has there been an accident?'

'It's your mother,' said Barbara, handing him the receiver. 'And I'm afraid there has been an accident ... Lady Martington has just had a call from the police, Darley.'

'The *police?*' repeated Darley. Then: 'Hello ... hello, Mother ... what is it? Quickly ...'

'Oh, Darley,' came Lady Martington's voice. 'Thank goodness I've found you. I'm so worried. Yes ... it's about Finella.'

'What! Quickly ...' repeated Darley in a tense voice. 'She's all right, isn't she?'

'She isn't dead if that's what you mean. But she's been injured slightly ... in a car accident.'

'What car? Where?'

'You won't like it when I tell you, my poor boy.'

'Oh, go on ... tell me ...' he said, his voice rasping.

'She was in a car with Gilfred Bryte,' said Lady Martington with slightly malicious pleasure. 'I don't know whether you *know* about it. But she was driving with him out of town and their car collided with a lorry somewhere just outside of Reigate.'

CHAPTER TWENTY-THREE

When, a moment later, Darley put down the telephone and turned to his sister-in-law, Barbara saw written in his hazel eyes a look of such pain and bewilderment that her heart sank.

'Oh, Darley!' she exclaimed. 'What is it? What has happened?'

For an instant it seemed that he could not speak. Barbara saw the muscles of his neck working. He took a cigarette from a packet and lit one. His fingers shook as they clicked his lighter. Barbara repeated:

'What has happened?'

He said:

'I can't believe it. I just *can't* believe it. After all we said and did ... good heavens...'

Then Barbara began to feel frightened.

'Darley, for goodness' sake don't keep me in suspense like this. Has Fin had an accident?'

He told her then.

'Yes, she was in a car smash. She's in a hospital near Reigate. She has slight concussion—nothing very serious ... and some cuts and bruises.'

'Why Reigate?'

'You may well ask...' Darley gave a rasping laugh. 'Well, my dear, she was driving out of town with her friend Gilfred Bryte. That b—y fellow!' He used a word Barbara had never heard from her brother-in-law before. She stared at him, aghast. He added: 'Well. That ends it. Now I know where I am. If Finella could do a thing like that ... not even bother to let me know ... and after what happened between us ... Heavens!'

Barbara caught him by the arm and shook it.

'But Darley ... what happened? You're speaking in riddles. I don't understand.'

'Neither do I...' Again Darley laughed, but his face was grey. 'And don't ask me to explain any further because I'm as much in the dark as you are.'

'But there must be a mistake.'

'Nice of you to be so loyal, but there's no mistake. The Reigate police 'phoned the Manor ... found Finella's identity card in her bag.'

'In Reigate ... with Gilfred Bryte?'

'Yes. Isn't he her boy-friend?' There was an ugly note in Darley's voice now. He turned his back on Barbara. 'Once I had a few doubts about the chap and about Fin, I may say. Now I have none. And the pair of them can go to hell for all I care.'

Barbara's round blue eyes looked horrified.

'*Darley!*' she exclaimed.

He swung round on her.

271

'What else do you expect? Naturally you don't understand everything that's been going on, but I presume you knew Finella had been having an affair with Bryte.'

'I . . . I . . . she used to go out with him when you were overseas, but n-nothing desperate . . . I mean . . . F-Fin always told me she l-loved you,' stammered poor Barbara. Inwardly she was seething with rage and bitter disappointment against her young sister. The fool . . . the little *fool* . . .

Darley laughed for the third time.

'My dear Barbara—don't talk about love to me. She doesn't know what it means. A day or two ago we sort of reached a fresh understanding—she was perfectly charming to me—I was beautifully taken in, I assure you. Felt certain she was interested in me—only me—and all the time she was planning this . . . a get-away with Bryte.'

'I don't believe it!' said Barbara stoutly, despite her own misgivings. 'Honestly I don't. She. . . . she had no luggage with her, had she?'

'She didn't bring any up with her this morning. But perhaps she had decided to leave behind everything that *I'd* given her. Bryte is more or less a millionaire . . . one of these jumped-up fellows who've made a packet in the war. He can buy her anything she wants. I don't really blame her. I'm sunk financially, for the moment.'

Barbara's nice face flushed scarlet. Hotly she said:

'I won't hear that said of Fin. She isn't . . . she never has been a gold-digger. You know that, Darley.'

He shrugged his shoulders.

'It doesn't matter much. She was going off with him.'

Barbara said:

'Oh, don't be so positive. She may have been doing nothing of the kind.'

Darley gave a twisted smile.

'Just a joy ride in the lunch hour, d'you think? And having pulled the wool over my eyes about lunching here and being fetched at half past two. My dear Barbara, if this accident hadn't happened, she'd have been carrying on with her joy ride. Wouldn't she? Jolly for me . . . waiting for her. Of course, Bryte's Lagonda's a beauty. I expect that's the one they were in. A bit smashed up, the police told Mother. But Bryte's okay. *Damn* him!'

Barbara was nearly in tears now, full of anxiety about her sister. At the same time she could see how Darley was suffering. It was because he loved Fin so much and had believed in her, that he was like this. She said, gently:

'Oh, Darley, I'm sorry, my dear. But don't think the worst until we've heard Fin's side of it—please.'

He said:

273

'Nothing she can say will get away from facts. She arranged to meet me here ... she had a clandestine date with Bryte ... the second within a week ... only the first didn't come off ... and she was driving out of town with him when the accident took place. So she must be particularly interested in him. In which case ... I'm through. I'm not sharing my wife with any other chap.'

Barbara's throat felt dry.

'*Darley* ... don't ... don't say things like that until you know—'

'You'll probably go down to Reigate to see her,' cut in Darley. 'Tell her she can write to the Manor. I'll be there.'

'Do you mean *you* are not going to Reigate?'

Darley, raw with pain and resentment, snapped back:

'Why should I? The boy-friend is there. Not badly hurt ... not even detained in hospital. He can look after her—finish the job.'

Barbara began to lose patience.

'Darley, you're being childish. And you're throwing Finella into that man's arms. You've no right ... you're her husband—'

'That fact, my dear Barbara, did not concern her when she started out on the joy ride,' broke in Darley, harshly. 'And I'm not going to let it concern me now. Forgive me, my dear, if I cut along now and get a train back to Godalming. And by the way—you'd do me a favour if you'd ring Borrow and Christy of South Kensington and ask them if there's a chance of re-letting 18 John Place. We obviously won't be living there now.'

Tears sprang to Barbara's eyes. She felt terrified for Finella and wretched about the whole affair. How she wished Jack were home ... that she could consult him. Her Jack, who was always so wise and practical about everything. Whenever she indulged in what he called 'flapping', he would pat her hand and say, 'Keep calm, my pet ... keep calm ...'

Well, it wasn't easy to 'keep calm' over *this*. ... with Fin in a hospital ... and Darley talking as though he meant to divorce her as soon as he could. He was walking toward the door. Barbara walked after him.

'Look here, Darley—you don't want to do anything in a hurry. After all ... you don't *know* what's at the back of this ... anyone would think you'd found out that poor Fin had been unfaithful to you.'

He turned back and looked at his sister-in-law, his thin face tired, white and bitter. For a moment he felt choked—he could not find words. Barbara, poor old Barbie ... she was Fin's sister and bound to be loyal ... to help if she could ... but she didn't know what *he* knew ... for instance ... all about that glorious day in the country, under the oak tree ... when Fin had been so utterly sweet, had surrendered so completely to his lips and arms ... the sweet, poignant night that had followed ... his renewed faith in her ... in her love *for him* ... her wish to give him a son ... to be all in all to him. That was what hurt so profoundly ... the idea that after all *that* she had met Bryte secretly and driven off into the country with him. Perhaps she hadn't been physically unfaithful to him *yet*, he thought grimly, but mentally ... she had betrayed him ... by this very action of hers ... the whole business was so treacherous on her part ... so wanton ... so unbelievably cruel ... he felt like a man who had been flung from the dizzy heights of happiness down the very abyss of despair. It was as though every hope he had ever had of being happy with his young and beautiful wife, had been destroyed piecemeal in front of his eyes.

His faith was so shaken by the news his mother had just given him that he had not so much as a vague wish left to go down to Reigate and make sure she was all right. Her sister could go. Anybody but *himself*. If he were to meet Gilfred Bryte in that hospital there might be murder done. That was how he felt and why he walked out of Barbara's little house that afternoon ... and like a man sleep-walking, spiritually dead, found his way to Waterloo and waited for the next train to Godalming.

Perhaps it was only chance, perhaps a little more, that Rachel Webb should be at

Godalming station when he got there. She had just been to the bookstall to collect the *Spectator* ordered for the General. She saw Darley step out of the train alone. Delightedly she approached him, but her smile faded when she saw his face. He looked ghastly. For an instant, she thought it was his arm.

'Oh, Darley,' she exclaimed. 'Have you been taken ill? Where's Finella?'

He looked at her in a slightly dazed fashion. Then he pulled himself together and answered:

'I'm not ill. Just had a bit of a shock.'

'Where's Finella?' repeated Rachel.

'Had a car accident,' said Darley briefly.

'Good heavens! Where?' asked Rachel shocked. She had been out all afternoon, unaware of the news her godmother had tried to pass on to her on the telephone.

Darley walked with her out of the station. The fine day had developed, treacherously, into a wet one. A steady rain was veiling the countryside. It was depressing and felt chilly, and Darley shivered. He felt as cold as death, he thought, mentally and physically. Rachel was hurling questions at him which he only half heard. After an instant he stopped her.

'Drive me home, Rachel, there's a good girl,' he said.

She was only too ready to do so and her heart beat quickly with excitement. She had not the least idea what had happened to Finella but one thing stood out clearly. Darley had come back alone and had not bothered to stay with Finella *wherever* she was.

As they got into the car, Rachel slammed the door and impulsively put out a hand and touched his.

'My dear, I don't quite understand what this is all about but you know that if I can do anything ... well ... here I am!'

He turned to her and for a moment his hand touched hers spasmodically. His eyes were anguished. He felt a slight uplifting of the spirit because this nice dependable girl, who was such an old friend, gave him her sympathy. Yes, she was always here ... always had been ... and it was good to know that someone was sincere in their affections. Everything about Finella had been insincere ... her kisses ... her promises ... oh, *God*, how blind he had been and how ingloriously he had failed to hold her.

He said:

'Don't ask me to explain at the moment, Rachel ... but Finella and I ... something rather grim has happened ... it isn't her accident ... she's not badly hurt ... but I am ... I *am*, Rachel!'

Rachel's heart leapt again. This was more than she had ever hoped for. So these two had split ... at last! And an instant later she knew that it was Gilfred Bryte because Darley added:

'I want to get out of the Manor as soon as I

can but I'm not quite sure of my plans. But I tell you what ... I've no wish to sleep under that fellow's roof and it *is* his while the Manor belongs to him. If you and the General would put me up tonight I'd be terribly grateful. I don't much like Mother staying at the Manor either, but I don't suppose she'll want to move at a moment's notice. She'll have to make her own plans. Of course, if I'd known then what I know now, I'd have gone broke before I let Bryte take a lease of my home.'

Rachel listened in silence as she turned the car up into the road that led toward the Manor. She felt that it might be indiscreet to question Darley further. She could see that he was in a high state of nervous tension. But obviously he had found out about Finella and that man. She was selfish enough to be delighted rather than to pity him because he was so unhappy. She said:

'Of course, Father and I would *love* to have you with us—as long as you care to stay, Darley.'

It was not until they reached the Manor and Rachel had a word with her godmother that she received a fuller explanation about the situation. Darley had gone up to his room to pack. Lady Martington and Rachel discussed the matter excitedly.

'That wicked girl!' Lady Martington intoned on a jubilant note. 'She's cooked her goose with Darley. You can see that from the look in his eye. As for that Gilfred Bryte . . . I'll give him a piece of my mind when I see him. I shall tell his sister outright what I think of him. Fancy her going off with him like that and Darley in the house with that sister of hers, quite in the dark, poor dear, till the police 'phoned me, and I got on to him . . .'

'Never mind, Aunt Margaret,' said Rachel, patting her godmother's arm. 'Perhaps it was all for the best, dear. You see, already Darley is coming to us for the night. Wouldn't you like to come, too?'

'No. I shall leave him in your capable hands, my dear,' said Lady Martington, beaming at the girl. 'Besides, I want to tell that Mr Bryte what I think of him.'

But she was not given a chance to do that. For not long after Rachel had driven away triumphantly with Darley, Joanna Lucas received a telephone call from her brother's secretary; a peremptory command to go up to his London flat at once and to tell Lady Martington that he wished to sub-let the Manor.

CHAPTER TWENTY-FOUR

Finella was still unconscious when Barbara arrived at the emergency hospital on the outskirts of Reigate to which the pair had both been taken after the accident.

Before Barbara went to her sister, she saw Gilfred. They faced each other in the waiting-room. Gilfred was unhurt except for a few bruises. It was Finella who had caught the impact of the lorry which had crashed into them. He was a little pale and shaken—otherwise none the worse. But he looked a trifle nervously at Finella's sister.

'This is rather a poor show, I'm afraid.' he said.

'It's more than that,' burst out Barbara indignantly. 'I think it's absolutely *monstrous* of you both. You're an absolute cad, Gilfred Bryte, and my sister is almost as bad. And *you* are to blame. You've wormed your way into her affections and broken up her marriage. You always meant to break it up. She didn't. But the result's the same. You've smashed up her life and that of the nicest man I know.'

Gilfred raised his brows. For an instant, busying himself with lighting a cigarette, he eyed Barbara with some interest. She was not a very attractive sight. She had been unable to get a taxi from the station and had walked through teeming rain to the hospital. Her feet were wet, her fair hair was bedraggled and her face was hot and pink with anger. Gilfred never had been attracted by Barbara ... she had neither Finella's glamour or looks, he told himself. But he was vastly interested by the inference of what

281

she was saying. His little plan for an innocuous picnic seemed to have turned out to be of much greater significance. Barbara had implied that he and Finella had been 'doing a bunk'. She *must* mean that, since she talked of smashed-up lives and marriages and so on.

Barbara added some more which satisfied Gilfred on that point.

'Poor Darley's absolutely shattered. I don't know how you could do this to a man who has fought all these years and been wounded in order to keep men like *you* in a cushy job. And I think it dreadful of both you and Fin to have gone off like that and not even warned him.'

Then Gilfred gave a twisted smile and inclined his head.

'Thanks for all the bouquets. However, I won't hold it up against you, my dear girl, for I can see you're very worried.'

Barbara made an angry gesture. She took off her hat and shook the rain from it.

'I'm disgusted about the whole business. Might I ask what you both intended to do before this smash? Were you heading for a honeymoon hotel and then going to wire the unfortunate husband?'

Gilfred put his tongue in his cheek and drew a deep breath of his cigarette. He was beginning to feel better and to enjoy himself, and was appreciating the sardonic humour of it all. If this is what Nella's family thought, let them go

282

on thinking it. He wouldn't trouble to deny it. The fat was in the fire and Nella would have to face it out with him, now. He was sure that she would be glad that her mind had been made up for her at last. She cared more for him than she admitted. He was confident of it. He was a man of huge conceit.

'Now, Barbara,' he said. 'Don't rant at me. You were lucky enough to find the right man when you got married. Nella didn't. But you don't want her to spend the rest of her life with the wrong one, do you?'

'I won't admit that Darley is the wrong one!' flashed Barbara. 'And if you'd let Fin alone she would have been quite happy with him.'

'My dear girl, she was without him for five years and he was a total stranger to her when he came back. A lot of war marriages will go the same way, I assure you.'

'Well, I'm not here to listen to your debate on war marriages,' said Barbara bluntly. She hated this man. She believed that he had ruined her sister and she had never admitted his fascination. In her opinion Darley was worth twenty of him. She added:

'This is just wasting time. I'm going to see Fin.'

'And isn't the devoted husband rushing to the bedside, too?'

Barbara scarlet with indignation, snapped back.

'Why *should* he when he knows that *you're* here?'

Gilfred shrugged his shoulders.

'Oh, well! I assure you we don't need him. I'll look after Nella, beautifully. You don't need to worry about her. And for your information, I'm not out to "do her wrong", my dear girl. I shall be only too delighted to marry her in due course.'

Barbara's blue eyes looked at him much as she would have looked at a noxious reptile.

'I hope and pray I never live to see the day you marry my sister,' she said, and swept out of the waiting-room.

It was then that Gilfred, highly satisfied at the repercussions of his accident, went out to the nearest telephone to give certain orders to his secretary. Certainly, he wouldn't go back to the Martingtons' home *now*. He had no wish to see either Darley or that old tartar of a mother of his. He must get Joanna up to town and soothe her down. She wouldn't be too pleased as she was crazy about the Manor. But he could always manage Jo. With his charm *and* his money. She'd stuck to him over the Vera affair and she'd stick to him now. The Manor didn't matter to him at all. It was Nella who mattered. The real difficulty, he knew, would be in persuading Nella to accept the situation which had arisen and to leave Darley for him. He felt a trifle uneasy when he remembered how frankly she had told him a few hours ago that she had fallen in love with her husband again. Well, from what Barbara said, he could but hope that it wouldn't be all that easy for Finella to get back to Darley now. He was thinking the worst.

A nurse took Barbara to the casualty ward where Finella was lying. Now Barbara's anger evaporated as she looked down at her sister's pathetic little face from which the blood had been drained. She was as white as the bandages around her head. She looked like a beautiful nun, Barbara thought. And she lay so terrifyingly still—although the sister in charge told Barbara that Mrs. Martington would recover consciousness any time now. Concussion always made patients look worse than they were, she informed Barbara, reassuringly.

Barbara sat beside Finella for a long time, holding one of the slim hands. She was full of pity and concern now. Poor little Fin . . . life had not been too easy for her. In their mother's life-time, she had wanted so badly to get on with her painting—to find an outlet for her artistic tendencies. She had never had Barbara's 'domestic streak'; Barbara's capacity for settling down cheerfully to rather dull, homely jobs. Lack of money had stood in Fin's way. When she had met and married Darley Martington it had seemed to Barbara that the answer to all Fin's problems had been found. Fin would be happy ... with Darley ... who could afford to keep his wife in comfort and let her get ahead if she so desired with her art.

But the war had hit all those plans on the head. There had followed those devastating years of loneliness and anxiety ... all the temptations that pursue pretty grass widows ... the hectic, heart-breaking years of bombing and hardship ... years that Finella had stood with real courage in that hard driving job ... she had surprised her own sister by the way she had endured—kept faith with Darley. Until that wretched Gilfred appeared on the scene, pondered Barbara. He had been Fin's undoing.

Barbara thought of her own good fortune; her marriage with Jack. Their love and little Mark. How lucky she was indeed ... when she thought over Finella's misfortunes. Two tears rolled down Barbara's cheeks. She wiped them away and tried to look on the bright side of things. Perhaps she could persuade Fin not to carry on with this madness—perhaps she would make it up with Darley yet. She was sure that Darley loved Fin with all his heart. Of course there was always that wretched mother-in-law in the background. *She* wished no good to Fin. Barbara knew that. She would never help the young couple patch things up. On the contrary—she would make mischief if she could. It was such a pity. A mother-in-law could be such a help; and had she loved Fin and won

Fin's affection and respect, perhaps none of this would have happened. Barbara was quite sure that the Bryte affair had evolved largely because Fin was so lonely and in need of love. She was such an affectionate person. Barbara felt a trifle guilty as she looked back ... she had been so taken up with Jack and their little son ... maybe she hadn't given Fin all the attention she should have done. Poor Fin had literally been thrown into that hateful man's arms.

At the end of an hour, just when Barbara was beginning to wonder what next to do ... for she must get back to her small son as Jack was not at home ... Finella stirred. Her heavy lids lifted. Her dazed eyes stared up at Barbara without recognition.

'Gil ...' she whispered. 'Gil ... take me ... home ...'

Barbara hardened her heart against her sister again. She disliked hearing her call for that man. She bent over her.

'Fin ... do you realize what you've done?' she began severely.

'Gil ...' repeated Finella stupidly, then shut her eyes again. Her moment of consciousness was transient. And she had fancied herself in that car driving away from London. Her main object was to make Gil take her back ... back to Barbie's house.

'Fin!' Barbara spoke sharply to her sister again. 'Don't you know me?'

287

But Finella said no more. In despair, Barbara fetched the sister. The woman tried to comfort her.

'That's all right. If she came to just for a moment it's a good sign. Don't worry, my dear. A few more hours and she'll be herself again.'

Barbara sighed.

'I'm afraid I must get back to my little boy, or I'd stay here.'

'Don't worry,' repeated the nurse kindly, then added: 'Isn't that her husband who is here with her?'

'No,' said Barbara, tightening her lips. 'Just a . . . friend.'

'I see,' said the woman tactfully.

'I'll have to go,' said Barbara. 'But I'll ring up later tonight to see how she is.'

'Very well, and I assure you you needn't worry. I'll let Doctor know straight away that Mrs. Martington has spoken,' said the nurse.

In the main corridor Barbara met Gilfred Bryte again. She told him, briefly, that she had to get back to her child and that it appeared that Finella was in no danger.

'Well, that's fine,' said Gilfred brightly. 'I'll be here to look after her when she comes to properly.'

'We'll see about that,' was Barbara's abrupt reply. 'I shall report to Captain Martington and meanwhile I'd be obliged if you'd remember that Fin is *his* wife and not yours.'

Gilfred smiled and bowed.

'Okay. You *do* like me, don't you, Barbara?'

'No. Quite frankly I do not,' said Barbara. And with those few words she departed.

Then Gilfred got busy. He saw the Matron, made himself utterly charming, introduced himself as a big business man, talked blithely of giving a big donation to the hospital; and asked if Mrs. Martington might be moved at once into a private room.

The Matron, suitably impressed, complied. Mr. Bryte intimated that he and Mrs. Martington were 'more than ordinary friends' and that he could and would pay. She saw no reason to doubt it. And she was much too busy to concern herself with the personal affairs of 'casualties'.

Forty-eight hours later, when Finella really recovered consciousness and became aware of her surroundings, she found herself in a small white room which was full of expensive flowers. Barbie was sitting beside her.

Barbara, quite aware that it was necessary for her to look after Fin's welfare, had taken young Mark to Jack's mother who had come to the rescue and offered to take care of her grandson. So Barbara was free to come down here and sit at Fin's bedside—much to the irritation of Gilfred Bryte, who took himself back to his London flat and his job.

Finella put out a hand to her sister.

'Barbie . . .' she whispered. 'Oh, *Barbie* . . ."
and then touched the bandages on her head and
groaned. 'Barbie, where am I?'

Barbara explained. Finella listened dazedly.
She remembered driving with Gil all right . . .
but about the accident, nothing. She felt sick
and weak.

She listened in horror when Barbara told her
that she had been in the hospital for two days
and two nights. She struggled to sit up, and
gasped:

'But where's Darley?'

A queer look came over Barbara's face and her
cheeks flushed. She took a note from her bag
and handed it to her sister.

'Oh, Fin,' she said sorrowfully. 'You *have*
torn things.'

'But where is he . . . why isn't he here with
me?' demanded Finella. Her head buzzed and
hurt and she put a hand gingerly to touch the
bandages again.

Barbara said: 'My dear, you can hardly expect
him to . . . when you rushed away like that with
Gilfred Bryte.'

Finella looked as startled as she felt, now.

Barbara added:

'All these flowers . . . even this private room
. . . everything being paid for by Gilfred, and
him telling everyone in town that he's ready and
willing to be co-respondent whenever Darley
likes to sue for a divorce. It's really awful, Fin!'

It was so awful to Finella that she could not, for a moment, quite grasp what her sister was saying. But gradually, as Barbara went on chatting in an artless fashion, Finella gathered that Darley believed that when the accident took place she had been running away with Gil . . . *and Gil had let him think so* . . . let everybody think it. Shaken to the core Finella felt for one moment that she would faint. Then she pulled her whirling senses together, lifted the letter Barbie had given her and stared at it. It was addressed to her in her husband's handwriting. In a frenzy she tore open the envelope.

The small neat writing was familiar . . . typical of Darley's well-ordered, soldierly mind. She had not received a letter from him for months now . . . but she remembered with sick apprehension how often he had written in the past five years and with what love and hope.

The words seemed to jump from the notepaper (headed '*The Manor*') and dated the previous day.

Finella,

I never was much of a chap at letter-writing and I hardly know what to say now. I'm too shocked. It was a bit unfair of you, you know, quitting me quite so suddenly and without a word of warning. It knocked me out for a bit. I felt nothing but contempt for you after all that had happened between us. My dear, in God's name, why did you go through that pretence when all the time you were meaning to leave me?

Now I've had time to think things over, I don't feel anything but mortally sick of the whole affair, and thankful to know the truth at last. But if you cared all that much for Bryte, why didn't you come into the open right away and say so? It would have been kinder. Anyhow, the thing's done and over. Everything for us is over. I realize now that our marriage was a mistake. I loved you, but you couldn't stay the course. All right. I'll set you free as soon as you like to send me the evidence. Meanwhile I'm staying with the Webbs, if you want to get in touch with me, or you may prefer to approach me through my lawyer. You know who that is.

I wish you all the happiness with Bryte you could not find with me. Good-bye, Finella. Sorry I can't write more.

Yours,
Darley.

When Finella had finished reading this letter, the contents of which both astounded and dismayed her, her heart was beating so violently that she could hardly breathe. Barbara hung over her anxiously.

'Fin—you look awful—are you okay?'

Finella tried to speak, but no words came. She stared at her sister with an expression of sheer anguish which the other girl could not

292

altogether understand. She took it for granted that this was a farewell letter from Darley but if Fin loved Gil Bryte, why look or feel *this* way about it? Really, Fin was unaccountable.

Finella choked and tried to say something. The room was going round and round. The pain in her head was growing worse. She thought piteously of Darley ... of what he had said in this letter. *Oh, this letter* ... saying good-bye to her ... talking about a divorce ... lawyers ... their marriage being a mistake. *A mistake, their marriage* ... when she loved him ... why, she had told Gil that she had fallen in love with her husband all over again. Told him. Darley ... Darley....

'Darley!' The name broke from her now in a great cry. Then the letter fluttered from her fingers. She fell back into Barbara's arms, once more drifting into unconsciousness.

CHAPTER TWENTY-FIVE

About a week later Finella drove with her sister in a hired car from the hospital back to Barbie's flat. Finella had more or less recovered except for a persistent headache and a few bruises. She felt stiff and ill, but it was with an illness of the mind more than of the body. The thing she had not been able to recover from was that letter

293

which she had received from her husband.

Barbara looked anxiously at the younger girl. Poor little Fin! Whatever she had done she had certainly paid for it. She must have lost weight even in that short week in the hospital, Barbara reflected. She was thankful that she would have Fin with her for a while under her own roof. She would 'nurse her up' and it was lucky, really, that darling Jack was not at home at the moment. She could give her full attention to the sister who had never been in more need of her.

As the car drove down the broad road past Croydon aerodrome, Barbara took one of Finella's listless hands and pressed it.

'Cheer up—I'm sure it will all come right, darling—it *must*.'

Dumbly Finella shook her head and the ready tears started to her eyes. She felt ashamed and brushed them away. Since her accident she had been nervy and overwrought and cried easily. She looked out of the car with an expression of hopelessness in her eyes. It was a fine day— London stretched before them in a golden mist of sunshine. A warm day with a breath of summer in the air. The sort of morning that usually made one feel glad to be alive. But Finella could feel nothing but misery. Sometimes in the hospital, lying awake, trying in vain to sleep, she had half wished that she had been killed in that car accident rather than have to face this mental pain. It was all so unjust . . .

for although she knew that she should, in the first place, never have encouraged any relationship with Gilfred Bryte, she had done nothing to deserve a punishment such as this.

It had been the blackest week of her life. Wretchedly she looked back on it. Once she had felt well enough to see Gil, there had been a scene, followed by several others. She had told him with bitter dislike that he had ruined her life, and he had merely argued that he loved her and that none of the present trouble mattered because as soon as Darley set her free he would marry her.

His charm for her had faded long ago and now she despised him. She did not hesitate to tell him so. She demanded that he should tell Darley himself why she had taken that trip in the car with him and how he had driven her right out of London against her will. But he had refused.

'I want you ... I've always wanted you, Nella,' he had said. 'Now that this has happened, can't you see it's Fate? Let things stand as they are and marry me.'

She had told him that she would not marry him if he were the last man on earth. The next time he came to the hospital she refused to see him and sent Barbara to tell him so. Barbara reported that Gil had left the hospital in a towering rage and that was the last they had seen of him. But Finella had since received urgent letters and daily telegrams from him, all telling her to be 'sensible', and announcing his readiness to stand by her.

She saw, in her despair, that he did not intend to let go nor to play the game.

Then there was Darley. . . .

She felt choked from the mere thought of what had happened between her and Darley. It all seemed so tragic and so ironic—that this should have happened now, just when she had learned to love him again.

Barbara counselled her to write to him and tell him the truth. She tried to . . . she started several letters and tore them all up. There was a stubborn streak in Finella, a hot streak of pride . . . if Darley had so little faith in her . . . she was not going to crawl to him for understanding. He had gone straight to Rachel. That knowledge bit deep into Finella.

The accident had left her head a little muzzy and her whole equilibrium unbalanced. When Barbara was not there to advise and sooth, she wrote to Darley . . . a foolish, unguarded and rather wild little note.

You seem in a great hurry to get rid of me and go to Rachel Webb, so you'd better stay with her, but I can assure you that even if our marriage was a mistake I am not going to supply you with evidence to set you free. You're wrong if you think I'm going to live with Gilfred Bryte. I am not, and if you're so anxious for a divorce you'll have to get it some other way....

Not at all what she had intended to write and it certainly did not have the effect of bringing Darley to her side.

This morning Barbara was trying to persuade her to send for Darley.

'You must see him! You must tell him that you weren't running away with Bryte. It's absurd to let him or your mother-in-law think so.'

Finella shrugged her shoulders in a hopeless way.

'I couldn't care less.'

'Don't be absurd, Fin,' said Barbara, in a crisp voice. 'You do care and you know it.'

Then Finella said in a choked voice:

'Darley has never loved me. He couldn't have, otherwise he wouldn't have been so ready to believe the worst. I shall never forgive him for it and I'm *not* going to be the one to make all the gestures. He hasn't answered my last letter.'

Barbara sighed.

'From what you tell me it wasn't a very tactful letter. It's no use you pushing Rachel down his throat as I don't for a moment suppose there is anything between them.'

'He rushed straight to her,' said Finella, hotly, and added: 'I loathe that woman.'

Barbara smiled.

'Don't tell me you "couldn't care less". You're still devoted to Darley and you're a little fool not to let him know.'

Then Finella burst into tears.

'I don't know what to do ... I'm too miserable for words,' she sobbed.

Barbara put an arm around her.

'Fin, you've always been so plucky, don't go to pieces now, darling. Let me see Darley for you.'

Finella shook her head.

'No! I don't want anybody to interfere. I'll have to see him sometime myself. I feel so ill at the moment. I just wanted to get home with you and have a few days' rest. It was horrid in the hospital. Everything's been horrid. I want to get back to normal before I start coping with things.'

Barbara made no further argument but she resolved that she, personally, would get in touch with Darley before any further harm was done.

That same afternoon Barbara saw to it that Finella was safely in bed and resting and that young Mark also was in his cot for his usual 'siesta'. She then got on to Directory Enquiries and asked for the Webb's number. Having found it she put through a call and without hesitation asked if she might speak to Captain Martington. She had quite decided that she was not going to let that hateful man Bryte ruin her sister's whole life.

A woman's clear cool voice spoke to her.

'This is Miss Webb. No, I'm afraid Captain Martington is not here.'

Barbara ruminated ... this must be the famous Rachel whom she had never met but whom she had heard about from Finella. Barbara was a girl of action and spirit, and nothing daunted she said:

'Do you mind telling me if Captain Martington is staying there and if I could get him later?'

Miss Webb answered cautiously:

'Might I ask who is speaking?'

'Yes. It's Mrs. Stevenson. Captain Martington's sister-in-law.'

An instant's pause and then Miss Webb's voice came again with a new sharp note:

'I'm very sorry, Mrs. Stevenson, but Captain Martington won't be here and I can't tell you where to find him. He's gone away.'

'Where . . .' began Barbara.

The telephone the other end went 'click'.

Barbara put up the receiver. Her fair face flushed slightly with annoyance. There and then she decided she would join her sister in disliking Miss Webb. But Barbara was not easily to be defeated and she at once put through another call to the Manor.

This time, she realized, she was indeed braving the lion in its den because Finella's mother-in-law answered, and upon enquiring who wanted her son and hearing the answer, became frozen and even hostile.

'I'm extremely sorry, Barbara, but my son cannot speak to you. No, he is *not* here. No . . . I cannot tell you where he is. What . . . ? I could if I wished to . . . ? I consider that an impertinence. Look here, young woman, that sister of yours has behaved abominably and—'

But Barbara waited to hear no more. She cut in with one of her rare flashes of temper.

'I'll trouble you to be careful, Lady Martington, in what you say about Fin. You are making a very grave mistake and so is Darley. Fin was *not* running away with Mr. Bryte. I never heard such nonsense and she is *not* guilty of anything more than a minor indiscretion, so if you're hoping to part her from Darley on that score, you'll be disappointed. Good-bye.'

With which she hung up and found herself trembling. Oh, how she wished Jack were here . . . her dear, dependable Jack, who was so rational and wise. Of course she knew he would tell her she had no right to interfere and must expect to get the sticky end of it if she did, but she felt so strongly about her sister and Darley. The whole thing was so out of proportion. She wondered where Darley had gone . . . or if, indeed, both Rachel Webb and Lady Martington were merely trying to prevent him from getting in touch with Finella. She had better confess to Fin that she had made this call and tell her the latest development.

When she took Fin a cup of tea later on and told her, Finella's white face flushed and then her lashes drooped. She said:

'You shouldn't interfere, Barbie, although I know you mean well.'

'Well, you can't allow the Martington family to get away with it like this,' said Barbara.

Finella gave a little smile which was so bitter that it positively hurt Barbara.

'Lady Martington hates me and will do everything she can to widen this breach,' she said. 'And Rachel Webb wants Darley.'

'Well, if Darley's anything of a man he won't let himself be pushed around by a lot of women,' announced Barbara.

Finella looked around the pretty little spare bedroom with its painted French furniture, the pretty striped silk curtains which Barbara, so clever with her needle, had made out of an old ball dress of their mother's. Her mind flashed to John Place and the curtains she had planned to make for No. 18 ... the little home she had hoped to share with Darley and begin a new enchanted existence.

A heartrending look came into her eyes. She put down her teacup and flung herself back on the bed, her shoulders quivering. She said with a sob:

'Darley won't be coerced by either his mother ... or Rachel ... he has lost faith in me. He'll be hard and bitter and refuse to believe a word I say. I've done it ... absolutely done it. Oh, I wish I had never kept that date with Gil. Oh, Barbie, where can Darley be now?'

Barbara shook her head, mutely, a hand stroking Finella's thick, silky hair.

'We must find him, darling, somehow,' she said.

It was at that precise moment that Darley Martington was walking up the long hill of Church Street, Kensington, on his way to Bedford Gardens. In his pocket lay the letter which he had only received this morning from Finella, telling him that she was not going away with Gilfred Bryte. When he had read it, he had been standing with his mother in her sitting-room at the Manor. He had driven over there from the Webbs' house after breakfast this morning, having ascertained that the coast was now clear. Not only had Gilfred Bryte sent for all his belongings and handed over the key of the house to the agents, but his sister, Mrs. Lucas, had also vacated the country home which had been hers for such a brief spell. Even Lady Martington had been sorry for Joanna.

'She's just a crude, simple person but I'm quite sure she knew nothing of what was going on and was entirely against it when she heard,' had been Lady Martington's verdict.

Darley, however, was not interested in Joanna Lucas. He felt but one crying need: to be done with the whole affair and get on with the job of making money and restoring the family fortunes.

After that first shock which he had received about Finella a new Darley had emerged from the pain and bewilderment—an embittered and cynical man who no longer believed in the love of women and he wanted no more romance in his life. He found that after a day or two at the Webbs' he could not even stand Rachel's flattering attentions. He was glad to leave and get back to his mother. But he had no intention of staying with her. Now that Finella had left him he decided to lead his own life in his own way.

His first reactions upon reading his wife's letter were far from happy. He did not really want to see his wife, but at the same time he was puzzled and felt that he had better go and see her. He was convinced that she would go to Bryte eventually and she was merely staying with Barbara as a temporary measure. When he discussed it with his mother she made every effort to prevent him from seeing Finella, which was not very clever of her because it had the effect of making Darley feel perverse. Added to which he was somewhat uncomfortably reminded that his mother had always disliked his young wife and had done nothing toward helping to make their marriage a success.

Lady Martington said:

'You're an absolute fool, my dear boy, to consider meeting her. I know what it is—this horrible man Bryte has probably had his fun and then walked out, and now Finella wants you to take her back, which you *certainly* mustn't do.'

'How you do jump to conclusions, Mother!' Darley said irritably.

Her eyes narrowed as she looked at him.

'Well, don't you be soft, darling. You can't trust that girl and—'

'All right, no need to enlarge on it,' broke in Darley, more shortly than he had ever before spoken to his mother (but this last week had tried his nerves sorely).

And it was soon after this that he went up to town, having decided to see Finella. No matter what she had done she was still, at the moment, his wife. He no longer loved her (he had told himself that every day since her accident because he no longer trusted her and without trust there could be no love). But her letter had definitely perplexed him. It did not seem that she was with Bryte after all if she was at Bedford Gardens with her sister. Of course, his mother might be right. Perhaps Bryte had walked out on Finella. He was that kind of a fellow. And what if that was so? And if Finella had decided that she had been a fool and wished to return to her husband? Darley was a mass of doubts and perplexities as he reviewed the situation, but he felt that he could make no decision until he had actually seen his wife face to face.

Then the door of the Stevensons' little house was opened. He saw Barbara standing there with young Mark behind her, clutching at the flowered overall which she so often wore while she was working about the house. At the sight of the small boy Darley's lips softened, but he barely smiled at his sister-in-law. Coldly he raised his hat and greeted her.

'Good afternoon, Barbara. If Finella's here I'd like to see her.'

He was unprepared for the warmth with which she greeted him in return.

'Oh, Darley, I am glad you've come! You don't know how glad.'

Without answering he walked into the house.

CHAPTER TWENTY-SIX

Husband and wife faced each other in the little Regency drawing-room. The golden afternoon had clouded over. On Darley's grey suit there were little drops of moisture from the fine summer rain which had just started. It was quiet and rather dim in this room. They stood apart like strangers sizing each other up in silence for a few seconds before either spoke. Finella saw no difference in Darley except that he looked stern ... sterner than she had ever seen him, and incredibly remote. But he was shocked at the change in her appearance. She was so very pale and shadowy-eyed. There was a piece of sticking-plaster on her temple. Her rich hair looked dank and lifeless. Her shoulders drooped a little. If she had not hurt him so badly he might have felt sorry for her. As it was he could feel nothing ... nothing but resentment because he believed that she had betrayed him.

Finella found her voice and said:

'I ... I'm glad you've come. I think we ought to talk about things. Do you mind if I sit down ... ? I ... I'm not very fit yet.'

'Of course,' he said, and then as she sank into the nearest chair he took out a packet of cigarettes and offered it to her. It was such a familiar gesture that it wrenched her heart. To see him, her husband, whom she loved as she had never loved him before, after this awful week, and to realize that she had lost him shook her to the core. For she *had* lost him ... she could sense that by his manner and the way he looked at her. Ten days ago she had been in his arms and they had seemed so close that nothing could divide them. This afternoon they were worlds apart.

She refused the cigarette, but Darley lit one. He did not sit down but began to walk with short nervy steps up and down Barbara's pretty room. The rain was pattering against the windows. The house was quiet except for little

Mark's voice and laughter floating down from the nursery.

Then Darley said:

'Well, I got your extraordinary letter and perhaps you'd come straight to the point,' then added: 'I would have come earlier this morning but I had to go and see my lawyers.'

Her heart gave a lurch and she wished she did not feel so weak and stupid.

'Your lawyers,' she repeated in a faltering voice.

'Yes, I asked them what I ought to do next.'

Shocked, she exclaimed:

'But it hasn't reached that pitch! I mean . . . if you're thinking of a divorce . . . you've no evidence.'

He turned and looked at her with a coldness and suspicion that smote her to the heart.

'So Mr. Arkell said, but I presumed that you would furnish me with some and that you would be living with Bryte now even if you hadn't done so already.'

She went scarlet and her pulses quickened with sudden anger against him.

'You've no right to say such things. You've no justification.'

'My dear Finella, you went off with this man—'

'You all seem to have jumped to that conclusion,' broke in Finella in a high-pitched voice.

'What else did you do?'

She choked for a moment and then tried to speak calmly.

'Look here, Darley, first of all I want to make this quite clear. I have *not* been unfaithful to you and you have absolutely no cause to start all this nonsense with lawyers. Why ... why, it's absurd!'

He stopped in front of her and looked down at her with an almost sullen gaze.

'That may be true at the moment ... not that I believe a word you say.'

'Thanks,' she said between her teeth.

He went on:

'Oh, it's no use you riding the high horse like this, my dear girl. You've lied to me consistently ever since I came home. You were having an affair with Bryte while I was away. Oh yes, I knew it all right but tried to shut my eyes to it, because I realized we'd been separated a long time and I couldn't expect you not to have a little innocent fun, but it's scarcely innocent when it reaches the pitch of the fellow taking my own house so as to be near you and arranging secret assignations and then you lying to me as you lied about the other day ... letting me think you were with Barbara and that you'd be here to meet me, whilst all the time you were on your way out of the town with Bryte. Good lord—' He broke off, red, furiously angry.

And now Finella stood up and she too was

scarlet and shaking.

'Don't go on like this!' she flared at him. 'I know you can make it all sound absolutely awful and it does want a lot of explaining . . . but—'

'It wants a hell of a lot of explaining,' it was his turn to break in.

'You seem very ready to think the worst!'

'I hate lies and deception,' he said. 'And above all I detest hypocrisy. You've been nothing better than a hypocrite pretending to love me the way you did on our picnic while all the time you were arranging to see that fellow again. It's unbelievable . . . how you made love to me and—'

'Oh, for heaven's sake!' she broke in, distracted. 'Stop saying things like that. They're not true. I haven't been a hypocrite. I've been a fool. I've messed everything up . . . I know that and I realize now that I ought to have been honest right at the start and told you about Gil, but I didn't because I hoped it had all ended. It *had* ended so far as I was concerned, but Gil wouldn't let go and I was trying to put a stop to it. And I didn't want to hurt or worry you so I . . . said nothing. That's been the whole trouble.'

He wanted to believe her but could not. This last bitter week had been too disillusioning, and doubts of her integrity had grown apace within his very soul. He could not easily trust her again. He said:

'The long and the short of it is that you were keen on this fellow. I can see it all now. You didn't love me when I came back. You didn't even want to have a child by me. Isn't that true?'

Crushed, she had to answer that with truth. (Whatever the issue, she was never going to lie to him again.)

'Yes, *that's* true, or it was, anyhow, right at the beginning.'

'There you are,' he said with bitter satisfaction. 'And I was fool enough to believe in you. All those years I was overseas, I built up an ideal around you. And look what I came back to!'

'But Darley,' she said in anguish, 'I never meant it to be like that, I swear. And I do ask you to believe that I . . . finished with Gilfred Bryte and that I . . . I wasn't a hypocrite that day you took me out to the picnic.'

He began to pace up and down the room again, scarcely looking at her.

'I find it hard to believe anything you say now.'

In despair she shrugged her shoulders.

'Then what's the use of me trying to explain? I suppose you won't believe it, either, when I tell you that I arranged that last lunch in order to finish with Gil for good and all.'

He swung round and faced her, eyes bitter.

'Did you have to finish with him miles out of town in the country when you had fixed to meet

310

me here?'

'No. That was never my intention. He . . . he wouldn't stop the car.'

'Oh, my dear Finella, what a weak explanation.'

Then something seemed to die in her. Love and hope together. She felt as though every emotion had been drained out of her by such cruel disbelief. White to the lips, she said:

'I can see you don't want to believe it and that you're anxious to get rid of me, Darley. All right. Your mother has won and I'm not going to fight any more.'

He stared at her.

'What on earth has my mother got to do with it?'

'Quite a lot,' said Finella bitterly. 'And Rachel too. Oh yes, you're not so guiltless yourself, Darley. You can't deny that you've had an affair with *her*.'

'Nothing of the kind!' he said hotly. 'One kiss. Nothing more. You're merely trying to shift the blame from yourself to me.'

'Oh, what's it matter?' she said wearily. 'I suppose what you want is for me to tell you that I'm ready to go to Gil and be divorced. But I'm just not going to do so.'

'Has he walked out on you?' asked Darley, but regretted the words as soon as they had left his mouth, for he knew instinctively that that was not the case and it made him uncomfortable

311

to see the look that sprang into Finella's large eyes. A look of horrified surprise as though he had hit her. Then, in a choked voice, she said:

'I'll *never* forgive you for that. It isn't true. I know I've hurt you and that some of the things I've done have been stupid and wrong, but I've never done *anything* really bad and to make you so hard and cruel to me now. I—Oh, I don't care if our marriage *does* break up. I'm through . . . absolutely through . . . !'

She burst into tears and rushed out of the room. She left Darley standing there. For a moment he stared after her vanished form, a host of fresh doubts and perplexities disturbing his consciousness. He still felt as resentful and bitter as when he had entered this house and yet . . . if what Finella said was true . . . if she had never really betrayed him and it had all been a mistake . . . just misguided folly on her part . . . ought he to have been so hard? Ought he not to call her back and try to put things right?

Then he flung his cigarette end into the empty grate. He thought:

'No . . . I'm not going to be weak . . . Finella has behaved abominably and I won't believe a word she says. It's time I took a strong line.'

Picking up his hat and gloves, he walked out of the house.

CHAPTER TWENTY-SEVEN

Darley sat at his desk in the library at the manor trying to grapple with a correspondence long overdue. He was not fond of letter-writing (the only person he had ever really written to, fluently and continually, was Finella). But there were one or two business letters which he must get done. There was 18 John Place to be sublet—he had not yet had the heart to go to the agents and tell them that he no longer wanted the house—but he had decided to write to them this morning. There was that Army form (connected with his wound gratuity) to be filled up, and a letter to be written to Jack Pelham who had been at Sandhurst with Darley and had just been invalided out of the Army. Jack had a flat in Sloane Street and Darley thought of asking if he might share it. There was no getting away from the fact that he could not stay at the Manor. Particularly not if he, himself, were going to leave the Army and settle down to serious work for Wychless. Last night he had talked things over with his mother. They had decided that this time they had better let the Manor as soon as possible for a large rent for the summer months only. They might be able to return to it in the winter months. Lady Martington now had fresh plans for herself.

General and Mrs. Webb had asked her to stay with them as a paying guest for the summer. They were devoted to her—particularly Rachel.

Darley, pen in his hand, feeling in no mood to put a single word on paper, sat looking out at the garden with brooding gaze. The sun was still shining brilliantly, but it was past six o'clock.

He could see the tall, dignified figure of his mother. She had been watering her special plants in the conservatory. She had a passion for cinerarias, but had given up growing them during the war because she considered it more patriotic to devote her time to other things. Now that the war was over, she was gradually paying less attention to the old war committees and was drifting back to her gardening.

There was pain in Darley's eyes as well as weariness as he watched his mother walk across the lawn with a watering can in one hand and a basket in the other. She wore a straw hat with a veil tied under the chin; a strangely Edwardian figure. He had so often seen her in hats like those. His father used to joke about them when he was a boy ... 'one of Mummy's hats' ... they were called. How sad it was that people could change so terribly with the years, thought the young man in bitterness of spirit. Not only had Finella changed, but his mother, too. Her love for him, no. That was as heart-whole as ever. But unfortunately it was the wrong kind of love, possessive, wholly selfish. She did not

314

want his happiness as much as her own. She only wanted him to be with the girl of *her* choosing. She had changed from the loving tolerant 'Mummy' of his boyhood days. This difficult, scheming woman had helped to destroy his marriage. He realized that now. He 'handed it' to Fin that she had never complained in any of her letters, but had suffered his mother's unkindness in silence. At least she had been sporting about it all. He could not fail to realize that, devoted though she was to him, his mother had a very unpleasant side to her and it showed itself in her treatment of Finella. Incidentally, in her behaviour generally since the Bryte affair. She no longer made any pretence of liking Darley's wife these days. Last night, when they had discussed the present situation, Darley had tried to defend Finella, and the result had brought forth insulting remarks from Lady Martington. They had ended with a short, sharp row, after which it was agreed that Finella's name should not be mentioned between them in future.

'Why should you, of all people, defend Finella?' Lady Martington had demanded.

He had answered unhesitatingly:

'Because I see how hard it must have been for her all those years I was away, and I don't really believe that she meant to run away with that fellow. I don't think she meant any harm. The thing just developed that way, unfortunately for us all.'

'You've no proof of that,' Lady Martington had flashed back.

'No,' he said, 'but I'd like to give Finella the benefit of the doubt.'

'Do you intend to take her back, then?' his mother had asked, with such utter dismay in her voice that Darley had felt exasperated to the pitch of snapping at her.

'That remains to be seen, and if I do try to patch things up, for heaven's sake don't, on your part, try to make them worse, Mother.'

Needless to say she had marched out of the room then, furious with him. They had scarcely spoken to each other since.

It seemed to Darley this evening, as he sat brooding over his affairs, that he had had a poor deal all round. He had lost the illusions he had cherished both in mother and wife. Of course Rachel had been very nice to him—unfailingly so. During the few days he had spent with the Webbs they had all done their best to be tactful, to help. But he had felt raw even there. It had been a humiliating position, and Rachel's solicitude, even though balm to the bruised spirit, had its drawbacks. He could not fail to know what she felt about him these days, and it was an awkward position for a chap if he could do nothing about it when a woman showed that she was in love. He had felt the only decent thing for him to do was to keep away in future.

That was really why he had left the Webbs' house rather abruptly and returned to the Manor.

There was something else on his mind which was depressing him just now. His luck was certainly 'out'. Old Sue, his spaniel, was mortally ill, at a time when he would have appreciated the old animal's familiar company. He was so used to her following him about. It was always a comfort to see her curled in her basket by his bed, to keep the choice morsels for her at table, to take her for the last walk after dinner at night and watch the old spirit leap within her when she scented a rabbit, and went dashing into the hedgerows as she used to do in her puppy days. But that was twelve years ago and old age had got Sue down. He had had to send for Jackson, the vet, yesterday, and it seemed that Sue was suffering from an incurable malady and that unless she showed signs of improvement in a day or so it would be necessary to put her to sleep.

That would mean parting with a very old friend and Darley was astonished at how much the mere idea hurt him. It didn't seem that he could lose much more that he loved.

Lady Martington looked into the library, saw her son at the desk and gave a half-nervous cough.

'Going to have a glass of sherry, dear?'

He stood up, aware that she was making an

317

effort, in her own way, to stage a reconciliation.

He felt really too tired and depressed for further fight. He gave her a faint smile back and said:

'Yes, why not? Come and have one, Mamma.'

Lady Martington's face brightened. That was his old pet name for her. In her own way she adored Darley and she had felt keenly their painful difference of opinion over Finella. She also felt a bit guilty about the whole thing, of course, but at the same time she could not reconcile herself to the knowledge that Darley still loved Finella and would gladly take her back. But she was also well aware that if she showed further hostility she would lose her son altogether, so she had told herself that she must 'climb down' no matter how much she disliked the process.

'I'll just go and wash my hands,' she said, brightly.

The sound of an approaching car made Darley glance out of the window. He recognized the car and its occupant and gave a sudden frown.

'It's Rachel. What on earth does she want? That girl's never out of this house.'

Lady Martington bit her lip.

'I'm sorry if you don't want her, dear,' she said, in an unusually humble manner.

'I suppose you asked her?' Darley answered gruffly.

'I told her to look in if she was passing.'

'She seems to do nothing but pass the Manor.'

'Oh, dear' said Lady Martington plaintively. 'You used to like Rachel, and after all she *is* my god-daughter and *so* fond of you, Darley. I do feel—'

'That I ought to be grateful, yes,' broke in Darley. But his jaw set in the stubborn line which his mother had grown to dread lately. 'And so I am, but to be quite candid, it's no use my seeing a lot of Rachel and no use your throwing her across my path on every single occasion. Even if Finella and I split, I shall *not* marry Rachel—or anybody else. You might as well face that fact.'

Lady Martington swallowed this, and her pride, with a gulp, and said meekly: 'Yes, dear ... I understand' ... and went up to her bedroom feeling a most disappointed and thwarted woman.

Rachel Webb, with the familiar air of one accustomed to being *persona grata* at the Manor, greeted Darley with a cheerfulness which even he could see was forced.

'Hullo! How's everyone? I've come to cadge a drink as I'm just on my way home from the station.'

'Good show,' said Darley, mechanically. 'Mamma and I were thinking of having a sherry. You must join us. She'll be down in a moment. Sit yourself, Rachel.'

She remained standing, looking at him, drawing off her gloves. She was trying to get his measure. She wondered what mood he was in this evening. He had been very difficult while he was staying with her family . . . one black mood after another had descended upon him. All the result of Finella's behaviour, of course. It infuriated Rachel to see how far that girl affected Darley. She had worked hard to get him back to normal but had not, she was well aware, succeeded. Bitterly she had had to admit to herself that she was fighting a losing battle against Finella. Darley was not to be comforted by her, Rachel, or by any other girl. Such a realization was a considerable blow to her vanity and yet Aunt Margaret still encouraged her to come here and told her to do everything she could to 'help' Darley. Of course Rachel knew what Aunt Margaret meant by that! And it seemed as though Lady Martington was wrong. Darley was not to be seduced from his long-standing adoration of Finella. It was a sickening disappointment to Rachel.

The two of them exchanged covert glances. She thought that he looked fatigued and drawn but still so very desirable (she had never for a moment forgotten that day when he sufficiently lost his head to take her in his arms and kiss her, here in this very room. Finella had been ill in bed at the time). Could she not make him kiss her again? Could there be no way in which she could break down his defences and make him realize how right she was for him and how wrong was Finella?

Darley, on his part, read the unspoken passion in Rachel's dark eyes and shrank from it. He could not deal with any more emotional scenes in his present raw condition of mind and heart. Neither was he a vain or selfish enough man to enjoy the knowledge that this girl was his for the asking. On the contrary it embarrassed him and made him less friendly than he would have been otherwise. Yet she was looking attractive enough, in one of the well-tailored suits that became her so well, and with a bright coloured scarf tying up her hair. She said:

'How are you, Darley dear?'

'Fine, thanks,' was his brief reply.

'Have you made any plans for the immediate future?'

'I am thinking about sharing a flat with my friend, Jack Pelham,' he said, dropping his gaze. It made him too uncomfortable to look into those eyes that asked in plain words that he should embrace her there and then.

A slightly pleased look passed Rachel's face.

'Oh! then you and Finella are not—'

He cut in swiftly and more coldly than he had meant.

'Oh, I haven't really come to any definite decisions. I have not seen Fin. It is still quite possible that she and I may reach an understanding, although I am well aware of course that there are a great many people who would like to see us in the divorce courts.'

Rachel went crimson.

Darley, glancing at her, saw what he had done and was immediately contrite, although the effects of his contritions were such that he cursed himself afterwards for being such a soft-hearted fool. (What were those lines about *'the brave man does it with a sword and the coward with a kiss*...'Something by Wilde. He had known his stuff! ...)

'Oh!' said Rachel, *'Darley.'*

He put out a hand.

'Sorry, Rachel, but honestly I'm rather tired of the general atmosphere down here ... everybody so dead against Finella, and you must admit you're one of the worst offenders.'

She caught at his hand and her strong, lithe fingers gripped his convulsively, showing the force of her feelings.

'Why, Darley,' she said in a choked voice. 'I'm sorry if I've given you offence, but you know what I feel about Finella. . . .'

'Yes, I know very well,' he said.

'Well, surely you understand. . . . Oh, don't make me say it! But you know how I resent anybody hurting *you*. . . .'

'Oh, my dear,' he said in a softer voice and with real regret in his eyes, 'you're very charming to me and I was only saying to mother just now that I do appreciate your friendship. But, Rachel, it's friendship I want and nothing else. I don't want to be made to say things, either. I think it would be much better for us both to keep off discussions like these. Things were much better between us when we were just pals, and it must be that way, Rachel. I'm not going to mince words, my dear. I still love my wife and I always will, and I'm going to do my damnedest to put things right between us.'

There was a moment's deadly silence. Rachel had torn her fingers away from his. She stood there, struggling with herself. Her face changing from red to white, and white to red again. Her lips were quivering, and Darley saw a gleam of tears on her lashes. Once again his kindly heart got the better of his judgment. Poor old Rachel! He ought never to have encouraged her even for a moment and the sight of her like this made him feel all kinds of a cad. She had always been so sane and practical and sporting . . . not the emotional type at all. Heavens, what a curse human emotions were! They were at the root of all the troubles in the world. It seemed to him in this moment, love was responsible, at any rate, for three-quarters of the miseries that assailed mankind.

He took her hand again and kissed it.

'You're a dear, Rachel, and you've been a grand friend to me. I'm not forgetful of that, I assure you.'

The kiss and the softness in his eyes broke down her pride and reduced her to a level of sentimentality that she would normally have despised. But she was madly in love with him and only too bitterly conscious that she would never get him now, *never*. She flung herself into his arms and burst into tears.

Darley, red and uncomfortable, held the quivering figure and tried to comfort her.

'Oh, my dear, don't ... don't. Rachel, you mustn't feel like this about me. Really you mustn't. It's bad for you and you put me on a spot. Don't, dear, *please*. Pull yourself together. I'm not worth your tears, and you should never be feeling this way about me. I'm a much married man...' He made a poor attempt at humour and added: 'We can't have our little Rachel fooling round with married men, you know.'

She raised a tear-wet face, with eyes flashing.

'You're laughing at me, I know. And I shall despise myself for this afterwards, but I love you and I've always loved you ... *always*.'

'Oh, Rachel, please!'

'Yes, I don't care if it does embarrass you. I fully see that I shan't see much more of you.'

'Rachel...' Darley began again, helplessly.

But she had lost her head and raged on:

'It's been hopeless from the start, I've known it. You *would* marry Finella even though Aunt Margaret warned you. I wouldn't have minded so much if she had made you happy, but she hasn't and she isn't any good to you. She's just a rotten—'

'Rachel!' Darley cut in again and this time without kindliness in voice or expression. He let her go abruptly. His young face was granite-hard. 'I refuse to hear anything more against Finella. She is far from rotten. Neither you nor my mother understand her. She's lovely and young and she's been alone all these years with men rushing after her and I'm only just beginning to understand how difficult it must all have been for her, especially with you two against her, down here. If you had really cared about me, Rachel, you would have shown a greater friendliness toward my wife. You might have been a real help to her ... Oh, what's the use? It's all too late and talking doesn't really get us anywhere.'

There was a long silence. Rachel was gasping for breath, trying to control herself. At that moment Lady Martington came into the room. The bright greeting she had prepared for her god-daughter died as she saw Rachel's face.

'My darling child, what is the matter ... ?' she began.

But Rachel did not wait for her to go on. She flung a look of intense bitterness at Darley, avoided her godmother's hand and rushed out of the house. They heard the car being started up and then driven away at a furious pace.

Lady Martington blinked and eyed her son with concern.

'Oh, Darley, what happened? Oh, poor Rachel!'

Darley, his nerves frayed, looked at his mother with resentment and snapped:

'Don't worry so much about "poor Rachel". Your poor Rachel and you, between you, have done everything you can to hurt Finella. You might start thinking about "poor Finella" and "poor me" for a change.'

Lady Martington's face screwed up.

'Oh, Darley!' she wailed.

'I'll come back for my sherry later,' he said. 'I'm going to see old Sue.'

He arrived at the gardener's cottage where Mrs. Wilkins, the kindly woman who was fond of Sue, had been nursing the sick animal, only to be told that half an hour ago old Sue had suddenly died of heart failure. It must have been while he was having that painful scene with Rachel that Sue had breathed her last.

He bent over the basket in which his old favourite lay so still and was unashamed of the stinging tears in his eyes as he touched the brown, quiet body for the last time.

'Sleep well, old friend,' he said. 'You've gone to a good place where there'll be lots of rabbits and bones. Good hunting, Sue. . . .'

He was glad that she would know no more pain and that he would not now need to have her put away. Queer, but at that moment he thought of Fin. She had been fond of the dog. She would be sorry to hear about this.

He walked slowly back to the Manor. Dusk had fallen. An almost intolerable sense of loss and loneliness weighed him down. That night he and his mother avoided any mention of Finella or Rachel, although Lady Martington did once mention the fact that she thought it would be 'rather awkward' for her to go and live with the Webbs now that he and Rachel had quarrelled.

To this Darley replied:

'It wasn't exactly a quarrel. And she and the General and Mrs. Webb are devoted to you, so what I do or don't do shouldn't have any bearing on your arrangements. All I know is that the sooner I get away from this district, the better, and I wish to heaven Rachel would meet some nice fellow and get herself married.'

Lady Martington made no reply to this, but thought dismally what a disappointment one's children can be and how rarely they fulfil their parents' ambitions for them. She was still convinced that Rachel would have made him the perfect wife and 'that girl' Finella had ruined his life.

The morning brought Darley a letter from his sister-in-law.

Dear Darley,

Finella wants me to let you know that she has decided to stay with me for the present and go back to her painting. She hopes to find a job as a commercial artist. As soon as she has got one, she says she does not wish you to support her. Of course, I think you are both crazy to go on like this when it's all a mistake. Fin is most unhappy and I am sure you can't be anything else.

Yours,
Barbara.

This worried Darley and gave him to think a great many times. The implication of it somehow made him feel guilty . . . as though he alone were responsible for the breaking up of this marriage. Finella was certainly not behaving like a woman in love with another man. She showed no signs of going to Gilfred Bryte. . . .

Whatever she had done, it was like her to show such pride, he thought; to refuse financial help if she wasn't going to live with him.

Damn it, there were so many fine things about Finella.

Damn it, he was still in love with her.

'Fin is most unhappy and I'm sure you can't be anything else.'

God alone knew that was true.

He got up from the breakfast table and walked to the window. Standing there a moment he did a few exercises with his injured arm. It seemed to be healing up nicely this time but it was still painful when he moved it.

He saw a car coming up the drive. Darley stiffened and his cheeks flushed slightly. This was Gilfred Bryte's big car—familiar to all of them at the Manor. Good lord! What effrontery, that fellow coming *here*.

Darley turned and walked out of the room and, moving to the front door, opened it. Bryte wasn't coming inside this house . . . and then he stood still. For he saw not Bryte but Joanna Lucas, his sister. She advanced toward Darley, smiling a trifle nervously, and with none of her usual heartiness.

'Oh, Captain Martington, I'm glad you're here . . . I *particularly* wanted to see you,' she said.

Always courteous, Darley asked her in. He had nothing personally against Joanna Lucas. He did not care for her type but he had always found her agreeable and he thought her much more genuine than her brother.

In the library she said:

'You must wonder why I've come. No . . . it's not because I've left anything behind but because I *must* tell you something that is on my mind. My . . . brother is away and I've taken his car. I'd get into trouble if he knew but I felt it my duty to see either you or Lady Martington. Only I'm glad it's you, Captain Martington. It really concerns *you* more than your mother.'

She made this speech with obvious nervousness, her rough North-country accent showing itself rather more than usual. Darley was puzzled but he looked at her with kindliness, trying to put her at her ease.

'What is it, Mrs. Lucas? Tell me.'

She fumbled with the clasp of her bag and lowered her gaze.

'It's to do with *my* brother and *your* wife, Captain Martington.'

Darley felt his heart plunge.

'Oh?'

Joanna Lucas raised her eyes to his. They were honest, and, at the moment, ashamed.

'I'm very fond of Gil, Captain Martington. He was my hero even when I was a child up at home. I always stood up for Gil when there were family rows. And since my husband's death he's been more to me than ever. But I'm not blind to his faults, I know his trouble is women ... it always was women ... and his selfishness. When Gil wants a thing he tries to get it at any price. That's the worst part of him. He doesn't stop to think how unhappy he may make others.'

She paused. Darley, brows knit, stared at her, wondering what was coming next. He wanted to tell her that he was not really interested in her analysis of her brother but he knew that he must listen ... she was going to say something vital ... something that he *must* hear.

330

She continued:

'I didn't really know until the other day what was going on between Gil and your wife. I was flabbergasted when I found out. I knew he admired her and that he used to take her out when you were overseas, but it never entered my head that ... that—' She broke off, stammering.

Darley tautened. He had been in the act of lighting a cigarette but he held the match suspended in his fingers.

'That what?' he asked tensely.

She gulped.

'That my brother was so mad about Finella,' finished Joanna.

Darley relaxed again.

'Well?'

'Well, it's like this ...'

And then Joanna Lucas poured out her story, every word of which interested Darley Martington more than a little. He was impatient when she started apologizing for Gilfred's behaviour. But the poor soul was so attached to Bryte ... trying to excuse him on the grounds that the money and successes he had made had gone to his head; that he thought all women in love with him and always had been mixed up with some girl or other. But Finella had fascinated him more than most, Joanna said, and he had wanted to marry her. She had refused to do anything definite about him because she still cared for the husband who was fighting for her. She had wanted to be faithful to him. She had told Gil to leave her alone and he had refused. On that fatal day of the accident she had asked Gil to lunch with her for the last time, and she had told him that she was in love with her own husband. She had only meant to spend a short hour with Gil. But he had lost his head and in a moment of frustration and anger had driven her out of town. It had been against her will but he had gone on and then they had crashed.

'Even then,' added Joanna, 'my brother wasn't going to give up hope, but Finella seems to have made it plain that she wouldn't have any more to do with him and so at last he's given it up. That's the whole truth, Captain Martington, and I feel you ought to know it. I'm so afraid Gil's put wrong ideas in all your heads down here about Finella. She's young and beautiful but she's really a very good girl, I-I'm sure of it. . . .'

Her voice died away. Darley stood up. His face was crimson. He said:

'Just one moment, Mrs. Lucas. I want to know how you know all this.'

She explained that she had found out most of it this last week. She was living in Gil's flat in London. After his last meeting with Finella . . . or was it her sister? . . . he had come home in a towering rage and the whole story had tumbled out. He hadn't hesitated to let her know how badly he was 'bitten'. He had raved and ranted about his failure to win Finella's love.

As for the business about motoring her out of town against her will, Joanna knew *that*, she stated, because Finella had written to Gil and she had seen the letter. Gil no longer cared what she knew. He was 'through' and admitted his defeat. Finella had said in her letter that he had behaved like a cad and that it was his duty to tell the Martingtons the truth. But he had flung the letter at Joanna and said;

'To hell with that. I'm not having any more to do with any of them. I hate the whole lot as much as they hate me. And Finella has disappointed me. She's too good to live. Let her stick to her husband. She isn't the only girl in the world. *I'm* not going to sit down and cry over her.'

Joanna repeated this to Darley and then added:

'So you see, Captain Martington, there is no need for you to be angry with Finella. And I can't *bear* to think you two have separated through my brother, when there is really no cause.'

There was a long pause. Darley seemed to be struggling with his emotions. His face was quite white now. Then he went up to Joanna and held out his hand.

'Thanks, Mrs. Lucas,' he said huskily. 'All

333

my thanks, in fact. You've been perfectly marvellous. You don't know *what* you've done for us.'

She gripped the hand and her honest eyes filled with tears.

'Oh, Captain Martington, I do wish my brother would behave himself,' she said with a half-sob. 'He's so clever. So delightful when he wants to be. You don't know how it hurts me . . . to know he does things like this.'

'Cheer up,' said Darley. 'And take my advice and strike out on your own. Don't let him get you down.'

Joanna wiped her eyes.

'I'd dearly like to think you and your pretty wife are going to patch things up.'

Darley said:

'We are. If I die in the attempt, I'll get Finella back and we'll start again. Don't worry.'

CHAPTER TWENTY-EIGHT

'The point is,' said Finella, 'how I'm going to get my clothes and things. I refuse, absolutely, to go down to the Manor myself. I don't want to meet Darley and I *never* want to see his horrid old mother again.'

She made this declaration, walking up and down Barbara's bedroom, whilst Barbara finished brushing her fair hair back from her fresh, pink face. She was dressing with greater care than usual this morning. She was meeting Jack for lunch. Her beloved Jack. He had telephoned to say he would be in London on a 'job' and would snatch lunch with her. She was still very much in love with her tall sailor husband and her eyes were shining with the excitement of seeing him again, even though they had so recently spent his last leave together. But as she told him, every time she said good-bye, though only for a week or two, it was like 'having a tooth pulled out'. It hurt . . . and it left a horrid aching.

The only thing to spoil her happiness today was the disaster which apparently faced her sister. Finella looked so thin and miserable, and despite all her defiant talk about earning her own living and being glad to separate from Darley, etc., Barbara knew perfectly well that Fin still loved her husband. She deplored this present misunderstanding, and she could willingly have murdered Gilfred Bryte for the part he had played in it all. She turned round from her mirror and looked at her sister.

'Darling,' she said, 'don't be such a mug. Go on down to Godalming and face them. You're innocent. You know it. Let *them* know it. Go down and pack up and be hanged to old Lady What-Not.'

Finella gave a bitter smile. She sat down on

the edge of Barbara's bed and lit a cigarette.

'You don't know my mother-in-law, Barbie. She'd probably lock the front door if she saw me coming down the drive, or let me in and then insult me—call me an immoral woman or something. I won't risk it. I'll have to write to Darley and ask him to ask Rose to pack a trunk for me and send it up here.'

'But have you quite made up your mind that you're not going to live with Darley any more?'

'Quite.'

'Oh, Fin,' said Barbara with a sigh. 'It's such a tragedy. I'm sure if you had it all out together—'

'We had it out here the other day,' broke in Finella, on a hard note. 'I shall never try again to clear myself in Darley's eyes. He thinks the worst, and that's that.'

'I'm sure he doesn't in his heart, Fin.'

'Yes, he does.'

'It's only pique . . . on both your parts.'

Finella shrugged her shoulders, puffed at her cigarette, then flicked the ash from it nervously with a little finger. Her young face looked gaunt and her eyes were strained. She had not taken so much trouble with her hair this morning. A loose strand hung untidily against her cheek. Even the bright red-gold of it seemed tarnished, lifeless. And as she watched Barbara dress for her meeting with her husband, she envied her with a bitter, passionate envy. Lucky, *lucky*

Barbie, to have made such a success of her marriage; to be sitting there, making up her face in joyous anticipation of a meeting with her Jack. Of course Finella knew that she, herself, was to blame in the original instance, for a great deal of her own troubles. She had been too impatient . . . while Darley was overseas; she had, in truth, been disloyal to him in *thought* . . . by associating with Gilfred Bryte and considering, even for a single instant, a serious love-affair with him. She had never had the placid, steady temperament of dear old Barbie. It *was* largely her own fault if at first things had gone wrong. But it was Darley's fault *now* . . . he had been so ready to believe ill of her. He, too, had failed in faith and loyalty. Oh, thought Finella, what a miserable waste it had all been . . . and what mistakes they had both made. Yet she had been so sure, just before the accident with Gil, that she and Darley could make a 'go of it' . . . and that she had fallen in love with him . . . madly in love again.

She missed him. She had missed him all this week. But nothing would induce her to take Barbara's advice and try to put things right again. She was going to the Art School tomorrow. She must start to earn her own living . . . get a job for instance on some woman's magazine. Good illustrations were always in demand and she had a 'flair' for that sort of thing. It was what she had meant to do just before she met Darley, in those days when Mummy had been hard up and she had known that she could not afford to study and become a serious painter.

At length she rose from the bed and, walking to her sister, leaned down and dropped a kiss on one of Barbara's smooth cheeks.

'Don't you worry about me, Barb ... just go and meet old Jack and be happy,' she said. 'I only hope he won't mind me living with you for a few weeks until I find my feet.'

'Of course he won't—you know he adores you, Fin, and it's lovely for Mark and me,' said Barbara.

After her sister had gone, Finella spent an hour playing with young Mark, then left him to the nurse-girl for his lunch and wandered into the drawing-room.

It was another golden day ... June in London was a lovely month and the city looked enchanted, thought Finella; trees so green and fresh in the parks; sun glittering on the great white blocks of flats. But Finella thought of a quaint 'blind-alley' in Kensington; of a row of little houses; 18 John Place ... the little house she had meant to make beautiful for Darley ... their first real home since their marriage. Oh, she had wanted to make such a success of housekeeping for Darley there. It was all to have been so thrilling.

Suddenly Finella sat down on the sofa, leaned

her forehead against her folded arms and wept. Slow, hot tears of misery, of regret, rolling down her cheeks.

When that crying fit came to an end, she reached a sudden decision. She bathed her face, made it up hastily, put on the short jacket which belonged to the linen frock she was wearing, seized a pair of gloves and a bag and walked out of the house. As though impelled by something stronger than herself, she went to South Kensington Underground, then found her way to John Place.

It gave her a queer nostalgic feeling when at length she faced the quaint little *cul-de-sac* which had reminded both her and Darley, when they first saw it, of a street on the Continent. This was not London at all ... it was Italy ... or France ... or Spain ... with the flat roofs and dirty white façades against the clear blue of the summer sky. True it was all spoilt by the ugly tenement at the bottom of the road, but there was beauty in the window-boxes and tubs full of gay flowers, and each little window proudly displaying snowy curtains of freshly laundered net. Most of the little painted doors stood open on a morning like this, letting in the sunshine.

Desolately Finella looked at each small house as she passed, and wondered what story lay behind those doors ... who the people were ... if they were happy ... or if their world had ever crashed in pieces as hers and Darley's had done.

She had not realized until this morning how much she had wanted to live here; to begin that home-life which she had missed all through the years of the war.

She stopped in front of No. 18. The windows were closed and the door was locked. The casements looked dusty and the little house had that forlorn, solitary air of the unoccupied building.

A brown and tan terrier came bounding up to Finella, wagging its tail in a friendly way. An attractive woman across the road called to him:

'Jackie, come here . . .'

A moment later Finella saw the woman and a man emerge from their house and walk up the street, arm in arm, the dog following them. They were laughing and talking animatedly. And Finella, who always wove romances around everybody, thought:

'I expect they're a happy married couple. Oh, why, *why* did things have to go wrong for *us*.'

Today, more than ever, she loathed the memory of Gilfred Bryte, and reproached herself for that foolish emotional affair which had done so much to spoil Darley's return.

Somehow she felt that she must go into the little house and look at it. It might be for the last time. She went across to the corner house and asked the caretaker for the keys. A moment later she was in No. 18. It was hot and stifling, for the sun poured through the windows at both ends. Finella opened some of the casements and let in the fresh air. She stood a moment looking at the empty bookcases beside the fireplace. Here she had meant to put her and Darley's books. Over there, where there was a good light, she had planned to sit and paint in her spare time ... longing to get back to her old artistic career. They had even discussed colour schemes ... washing down the walls with pale-green distemper, finding some gay rose and green chintzes for the windows and chair covers. The carpet was going to be green, too. And Darley had talked about bringing some of the smaller pieces of oak furniture up from the Manor ... things his mother did not want....

There was a tightness in Finella's throat, and a look of real misery in her eyes as she wandered about the house ... into the kitchenette where she had meant to learn cooking ... up to the bedroom which she would have shared with Darley, and that little spare room next door, which would have been for their friends.

She was terrified that she was going to cry again. She stood a moment with both knuckles pressed against her eyes.

She heard the sound of a taxi scraping down the road and going back into the front bedroom, peered down. The taxi drew up in front of No. 18. Her heart gave a tremendous jerk as she saw the slimly built figure of the man in grey flannels who stepped out. It was Darley. *Darley* had come here, too.

She turned, ran down the little curved staircase and opened the front door. Darley took off his hat and stood staring with astonishment and a dawning pleasure in his eyes as he looked at the tall slender girl who was his wife.

'Good heavens, Fin,' he exclaimed, 'you're the last person I expected to find here!'

She coloured and felt suddenly at a disadvantage because she knew she had not taken much care with her appearance. Her red-gold hair was untidy and her nose, she felt sure, was shining. Her eyes, too, must be swollen after all that crying that she had done before she came out. Swallowing hard she said:

'I—What on earth are *you* doing here, Darley?'

He closed the door and stood leaning against it, looking past Finella, at the sunny room which had that pungent warm smell of sun baking on bare wooden boards.

'I . . . I just thought I'd have a look at the house . . .'

'So did I,' she said.

An embarrassing pause. Darley added:

'I was thinking of sharing a flat with old Jack Pelham, you know, but I'm not all that keen on it, and I wondered whether I'd get rid of this place or keep it on.'

Her lashes dropped.

'I see,' she said.

Now he turned his gaze to her again. A sharp pang of pity for her gripped his heart. This was no hard, unforgiving 'glamour girl'. This untidy Finella whose face bore traces of tears was pathetic and vulnerable, and somebody who appealed for a man's protection. He had an infinite wish to become her protector, to shield her against the onslaughts of people like his own mother—or Rachel Webb—or fellows like Gilfred Bryte.

'Why, Fin,' he said gently, 'perhaps you came here really for the same reason that I have done ... because I damned well hated the idea of chucking up our little place and all that it meant.'

Her heart leapt again as it had leapt when she saw him step out of the taxi. But she shook her head and muttered:

'What's the use ... ?'

There was a sob in her voice, and the implication of that sound and of the unhappiness that was written all over her drove every thought from his mind save one ... the knowledge that he loved her ... that he had always loved her ... and always would.

'Oh, darling,' he said, *'darling ...'*

He walked up to her there and then and took her in his arms and began to kiss her; kiss every inch of her bewildered face. (Poor little face ... so much too thin and changed, he thought.) In

343

between the kisses, he murmured:

'I love you. Fin, I love you. I've always loved you. We've both been mad. We could never separate, you and I. Fin, Fin, forgive me . . . please . . . darling. I love you so much . . .'

For the fraction of a moment she resisted. Then his passionate kisses woke response in her. She went limp in his arms, and kissed him back . . . with mad abandon. For oh, it was blessed relief to feel his arms about her . . . to see him here . . . not the ghost of the Darley she had loved, but the flesh-and-blood man . . . warm, vital, lips upon hers, hands threading through her hair. Without speaking, for a long time, she clung to him and let him kiss her. Like two people starved, hungry for love, they kissed and clung. And when finally he released her, her cheeks were burning pink and her eyes like stars. He smiled at her tenderly.

'Darling,' he said. 'We must talk.'

Still bewildered, she looked up into his eyes.

'Darley,' she said breathlessly. 'Why . . . *why* this? What's changed us both?'

'I know what's changed me,' he said.

'What?'

'The knowledge that I've been a goddam fool, darling, to imagine for one single moment that you could play such a really scurvy trick on me . . . or to doubt that you spoke the truth when you told me about that day with Gilfred Bryte.'

'But what's made you know it all of a sudden,

Darley?'

'Bryte's sister drove down to the Manor first thing this morning to see me, Fin. What she said pulled me up with a jerk. Though I swear I didn't need much pulling ... I knew inside me, somehow, that I'd been a fool to doubt you ... but she proved it.'

'But what on earth could Mrs. Lucas say to prove it?'

He told her. Finella listened in amazement. Then, when he had finished the story, she sat quietly, and the rose-red seeped a little from her face, and she looked pale and sad again.

'I see,' she said. 'Well ... now you *do* know. But I'm a bit fed up to think you had to have it proved beyond doubt before you trusted me again.'

He said:

'Don't judge me too harshly for that, Fin. I dare say I ought to have believed in you from the start and all that ... but there were a lot of reasons why I had doubts. You *had* gone behind my back with that fellow, after all. And what with one thing and another, I must be excused if I lost faith and all that ... but oh, my Fin, I never stopped loving you,' he added on a deep note of sincerity. 'I swear to that. It just about broke my heart when I thought you'd walked out on me. I wanted to make it up with you, and then I came to see you and we had that stupid scene and started the trouble all over again. Fin,

345

we've both been fools. But don't condemn me if I've had a few suspicions. Good lord . . . you did ask for it, darling.'

Her head sank. Her lower lip began to tremble . . . mid-way between a smile and the desire to cry. He was so touchingly boyish in this moment, she thought. Far from the hard, relentless Darley she had walked out on a week ago . . . and whom she had almost hated. How narrow was the margin between love and hate! But she did love him. Of that there was no doubt. And what he said was perfectly true. She *had* 'asked for it'. She could not altogether play the injured party. If he had suspected her, he had had cause. She had lied to him and there *had* been Gil . . .

She said:

'I've done a lot of silly things, I know it. But I swear I was never unfaithful to you, Darley.'

He flushed.

'I'm sure of that. You needn't say any more, darling.'

'I never really loved Gil either,' she added in a low voice. 'It was a sort of infatuation . . . I was lonely . . . and wanting love. But fundamentally I wanted *you*. Oh, Darley, do believe me when I say that when you came home I had no desire in my heart save to finish with Gil and make a success of our marriage.'

'I do believe you now. Only you went about it in such a silly way, if I may say so, darling.' He

346

gave a short laugh, picked up one of her slender hands and brushed his lips against the palm. 'You ought to have told me ... right away, about the whole show. Then none of this would have happened.'

'I see that, in retrospect. But at the time I thought I could manage Gil and end it all and spare you from knowing I had ever strayed a little, even in my thoughts,' she whispered. The hand he held trembled. She added: 'Darley, I would have *died* if you hadn't come to me today. I *have* been half dead. Oh, Darley, have you wanted me?'

'Unbearably,' he said and took her in his arms again. He told her then about Sue.

Her lips quivered with pity. She said: 'Oh, poor Sue—and poor Darley. How miserable for you.'

'Never mind, darling, we'll have each other,' he said.

'Darling ... that day of our picnic ... I *was* genuine, I *was* in love with you again. I *am* ...' she choked the words. 'And I do want children, Darley.'

He raised his head and looked into her eyes.

'Angel, I believe you. But don't say any more. Let's wipe the past right out. We're going to start again ... make a terrific success of our marriage ... from today, my darling one.'

She nodded, her eyes full of tears.

'Yes ... please.'

Their lips met and clung again ... salt with her tears. He said:

'Don't cry. No need to cry now. Be happy. And listen, darling. I won't ask you to go down to the Manor. I'm fed up with the way Mother's behaved toward you and I *don't* want to see Rachel for the moment. By the way, I can assure you there was never anything between Rachel and me.'

She nodded her acceptance of this.

He added: 'I've brought up a suitcase. We can stay the night ... at the Berkeley ... if we can get in ... it's where we meant to have our wedding night. And this time, we'll really belong to each other ... body and soul, shall we, my Finella?'

'Yes,' she said on a breathless, rapturous note. 'Oh, darling, *yes* ... !'

'And tomorrow ... we'll set to work to get this house ready, shall we? Would you like to, Fin?'

'Oh, Darley!' she looked at him with shining limpid eyes. 'Then you haven't got rid of the lease?'

He tapped his pocket.

'No. Got it in here. We've still got our funny little home. Shall we live here, darling, and I'll get down to my job for Wychless ... and shall we carry out all our plans ... and show John Place what a married couple should be like ... *shall we?*'

She nodded, speechlessly, and hugged him, her heart beating fast. The world was a lovely, lovely place again. She thought:

'I must rush home and change ... do my face and hair ... make myself look wonderful for him ... I'm an absolute *sight*.'

But Darley did not seem to think so. For he looked at her tumbled hair, her tear-wet face, and in a voice that shook a little, he said:

'Fin ... my adorable darling ... I'm crazy about you. You are so very, *very* beautiful."

Photoset, printed and bound in Great Britain by REDWOOD BURN LIMITED, Trowbridge, Wiltshire